A ROGUE COWBOY FINDS LOVE

A Hart Ranch Billionaire's Novel

STEPHANIE ROWE

COPYRIGHT

CHAPTER ONE

JACOB HART NEEDED to get away.

From people.

From his memories.

From noise.

Anger coiling through him, Jacob urged his horse faster, allowing the rescued gelding to unleash the monster that haunted him. Together, they raced across the barren terrain, both of them breathing hard as they sought the elusive peace that they could never find.

Farther and faster they went, carving their way across the massive Hart Ranch, heading toward the most distant corner where no one else ever went, where everyone knew to stay away.

Toward the remote hideaway where Jacob had chosen to build his home.

The massive pitch-black gelding galloped hard and free, a magnificent beast who hadn't been able to walk when Jacob had broken into that shack and pried him free of the life that had tried to claim him.

1

And now. Galloping fast. Free. The ultimate rescue success.

And yet all the shadows still clung to the horse's cells, his skin, his soul.

Just like Jacob.

He clenched his jaw, focusing on the wind whipping at his cheeks, knifing the front of his neck where his jacket had flapped open, but it was never enough to change his moment, his existence in this world that he couldn't embrace.

Ahead of them, Jacob's cabin loomed, with the luxurious attached barn that he'd designed and built for the horses he claimed, his own private rescue for the most damaged, the ones no one else could help.

His mount, who he'd named Freedom, eased off the frantic gallop as their home came into sight. Freedom, who would never be sent away from this new home Jacob had given him. Freedom, who didn't yet trust that he could put down roots and breathe deeply of the oasis he lived in.

Just like Jacob.

Freedom slowed to a jog, his breath like white bursts of angel breath in the cold, high desert early morning air of eastern Oregon. Jacob settled back in the saddle as he ran his hand along Freedom's shoulder. His hands were like ice, in need of the gloves he hadn't bothered to put on when he'd bolted from the house, desperate to get out and away from the noise that sometimes closed in on him when he was alone.

The only time it quieted was when he was with his family, his brothers and sisters, Harts by choice and not by blood, but even that relief only lasted for so long.

Especially after the news he'd just gotten.

Jacob needed to be in a place where conversation didn't need to happen, where meals could be taken with nothing but the sunset and the fresh air around him, where he didn't have to pretend he understood how to be social.

Not that the Harts asked him to be what he wasn't. They understood. They accepted. They loved him.

But still, he'd had to build his house at the far end of their massive ranch. Small. A fraction of the size of the others. Two bedrooms. One bathroom. An open living space. Sparse. No clutter. Just an oasis to breathe, to stabilize, to be alone.

His sanctuary was needed even more, now that two of his brothers had found partners, one of whom had a sixteen-year-old daughter. He loved both women, and the kid, but their presence at family events shifted the dynamic in a way he struggled with.

He pulled a remote out of his pocket. With the push of a button, the huge barn door began to slide open, and he rode Freedom straight into the entry of the barn. He paused the gelding in the foyer, waiting as the door closed behind him. The moment it shut out the cold air, the interior door opened, welcoming them. The motor was silent as the doors moved, cutting-edge technology that he improved and modified regularly.

Three of the four horses he currently had looked over their stall doors in greeting as he reined Freedom to a stop, the gelding's hooves silent on the state-of-the-art shock-absorbing mats that covered every inch of flooring for his horses. The fourth was a pony, too small to see over the door, but Jacob was going to fix that in the morning.

Every animal needed the freedom of being able to connect with the others, and the pony was no exception.

The air was fresh and clean, the barn sparkling with the best of everything for his animals. Literally everything. Organic food that he contracted out to be hand-mixed and delivered twice a week. Hay that he had privately grown in nearby fields, devoid of any toxic chemicals, stored in the most pristine conditions.

He breathed deeply into the silence, into the soft snorts of welcome, into the peaceful presence of living creatures that gave him companionship, but demanded nothing of him.

"Only the best for you guys," he told Freedom as he uncinched the girth to remove the saddle.

Did having only the best chase away their demons? He did all he could for them, for the fragile creatures who needed him.

Talking quietly to the horses, he stripped down Freedom and went to work brushing him, cleansing the dirt and cold and sweat they'd churned up. Freedom relaxed under the grooming, his back foot cocked and his head down, embracing the attention.

Jacob smiled, remembering how Freedom had been terrified of any physical contact when he'd first arrived. "I remember what that was like," he said. "It's a tough lesson to unlearn, isn't it?"

Freedom swung his head around and snuffled at Jacob's back pocket. He laughed softly. "I already gave you all the treats I have." He moved his hand slowly so as not to startle Freedom, and the horse didn't flinch as Jacob rubbed his ears. "They say time heals all wounds. You think that's true? That wholeness is possible?"

Freedom pressed his head against Jacob's side and sighed, his ribs expanding with the deep breath of contentment.

"I'll take that as a yes." The horses gave him hope.

Without hope, he had nothing.

With hope, he had a reason to get up every day, take care of his horses, and play with technology. Because maybe this time, something new would happen. Something would change. Inside him. Outside him. Whatever it took.

His phone rang, and he looked over at the feed room where he'd left it.

He didn't take it with him most of the time, because he didn't want to be found. Didn't want to have to talk when he didn't want to talk. He never let a call from his family go unanswered, but if he didn't have his phone, he didn't have to answer.

The ringtone echoing through the barn was the one he used for his family, which meant he had to answer.

He gave Freedom a little pat. "I'll be right back."

He kept his eye on the horse as he walked across the barn. He never cross-tied his horses, because he didn't want them to feel trapped. He asked them to stay for him, and they did.

The phone went into voicemail before he reached it, but he saw from the screen that it was his brother Dylan. He immediately called him back, because his connection with his family was something so ingrained in him that he never blocked them.

Dylan answered on the first ring. "You have to start taking your phone with you on rides."

Jacob smiled and sauntered back across the floor. "Nothing is ever that urgent."

"Except now."

Jacob's smile dropped off his face at the tension in his brother's voice. *Son of a bitch.* He gripped the phone with sudden alarm. "What's wrong? Who's hurt? Who's in trouble? I'm on my way. Tell me where." He started running toward the door, panic hammering in his chest, terror that his little family, his precious world, had been shattered.

"Stop." Dylan's voice was calmer now, but Jacob could feel he was concealing his urgency. "No one in the family. Everyone is fine. I need your help with something else."

"Fuck." Jacob stopped and leaned over, bracing his hands

on his knees, fighting to keep his composure as the relief swarmed him. "Don't do that to me."

"Shit. Sorry. I wasn't thinking. Look, I've got a situation."

Freedom walked over and blew in Jacob's ear. Jacob wrapped his arm around the horse's head and closed his eyes. "What kind of situation?"

"You know Eliana, right?"

Jacob nodded. "The woman you're in love with but will never make a move on because you're afraid you'll lose her friendship forever, and your platonic friendship is better than losing her? That Eliana?"

"Funny guy," Dylan said. "We're just friends."

"You know you'll never get her unless you tell her that you love her."

"Dating advice coming from the guy who hasn't gone on a date in years?"

"Yep." Jacob rose to his feet, then set his hand on Freedom's neck to guide him toward his stall. "What's going on?"

"You know how she helps women escape from abusive situations and then disappear?"

"I do." Eliana was an absolute badass. Jacob had the highest respect for her. She understood the edge that ate away at Jacob, and most of his siblings, because she spent much of her time in the same marshy world. That connection helped Jacob be comfortable around her. She'd be perfect for Dylan, if the two of them ever got out of their own way. "What's up?"

"She didn't give me the details—"

"She never does."

Dylan ignored his comment. "She has a woman and a young girl living not too far from our ranch, but some guy just got out of prison. She's worried that he's going to go after them. She needs them off the radar until she can be sure they're safe."

"You need to borrow my truck?" Dylan owned a private detective firm, and he often helped out Eliana with her clients.

"No, I'm out of the country right now. I need you to go get them and bring them to your house."

Silence reigned.

"Jacob?"

"Did you just say you want me to go get a woman and a child and bring them to my house and have them stay here? With me?"

"Yes."

"Here? Bring them *here?* For how long?"

"A few days? A week? I don't know. Eliana didn't tell me."

"I can't have them in my house."

"You can."

Jacob shut Freedom's door. "You need to know that I got a call that my dad got out of prison yesterday."

Dylan let out his breath. "You okay?"

"Yeah."

"Heard from him?"

"No." Not that he would answer if his dad did reach out. "I'm sure he has no idea that his son is the billionaire rancher Jacob Hart. He'd never expect I could have been that guy."

"And if he did, he has no power over you anymore."

"I know." But the release of his dad from prison brought back memories that Jacob had thought no longer controlled him. "So, yeah, not the best time for me to take on a woman and a kid."

"Crises never ask ahead to make sure the timing is good. I need you to do this."

Jacob swore. "Did you call the wrong brother? I'm not the guy who takes in women and kids."

"You're the guy who takes in horses."

"Hell, Dylan—"

"I've known you for almost twenty years. I know exactly who you are and how difficult this will be for you. So you know that if I'm asking, I don't have a better option right now."

Jacob leaned against the stall door and closed his eyes. "Fuck."

"Bring a gun."

His eyes opened. "A gun?"

"If this guy finds them, he's likely to try to kill them. So, yeah, a gun. He got out of prison an hour ago, and Eliana has already lost track of him. None of her contacts can find him, so he could be on his way right now. Apparently, he has money and connections."

Memories flashed though Jacob's mind, galvanizing him. He strode over to the cabinet, let it scan his face, then the door swung open for him. He reached inside and pulled out his gun. Then a second one. "Where are they?"

"The town of Blackthorn. It's about an hour away."

"I'll be on my way in two minutes. Text me the address and any info I need."

"Will do. And one more thing..."

Jacob was already running for the door, setting the alarm for the barn on his phone as he ran. "What?"

"This woman uses her phone about as much as you do. Eliana hasn't been able to reach her yet to tell her what's going on. So, when you show up, she might not know why you're there, or that you're a good guy."

Jacob burst outside into the cold night, his boots thudding on the frozen gravel as he ran for the garage where he kept his truck. "So, I'm supposed to sweet talk a woman and kid?"

"Pretend they're horses. You'll do great. And, Jacob?"

Jacob ducked under the garage door as it opened and

leapt into his truck, which he'd remote-started already. "What?"

"Thanks."

Jacob put his truck in reverse. "No little girl dies on my watch. Not ever again."

Then he hung up and hit the gas.

CHAPTER TWO

THE SHRIEK from the living room had Phoebe Sheridan sprinting toward the room even before she heard the resounding crash.

"Mommy!"

"Annie! Are you okay?" She burst into the living room, and then stopped, unable to stop the swell of laughter at the sight before her. "Holy cow, Annie. What did you do?"

"Mommy! Help!" A couch table was upended on the floor, Annie's hand was sticking out of a huge pile of pillows, and there was a furry, wagging tail sticking out from between the same pillows. "Cupcake's eating my braids!"

Still laughing, Phoebe started tossing aside couch cushions, until she found her six-year-old daughter and their eight-month rescue dog, a thirty-pound black-and-white shaggy whirlwind of chaos, destruction, and joy.

Cupcake did indeed have Annie's braids in his teeth, and he was tugging hard while Annie held the base of her braids and alternated between hysterical giggles and shouting at him.

"Cupcake, no." Unable to hold back her own laughter,

Phoebe hauled the exuberant puppy off her daughter. "Is every pillow in the house in this room?"

"Yes!" Annie bounded to her feet, her dark eyes glistening with merriment. Her sixteen little braids seemed none the worse for the wear, which was great, since it still took Phoebe about four hours to comb and braid Annie's hair. She was learning how to handle her daughter's tight curls, but it still took a long time.

"Mommy, we have a crazy dog."

"I know we do." Phoebe picked up the squirming dog and hugged him, laughing as he tried to lick every inch of her face. "I thought you were going to train him."

"I don't know how to train him! He won't listen!"

"Well, then we're in trouble, because I don't either." Cupcake went for Phoebe's necklace, and she felt his teeth hook the chain. She immediately grasped his nose and diverted him. "Okay, out in the yard, puppikins. Want to go out?"

Cupcake barked and shot out of her arms, racing toward the back door. She hurried after him and opened it. He bolted outside, chasing after a squirrel that had dared brave the fence.

With a sigh, Phoebe watched the black bundle of energy race across the fenced yard. She'd walked him for two hours already, trained him for thirty minutes, and he was still a maniac.

He was the wrong dog for their lifestyle. She'd known it from the moment they'd met him, but Annie fell immediately in love with him, so the choice was made. Phoebe had been desperate to help her daughter stabilize after the difficult childhood that had brought her to Phoebe's doorstep three years ago, a tiny little stranger who no longer had a mom or a family, or anyone to call her own...until Phoebe claimed her.

Having the dog sleep in Annie's room had ended the night

terrors, so Phoebe would love that dog forever and do whatever it took to keep him a part of their little family. She loved him, but there were moments when she was about at the end of her coping.

Three dog trainers had quit, declaring him untrainable and telling her to get rid of him.

Who says that in front of a six-year-old girl?

It had taken days to undo that damage and get Annie to trust that Cupcake wasn't leaving her.

"Mommy!" Annie beamed at her. "Ready to bake?"

Phoebe didn't have time to bake. She had so much work to do for her business. She'd been planning to spend the day working while Annie had been at school, but it had been one of *those* mornings, and Annie hadn't been able to cope with school. So, Annie being home, plus a dog maniac, meant Phoebe was once again going to have to stay up all night to work.

Because never, ever would she let her daughter feel or believe that she wasn't the most important thing in Phoebe's life. Annie used to push her boundaries all the time, trying to sabotage the new home she had, but Phoebe had been relentless in her love. Now, Annie was still a handful, but she had internalized that Phoebe wasn't leaving her and never would, no matter what Annie did, and that had started to give Annie room to start to trust and relax.

Still a long way to go, but progress was hope, and that kept her going.

So, baking it was. Phoebe smiled. "Of course, we'll bake. On one condition."

"I know! I'll help clean! Yay!" Annie bounded into the kitchen.

"Annie."

"Mommy." Annie didn't reappear.

Phoebe folded her arms over her chest. "Annie."

Her daughter peered around the doorway from the kitchen, her dark brown skin glistening in the midday light. "Mommy."

"Pillows?"

Annie's gaze shot toward the pile in the living room, then back at Phoebe. "They like being together. It makes them feel safe."

Safe. That word that Annie used a lot, because safe mattered to her. Phoebe didn't want Annie to think about "safe." She wanted Annie to think about being wild and free, about recess and gym class, about learning how to do math. Things kids should think about. "Well, what would make them feel safe enough to all go back to their rooms?"

Annie rubbed her jaw, thinking about it. "Nothing. They need to stay here."

Phoebe eyed the massive pile of pillows. "Forever?"

"Yep."

Phoebe sighed, trying to think. "What if we made sure that each pillow had a best friend? No one ever alone."

Phoebe rubbed her jaw. "Each little pillow needs a big pillow with it."

"Of course. Big pillows take care of the little pillows, but you know what?"

"What?"

"Little pillows are also super tough and they can take care of themselves. They don't need a big pillow. They can do it all alone."

Annie eyed her doubtfully. "Really?"

"Yep." Phoebe went over and picked up a little pillow. She tossed it to her daughter. "Throw it at me."

Annie's face brightened. "Really?"

"Yep." Phoebe braced her hands on her knees, bending low so her face was level with her daughter. "Throw that little pillow right at my face. You'll see how tough it is."

Annie giggled. "Can I come closer?"

"You bet." Lordy, Phoebe hoped this wasn't going be one of those parenting decisions she regretted forever.

Clutching the pillow, Annie inched forward. "Now?"

"Go for it."

"Okay." Annie reached back and hurled the pillow as hard as she could.

It barely brushed across Phoebe's cheek before falling to the carpet, but Phoebe let out a yelp and then dropped to the floor. "You got me!"

Annie screeched with delight, charged across the room, and flung herself on Phoebe's chest. Phoebe laughed and tickled her daughter, who screamed with laughter, giggling and snorting. Outside, she heard Cupcake barking, and she laughed. "Cupcake wants to play!"

"Yes! Let's get him!" Annie launched herself off Phoebe and raced to the door. She flung it open, then froze.

A man was in their doorway.

CHAPTER THREE

Tall, broad-shouldered, the man's face was shadowed by a cowboy hat.

He was immobile, standing there in her door, ignoring Cupcake jumping up on him and whipping around him in a frenzy.

Phoebe's heart jumped, and she scrambled to her feet, her heart racing. She didn't have her phone. Or her gun. Or anything to defend them. She'd gotten so lax, and now... "Annie," she said softly. "Come give Mommy a hug."

But her daughter didn't move, frozen inches from this massive, silhouetted man, her little face staring up at him.

Fear gripped Phoebe, and suddenly she couldn't breathe. She'd been in tough situations before, but she'd never felt like a victim, never felt like she couldn't handle them, but as she stood there, too far away from Annie to grab her if the man made a move, she felt absolute, raw terror for her baby's safety.

"Annie," she said cheerfully. "Let's go bake. Can you get the pans out?"

Annie startled, then spun around. "Yay!"

She turned and raced back to the kitchen, and the man made no move to grab her, leaving Phoebe alone with him.

"Get out of my house," she said softly, with as much menace as she could muster. "Now."

He cleared his throat, then muttered under his breath. "Eliana said to tell you that toucans eat chocolate bonbons on day seventeen."

Phoebe blinked, startled by how rich and sexy his voice was, and by the fact he'd just said something about toucans and chocolate bonbons. "What?"

"And snow leopards believe in unicorns."

Phoebe stared at him blankly. "What are you talking about?"

"Isn't that the code to tell you that Eliana sent me and that I'm here to help?"

"Unicorns and bonbons? Seriously?"

He swore suddenly and pulled out his phone. "Hang on a sec." He hit send, keeping his phone on speaker.

A man answered. "Did you find them okay?"

"You made up that unicorn shit, didn't you?"

The man on the other end started laughing. "You really said that to Phoebe?"

Her visitor glanced at her. "I did. She thinks I'm insane now."

The man laughed harder. "That was a joke. I was trying to break through all the internal tension that you were bringing with you so you didn't scare her. Did it work?"

"You're a fucker." Her visitor hung up his phone, then shoved his hat back and grimaced. "Sorry about the profanity. My brother brings it out in me."

She waved her hand absently, distracted by how attractive he was. Sculpted jaw, radiant blue eyes, just enough whiskers to make a woman take notice. He was pure testosterone, and yet, there was a calmness to his energy, as if he had nowhere to go, nothing else to do, and would be perfectly at peace standing in her doorway for hours.

It had been a long time since Phoebe had bothered to notice an attractive guy, so it was a little startling that she was noticing now. "It's fine. I believe in profanity," she said. "Who exactly are you?"

The conversation with his brother had been too genuine for it to be faked. The warmth in their voices had been real, despite the teasing they were giving each other. So, she wasn't exactly scared of him, but at the same time... Big, muscled stranger in her doorway needed to be addressed.

He took his hat off as his gaze went around the chaotic living room. "My name's Jacob Hart. My brother, Dylan, works with Eliana Tiernan. Apparently, there's a situation, and Eliana would like for me to escort you and your daughter to a new location for a little while." His words were light and calm, but there was an underlying edge to his voice that got her attention in a hurry.

"Now?"

He nodded. "Right now. Pack for a few days, I guess."

Alarm crept down her spine. "What's going on?"

"I don't know." The first smile she'd seen on him danced at the corners of his mouth. "Apparently, you check your phone less often than I do. Eliana has been trying to reach you."

"My phone?" Of course. Her *phone*. Phoebe dashed into the kitchen, grabbed her purse off the counter, and pulled out her phone. Her heart sank when she saw eleven voicemails and twenty-five text messages from Eliana. *"Oh, God."*

"Mommy?" She turned around to see Annie staring at her, her eyes wide, a mixing bowl in her hand. "Mommy? Is something bad happening?"

"Oh, no, of course not. This is my friend...Uncle Jacob." She quickly texted Eliana, not taking the time to read all the texts. The few she saw were enough to raise her adrenaline. She immediately texted Eliana. *Jacob Hart is here. Said you sent him. Send me a picture of him if he's okay.*

Jacob cocked an eyebrow from his spot in the doorway, from which he still hadn't budged. Cupcake had given up harassing him, and was now sitting by Jacob's side, staring up at him expectantly. "Uncle Jacob?" he repeated, a hint of amusement in his voice.

"Yes. He's a dear and trusted friend." Phoebe smiled down at her daughter with confidence she didn't feel. Her mind was whirling, and panic was trying to close in on her. "Jacob is a sillyhead," she said. "You'll adore him."

Her phone vibrated, and she looked down as Eliana sent a picture of the man standing in her doorway. *Is this who's at your door?*

Yes.

Good. He's Jacob Hart. Go with him. Get out now. I'll explain as soon as you guys are clear. High alert. Go!

Oh, Lordy. She couldn't believe this was happening. *Do we have time to pack?*

Three minutes. That's it.

Ok. She fought to hold off the panic as she shoved her phone in her pocket. "Guess what, Annie! Jacob's taking us on a vacation!"

Jacob's brows shot up, and Annie's eyes widened. "Disney World? Are we going to *Disney World?*"

Crap. She shouldn't have said vacation. "Um...not exactly...It's a surprise. Right, Jacob?"

Jacob looked at her, then looked at Annie. He seemed to wage an internal battle, then he got down on one knee so he was eye level with Annie, who was still in the kitchen. "Do you like horses?"

She nodded silently as she slid her hand into Phoebe's.

"Want to go visit a horse ranch? You and your mom can

help me take care of the horses. I have this new one, a pony, who needs a friend. She feels lost. Would you be her friend?"

Annie stared at him, then nodded once. "What's her name?"

"Her name is..." He paused, and then got a thoughtful look on his face. "She doesn't have a name yet. I need help naming her."

"I'll help!" Annie clapped her hands. "Can I see a picture?"

"Yeah, sure." He pulled out his phone as Annie ran across the room. She leaned against his shoulder as he scrolled through some pictures.

Phoebe felt her heart turn over as she watched Annie's face light up at a photo he showed her. Annie didn't trust men, and yet she'd warmed to Jacob immediately. *Yes.* Her throat tightened. *Maybe her baby would be all right.*

"Send it to Mommy so I can see it all the time." Annie grabbed his phone and pressed a kiss to the screen. "Pony, I'm coming!" She dropped the phone and started to run out the front door, but Jacob gently blocked her.

"I think you need to pack, don't you?"

She stared at him. "Yes! Mommy, come on!" She turned and raced toward the stairs, her little feet thudding as she ran up them. Cupcake barked and took off after her, yelping with delight. As they reached the top of the stairs, there was a crash, and then, "I'm okay," Annie yelled. "But you need a new lamp!"

Oh, God.

Jacob stared at the ceiling, a look of slight horror on his face as he listened to the chaotic sounds of dog and child feet racing around echoed through the house, and Annie's occasional shouts and Cupcake's constant barks.

Phoebe decided not to give Jacob a chance to decide to run for his life instead of helping them. "I'll be right down," she said, hurrying toward the stairs. "If you can grab the bin of Cupcake's food from the corner of the kitchen, and pack up a bunch of his dog toys, that would be super helpful!"

Jacob's gaze went to the torn-up couches. "The dog's coming?"

Phoebe paused on the bottom step. "He keeps Annie's night terrors away," she said, her voice calm but unyielding. "I wouldn't leave him behind for anything. He's family." She was long past apologizing for who she was or what she wanted, especially to a man.

This particular man raised his brows and met her gaze. She expected him to resist, or be grumpy, but instead, he grinned, the first genuine smile she'd seen on him. It lit up his face, nearly bringing her to her knees with how handsome he was. "Any dog that keeps away night terrors is a dog worth keeping. He definitely comes."

Phoebe smiled back, caught up in the light radiating from him. "All right then." She started to run up the stairs, then turned back as he stepped inside and shut the door behind him. "Annie is afraid of most men. How did you get her to trust you like that?"

He shrugged. "I know what it's like to be so scared you can't even make yourself crawl out of the shadows you're hiding in, even though you're cold, hungry, and wet. I feel it, and I feel it in animals, and I project the peace that I could never find, that I needed. I guess I did that with her."

He was so tall, so muscled, so...all-consuming that it was stunning to think of him hiding in shadows...and admitting it. "Wow."

He shrugged again, clearly unimpressed with himself. "Rehabbing traumatized horses is my superpower. My brother told me to treat you guys like horses, so..." he shrugged. "I guess it works."

She didn't know what to say to that. She'd never met a

man who would claim rehabbing traumatized animals as his superpower. Or who was advised to treat a woman and her child like horses...and have that make sense. "You're unusual, aren't you?"

"Yes." He didn't hesitate or try to explain. He simply confirmed it.

"Great." She smiled. "We are, too."

He stared at her for a moment, then grinned, that same heart-melting grin that he'd flashed once before at her. "All right, then. We gotta go."

"Okay." She cleared her throat. "We'll be down in a few minutes." She spun around and ran up the stairs, her mind whirling.

Her worst nightmare had happened, having to go on the run with her daughter...but Jacob...he was a surprise. A tempting, handsome surprise who seemed to surround her and Annie with a sense of calm, of protection, an answer to the chaos that permeated her life.

How this was going to unfold, she had no idea.

But she was going to find a way to make it work, because she was no longer the woman who hid in shadows. She was now a mom who would never give up, not for herself, and not for her daughter, and not for their trouble-making dog.

How much danger were they in? What did she need to do to make them safe? How much could she trust Jacob, and with what?

"Mommy! Help!"

"Coming!" Phoebe took a breath and headed toward her daughter's room, her mind whirring with possibilities, questions, and fear.

And determination.

Would it be enough to survive whatever was coming for them?

She would make sure it was.

CHAPTER FOUR

HOLY *CRAP*.

Jacob released his breath as Phoebe disappeared from sight, trying to regain his equilibrium.

Phoebe was absolutely breathtaking, in a way he hadn't been prepared for.

The woman he'd been sent to collect was wearing baggy sweatpants, an old tee shirt, and purple, fuzzy socks. Her ponytail was crooked, she was wearing no makeup...and she had rocked him to his core.

So real. So alive. So...vibrant.

Jacob had been shocked by the look of absolute terror on her face when he'd walked in and stood too close to her daughter.

He'd admired her fierce threat when she'd told him to leave.

She'd won his respect the way she'd claimed that dog to protect her daughter.

And his heart had been the victim when Phoebe's face had softened as she'd listened to him talking to Dylan. He'd speaker-phoned his brother on purpose, figuring it was the best way to get that look of terror off her face, and it had worked.

But...*shit*. No woman should ever have to be that afraid, especially not for her child. Her response had unleashed a fierce protective instinct in him that was usually reserved only for his siblings and his horses.

He needed more information from Eliana. He needed to know about the threat they were facing, and what he needed to do to prepare for it.

But first, to get them out.

Instead of collecting dog toys and food, Jacob strode to the window and edged the curtain aside to check the back-yard. Finding nothing suspicious, he walked to the side window and checked out the window there. Then to the front of the house, and then the other side. Only when he was satisfied that no one was poised to break in did he turn his attention to collecting dog gear...but at every moment, his attention was attuned to the sounds upstairs of his three charges gathering their items, and he was paying close attention to the noises outside the house, listening for any sign that danger was imminent.

Which meant he heard Phoebe's footsteps racing back down the stairs, and he was already turning to face her when she popped into the room. But his gut still dropped when he saw her again.

She'd changed into jeans that fit her like a gift, boots with a fleece cuff, and a black hoodie that she'd zipped halfway up, down just enough so he could see her pink shirt underneath. Her hair was brushed now, up in a messy bun, and she was wearing the faintest hint of makeup.

Not seeming to notice how she was affecting him, Phoebe flashed him a polite smile. "So, just a quick question. Are we going to a hotel? Or do we need to bring sheets and towels and stuff like that? Do we need to bring food?"

She was breathtaking. Did she have dimples? He kinda thought she might. Her eyes were a radiant blue. He'd never seen anything like them before.

She blinked. "Jacob?"

Shit. What was wrong with him? "Yeah. Sorry. I was distracted."

"By what?"

"Listening to the outdoors to make sure no one is outside who shouldn't be." A partial truth, but he wasn't going to scare her off by admitting how deeply affected by her he was.

Her eyes widened. "Did you hear anything suspicious?"

"Nope. We're good."

She smiled then, a genuine smile that made him want to smile back. "Okay, then. The sheets and towels? Are we going to a hotel?"

A few hours ago, he would have jumped on that idea. Stash them at a hotel and go back and forth between the hotel and his horses. Anything to avoid having to host these strangers in the private oasis he'd created for himself, away from people and noise and chaos.

But now that he'd met them, the idea of leaving them unattended in a hotel room for even a moment was intolerable. He shook his head. "Dylan requested I take you back to my place."

She blinked. "Your house?"

He nodded. "It's fully secure." Suddenly, he almost wished he was the kind of guy who'd created a place that others might decide felt like home. He knew how plain it was. "It's sparse. You might want to bring stuff to make Annie feel like it's a home." And Phoebe. But he couldn't say that.

She cocked her head. "How sparse is it?"

He shrugged. "I don't think you'll like it, but it's safe. Clean. Toss whatever you want to take down the stairs and I'll bring it out. I have a big truck, and can take a lot." What the hell was he doing? Inviting chaos and clutter into his home?

Yeah. He was. If Annie needed a dog to keep away the night terrors, then she was a kid who had a past like he had. He knew about night terrors, and there was no damn way he was going to mess up what progress she'd made.

Phoebe gave him a thoughtful look. "It could be a while that we're there then, you think?"

He shrugged. "Each night can feel like an eternity if it's dark enough. Take it one at a time. Each night matters when you're scared. So do whatever it takes to make each night okay for her."

Her eyebrows shot up, and he swore. What the fuck was he, a poet now? "Or whatever," he muttered. "I'll get the dog food."

He spun around and headed into the kitchen. What the hell was wrong with him? He was losing his mind. His focus.

But a traumatized kid with night terrors? A mom who got scared about her kid? It brought back memories he'd shut down a long time ago, memories that would haunt him forever. Memories that maybe could be silenced if he helped Annie and Phoebe.

"Jacob?" Her voice was gentle. Soft. *Compelling.*

He turned around to find Phoebe still standing there, her hand over her heart. "Yeah?"

"Thank you. With all my heart."

He heard the earnestness in those words, and he nodded.

He met her gaze, and he could tell she wanted to say more, that she wanted him to say more, but he didn't have words for what was going on in his head and his heart right now. "You're welcome," he muttered. "What's your timing?" he asked, trying to change the subject to one that didn't feel so fraught with landmines.

"Our timing?" She cleared her throat, and seemed to pull

herself back together. "A few more minutes. I'm going to fill a duffel with some of Annie's favorite things."

"Great. Get her blankets and comforter too. She'll like that." For a second, they looked at each other, and he was once again caught by his reaction to her. Stunning. Awaking the man inside him that he'd forgotten how to be.

Then, as one, they both turned away. "Can you come up in a couple minutes and help carry stuff down?" she shouted as she hurried up the stairs.

"You bet." He grabbed the dog food bin and carried it to the front door...but instead of moving it outside, he set it down inside the house. He'd take it to his truck when they were all together.

Because until he found out what the threat was, he was keeping them close.

And it wasn't because he found himself unable to tear himself away from them.

Or at least, it wasn't *only* because of that.

PHOEBE WATCHED Jacob's jaw tick as he drove.

Annie and Cupcake were asleep in the back seat of his extended cab pickup truck, stuffed in beside blankets, pillows, and dog beds. In the truck bed, beneath the cover, was the rest of their gear. Except for her computer, her camera, her microphone, her computer monitor, and all the other things she needed for her business. All of that was nestled at her feet, because she never let it out of her sight. It had taken them too long to get out of her house, and the tension of both adults was rising with each passing minute, not knowing what was coming or when.

But now they were on the road, and the miles were ticking by.

Jacob had taken a number of detours and roundabout routes to expose anyone who might be following them. He'd called his brother Lucas to drive a ways behind them, also watching to see if anyone was following them.

Jacob had stopped to cover his license plates with mud, and he'd given her a burner phone to use and made her turn hers off before they'd driven away from her house.

His attention to detail to keeping them safe was reassuring, but also alarming. She didn't want to be living a life where she had to rely on someone like Jacob to do what he was doing. "How come you're such an expert on this stuff?" she asked, trying to distract herself from how much she didn't want to be in this situation.

Jacob looked over at her. "My family takes our safety seriously."

She raised her brows. "Is your family in danger often?"

He shrugged as he pulled off a main road onto a dirt road, for what felt like the bazillionth time. "We have pasts."

"What kind of pasts? Do I need to be concerned?"

He looked over at her then. "Do you not know who I am? Who the Harts are?"

She almost started laughing at his surprise. "I don't, sorry. I have enough trouble keeping track of my own life. I'd never be able to keep up with someone else's. Fill me in."

He rubbed his jaw, drawing her attention to his forearm. It was so freaking chiseled. The man was strong, and she couldn't help but notice. "The abbreviated version is that we were all homeless kids. We found each other, lived under a bridge for a while, and became the Hart family. We invented some software and made some money when we sold it. We used the proceeds to buy a ranch and we all have homes on it. But when you're a teenager living on the streets, it usually means that you walked away from a situation that wasn't good, so yeah, we learned to protect each other from early on. The habit stuck."

Phoebe leaned back in her seat, digesting that. The truck they were in right now was clearly the top of the line. It was huge, leather seats, pristine condition, aftermarket super-elite technology in the dashboard. His brother's truck that was now following them up close was equally tricked out.

So, they'd done all right for themselves, the Hart home-less kids. "I like that story," she said. At his glance, she added, "The part about creating your own forever family. It gives hope to people who feel alone. I like that."

He glanced at her again. "You got family?"

She nodded. "I do. My parents are awesome, but I haven't seen them for a long time. I had to go off the radar, and it wasn't safe to contact them. And then, I adopted Annie, and had to make some more adjustments." God, there was so much more to it than that, but that was all she could share. And what was the point of dwelling on what she couldn't change?

Jacob cocked an eyebrow. "You have a great family? And you left them?"

There wasn't judgment in his tone, but it was rife with curiosity, as if, what could possibly compel her to walk away from family. "Yes. I did."

He glanced over at her, and she stiffened, waiting for him to push it, to try to force her to talk about what she didn't want to discuss. But to her surprise, he simply nodded. "Takes guts to make that kind of call. I know it's not easy."

To her absolute shock, sudden tears filled her eyes, and she turned her head away so he wouldn't see. What the heck? Since when did she let herself even think about crying? "I'm fine. I'm good." She *was* good. She was great, actually. "It's just that this little situation knocked my equilibrium a bit.

You don't need to worry that you need to take care of us. Just a place to sleep and we're good."

He was quiet for a moment, and the truck bounced along the dirt road. "We're almost there."

She looked around, but saw only trees. "Great."

"But I gotta tell you something before we get there."

This time, it was her turn to look at him. There was a tension in his voice that caught her attention. "Okay. What's up?"

He gripped the steering wheel, keeping his gaze on the road. "I'm not a people person," he finally said. "My place is off alone, because I need space. I don't always know how to interact with people. I can't always read what they want from me, and it can piss people off."

Her heart softened at his confession. She could feel the commitment it took for him to tell her. "That's okay," she said. "Annie doesn't do well around people either. I get that about her, and I work with what she can handle. We'll try not to rock your boat too much, but if we do, just tell us and we'll adjust."

He let out his breath. "I might not know how to be a good host, but I'll keep you guys safe. But just wanted to warn you that I—" He stopped, and swore. "I don't know. I just felt like I should warn you."

She laughed softly. "I appreciate the heads-up, but don't worry about it. Whoever you are, it will be exactly what we need." At his surprised look, she nodded. "That's how I believe the world works." She grinned. "And that also means that whatever you get from us is exactly what you need. And I say that knowing that I have a maniac puppy, an unpredictable daughter, and a truck bed full of chaos. Just wanted to warn you..."

He laughed then, a full-bodied deep laugh that made her

heart turn over. "I'll try to remember that theory when my couch gets eaten."

"You have a couch? Awesome. When you were all dramatic about how sparse your house was, I thought we were going to be sleeping on a steel floor. This is going to be great."

He laughed again as he eased the truck to a stop. "Great, indeed." He put the vehicle in park. "Welcome to your new home, Phoebe."

"We're here?" She'd been so consumed by their little discussion that she'd forgotten to look around. She quickly leaned forward to peer out the window, then her mouth dropped open. "Holy cow. Are you kidding?"

CHAPTER FIVE

JACOB TENSED at Phoebe's strong response to his house. "I know it's small. It's not much. But it's safe."

"It's beautiful!" She leaned over and patted her daughter's leg. "Annie! Wake up! Look at where we get to stay!"

Within moments, the two females and the dog were out of his truck, racing across the grass, literally bounding with excitement.

Jacob leaned on his steering wheel, completely flummoxed by their reaction. Yeah, he loved his house, but no one else did. Everyone said it was small, simple, and plain.

But this crazy trio was running around his lawn like he'd just brought them to Disneyland. Shaking his head in confusion, he got out of the truck as Annie collapsed onto the grass, rolled onto her back, and started doing snow angels.

Snow angels in the green grass.

Cupcake dove onto the little girl, and she started shrieking with laugher as the dog tried to consume her with kisses.

Phoebe stretched out beside Annie, and the two of them started doing matching snow angels on his grass.

What. The. Hell.

He walked over and stood there awkwardly, staring down at the trio.

Phoebe beamed up at him. "Join us!"

"No."

"Okay!" She didn't seem remotely upset by his one-word refusal. "Your lawn is gorgeous. Do you do it yourself?"

"Yeah. All organic fertilizer. It's safe for Annie." Safe for Annie. For horses. For birds. For rabbits. For whatever living creature decided to make use of his grass.

Phoebe beamed at him, her arms stretched above her head. The position made her shirt bunch up, revealing a few inches of her belly, including the cutest damned belly button he'd ever seen. A little gold stud was nestled in her belly button, making him grin.

He wouldn't have figured Phoebe for a belly piercing, but he liked it. It was hot as hell, actually.

Phoebe smiled. "Wow. You have a nice smile. I love that."

His smile immediately faded. "Don't get used to it. I never smile."

Her smile widened, undaunted. "I'll keep that in mind."

Annie got up and ran across the grass with Cupcake, laughing and shrieking as she dove and began to log roll across the lawn.

Jacob frowned. "Is she okay?"

Phoebe sat up, draping her arms across her knees. "Oh, yes. This is amazing for her." Her face was pure love as she watched her daughter, making something inside him turn over. The way she looked at her daughter was the way every kid deserved to have someone look at them. "Annie thinks grass is magical. She grew up in an apartment. It was a rough situation. Sometimes she doesn't want to be inside. I don't think she was outside much, and definitely didn't have grass or flowers or anything like that."

"I get that." He fucking loved that Phoebe clearly didn't give a shit that Annie wasn't her biological daughter. She loved that little girl with all-in mama bear fierceness. He didn't believe that family was based on blood, and the fact that Phoebe lived that truth put this little family right at the top of his priority list.

Phoebe sighed with contentment. "I think the grass makes her feel free to be able to enjoy the soft blades under her feet. We have a lot of shade at our house, so the lawn isn't great. Plus, honestly, I don't have time to spend trying to grow a stubborn lawn. Your lawn is heaven for her. She'll be out here a lot, I suspect." She smiled at him. "Thanks for bringing us here, Jacob. This is exactly what she needed."

"The rest of the place isn't so great," he muttered.

Phoebe looked past him to his little house. "It's an adorable log cabin with a wraparound porch, big windows, and a beautiful pasture. The barn looks like a castle for horses. Even the rose bushes under the windows are in bloom with the most beautiful pink blossoms. What on earth isn't great about your home?"

He stared at her.

She looked back at him. "What?"

"It's small. It's plain. It's sparse." He repeated what everyone always said when they came by, urging him to upgrade.

Phoebe smiled up at him. "Well, it seems to me that you need to start singing a different tune about your home. It's a treasure." Then she hopped to her feet, patted his arm, and then ran off after her daughter and dog.

He looked down at his arm where she'd touched him. Her touch had felt good. Amazing. Incredible. He was so confused. Why didn't this group feel like an invasion? Because they didn't. They felt good.

But they also made him want to be more, and he didn't like that.

He wanted to stay exactly as he was. It had gotten him this far in life, and his life was pretty damned good. "I'll get the bags."

He was pretty sure neither of them even heard him.

Now, that, he understood. He tuned people out as much as he could.

But he couldn't tune out Annie's shrieks of joy. The dog's barking. Phoebe's laughter.

And he couldn't stop checking the perimeter to make sure no one had followed them.

As he looked, his brother's truck emerged from the woods that concealed his long driveway. Lucas was driving leisurely, which made Jacob relax slightly. If there was an issue, Lucas would be driving differently.

Lucas pulled up behind Jacob's truck and got out. He paused to watch the gallivanting trio on the lawn, his jaw dropping open when he heard the barking and laughing. He swore under his breath and walked over to Jacob. "Look. I know Dylan wants them with you, but none of us want you to shut down again. If they're pushing you over the edge, I'll take them."

Possessiveness flooded Jacob, surprising him. "Nah. They're good." He wasn't giving them up. Dylan had asked him to keep them safe, and he was going to do it.

"They're good?" Lucas frowned. "There's a kid, a dog, and a woman, screaming and running around your lawn. How is that good?"

"I don't know." That was the truth.

Lucas looked over at him. "You're serious."

"Yeah. They fit okay here."

"Well, hell. I didn't think anyone would ever fit in your space." Lucas got a speculative look on his face as he watched them. "Aren't you surprised?"

"I never thought about anyone being here." Jacob didn't know quite how to explain it. He wasn't surprised, because it wasn't something he'd ever considered long enough to have an opinion on it. He didn't spend a lot of time thinking about the future or a life he didn't have. He kept his world focused, controlled, and in balance. Annie, Phoebe, and Cupcake had clicked in, and that was that. "They're fine."

"Well, let me know if that changes."

"It won't."

Lucas put his hands on his hips and turned to face him. "You all right? This isn't you. You're not okay with people."

He shrugged. "I'm okay with our family. And a few others. Every person has an energy. A vibe. They either fit me or they don't. Most people don't fit, but Annie and Phoebe do. It won't change."

Lucas grinned. "Well, damn, then. If you're going to keep them, you'll need some more furniture. You have one bed."

"They can have the bed. I'll sleep on the couch."

"The couch is hard as rock and too short."

Jacob narrowed his eyes. "I like my house the way it is."

"I know. We'll take the extra furniture out when they leave. It'll be back the way it was. But you can't have them living with you and not make a few adjustments."

Jacob tensed, resistance building inside him. He didn't like change. He didn't like anyone trying to make him into what he wasn't. "They won't care."

"They won't complain, but that doesn't mean they won't care. It's a mom and a kid on the run. Having some comforts in the house will be good for them." Lucas softened his voice. "Maybe try it, at least, for their sake. If it stresses you out, we can adjust. But remember when you were at your worst. The mattress Brody gave you felt like a gift, even though it was under a bridge. You can give that to these two. Don't you want to do that?"

Hell. Lucas was right. Annie needed to feel safe, and his cold bare floor and barren home wasn't a warm and cozy place for a little girl. Jacob grunted. "I hate it when you make sense."

Lucas laughed. "I know how to get to you, that's all." Lucas patted his shoulder. "I'll grab a few things, and bring them over."

"Get rugs." Jacob watched them play. He didn't remember ever playing like that, not even as a kid. It was foreign to him, but also relaxing. His lawn needed that joy, he realized. Just like fertilizer and water, his lawn needed the positive energy. He thought of his horses. Would they benefit, too? He was going to find out. "No delivery men. This is a high-alert situation. No strangers get onto my land."

"Absolutely. I'll get everything and bring it myself." Lucas pulled out his phone. "I'll have Bella bring some dinner over. Cool? And some groceries. You can't leave Annie and Phoebe unattended to go shopping. Dylan made it clear that you needed to stay with them all the time."

"Okay." Jacob smiled, thinking of how Annie and Phoebe would respond to one of Bella's meals. His sister was a culinary genius. "Yeah, I'm not leaving the property as long as they're here."

"We'll bring stuff in."

"Thanks." He let out a breath and finally took his gaze off his visitors to look at his brother. "I appreciate it."

Lucas nodded. "We're all in this together, bro. Like every other situation. When Dylan gets back, maybe we'll get more info. But for now, we know our job, and we'll work together to keep them safe. You need a break at any point, give me a ring and I'll come stand guard for you."

Jacob nodded. "Thanks." He and his siblings were all great

with guns, self-defense, and anything else that would help keep them safe. He'd trust any of them with Phoebe and Annie's safety—

He suddenly noticed that Annie had stopped playing. She was standing stock still, staring at Lucas. Her body was tense, and her eyes were wide. Phoebe was scrambling to her feet, alarm on her face as she saw the change in her daughter.

Shit. He knew fear when he saw it. "Lucas. Stay there for a sec."

Lucas followed his gaze to Annie, and swore under his breath, also recognizing the fear in the little's girl's stance. "Yeah, okay."

Jacob headed across the lawn toward his charges. "Annie," he said. "Look at me."

Annie was still fixated on Lucas, frozen in fear as Phoebe hurried over and put her hand on her shoulder. "Annie," Phoebe said. "It's okay."

Jacob knelt in front of Annie, blocking her view of Lucas. "Annie," he said softly. "Who do you see across the lawn?"

Her gaze went to him, because his body was blocking her view. "Frank. Is that Frank?"

Anger ripped through Jacob, and he suddenly wanted to find this Frank and kill him. Right then, right there. "No, sweetie. His name is Lucas. He's my brother. One of my best friends. He's a superhero, always taking care of others and protecting them."

Her gaze finally focused on Jacob's face. "Like you? Is he a superhero like you?"

His chest tightened. Him a super hero? Mother of hell. "Yes," he said. "Like me. If you ever need help and I'm not here, you can always ask him. He'll slay dragons for you."

"Like you will?"

He nodded. "Like I will. And your mom."

"I want to slay dragons," she said. "I want to be a big

37

pillow, not a little pillow."

Jacob wasn't sure of the reference, but he nodded. "I can help with that."

She nodded. "Okay."

"You want to meet Lucas?"

"No."

Jacob thought about that for a second. "I think you should."

Her gaze sharpened. "Why?"

"So, you can recognize him when you meet him again. So you'll know the difference between him and Frank. It's important to know who you can trust. What do you think?"

Annie looked at Phoebe, who nodded. "I'd like to meet him," Phoebe said.

"Okay." Annie stepped backward into her mom's arms, and tucked herself against Phoebe's chest.

What a freaking brave kid. He fucking loved her already. "Lucas," he said, raising his voice slightly. "Annie would like to meet you."

"All right." Lucas walked up beside Jacob and went down on his knees, so he was lower than Annie, who was still trying to disappear into Phoebe. "Hi Annie. I'm Jacob's big brother."

She said nothing, staring at him with wide eyes.

Jacob put his arm around Lucas's shoulders. "Did you know that Lucas has a pet unicorn? His name is Rainbow Sparkle." Rainbow Sparkle would suffice, he was pretty sure.

Annie started giggling. "He does not."

"He does."

"I sure do." Lucas played along. "Rainbow Sparkle is a great unicorn. Would you like me to bring him by sometime to meet you?"

Her eyes widened. "Yes. Does he poop sparkles?"

Jacob grinned and winked at Phoebe, who was trying not

to laugh.

"Sometimes, but not always," Lucas said. "You just never know when it comes to Rainbow Sparkle. He's very unpredictable."

"Unicorns usually are," Jacob agreed.

"When can you bring him?" Annie asked.

Jacob raised his brows at his brother, and he knew that his brother, like him, was quickly going through the list of horses currently on the Hart ranch to decide which one would make the best unicorn. Because there was no way they weren't going to bring Annie a real, live unicorn. Lucas needed to figure out which horse, and how to attach a unicorn horn to its forehead. And maybe some sparkles on its rear end.

"I'll need to check his schedule. Hopefully on Saturday," Lucas said. "But today I'm going to go get some furniture for Jacob's house, because he doesn't have much stuff for you and your mom. So, I'll be back and forth with that. How does that sound?"

Annie nodded. "When on Saturday? What time?"

Jacob grinned at Annie's persistence. He understood that. He'd spent a long time trying to control the world around him to make himself feel safe. Now he just retreated from it.

"Noon," Lucas said. "I'll be here at noon."

"Promise?"

He glanced at Jacob, and Jacob knew what he was asking. Jacob nodded, giving him permission to tell Annie about the Hart Promise. The kid needed it.

Lucas focused on Annie. "Our family, the Harts, weren't born from the same mom and dad, but we found each other and made a family when we were kids."

Annie glanced at Phoebe, and her mom hugged her.

"We have a secret handshake just for us. When we do it with each other, it's a Hart promise, one that we'll never break, that we can always count on."

Annie looked fascinated. "Really?"

Jacob and Lucas both nodded.

"Show me," she demanded.

The brothers looked at each other, and then they bumped elbows.

"That's it?" Annie frowned.

"It's perfect because you can do it any time, and you can do it secretly and no one sees it, or you can do it big and obvious to tell the world," Jacob said.

Lucas held up his elbow. "I promise I'll bring Rainbow Sparkle here Saturday at noon. Hart Promise."

Annie grinned and lifted her elbow. She bumped it against Lucas, then collapsed back into Phoebe, giggling.

"Right on." Lucas grinned. "I'm going to go get some furniture. I'll be back later, okay?"

Annie nodded. "I won't be scared."

Phoebe's arms tightened around her, and Jacob saw the emotion in her face.

Lucas stood up slowly so as not to spook Annie, gave them all a wave, and headed back to his truck.

Annie watched him go, and Phoebe looked at Jacob. "You Harts are good people."

Jacob grinned. "My family is fantastic." He didn't get up. "Annie."

She tore her gaze off Lucas to look at him.

"I have a sister named Bella. She's an amazing cook. She's going to come by today and bring us food and groceries." He pulled out his phone, scrolled to a picture of Bella, and held it out to her. "This is what she looks like. If you see her, you don't need to be scared."

Annie took the phone and studied it. Phoebe leaned over her shoulder and studied it as well. "She looks nice."

"She is nice. I have a bunch of other siblings, but I told

them to stay away," he said. "If you two see anyone except Bella and Lucas, tell me right away. Okay?"

Annie looked at him. "Why? Is someone after us?"

Jacob didn't like that Annie was quick to ask that question. A kid her age shouldn't be thinking about men coming after her, but every Hart had had the same childhood, so it was what it was. Jacob looked at Phoebe, and she shook her head once to tell him not to tell Annie what was going on.

He wasn't sure he agreed with that, but he smiled at Annie. "I just don't like most people," he said. "I need to prepare myself if people are visiting to get in the right mood, or I'm super cranky. So I need to know as soon as someone shows up."

Annie nodded. "I don't like everyone either."

Jacob laughed. "Then we're going to be good friends." He leaned forward. "You know what's weird?"

Annie shook her head, staring at him.

"I don't like most people, but I like you and your mom. And Cupcake."

Annie burst into a big smile. "I like you, too."

"Me, too," Phoebe said. "I guess we're all weird, then."

"I love being weird," Jacob said.

"Me, too," Phoebe agreed.

"Me, three!"

Relief rushed through Jacob at Annie's exuberance. They'd pulled her through the stress of the transition and meeting Lucas. The kid was relaxed and happy. He made a promise to himself that he was going to make sure she stayed that way. He was going to keep her safe, both physically and emotionally. Maybe he could save her from a life of shadows in a way he'd never been able to save himself. "Anyone want to go meet the horses?"

"Yes!" Annie clapped her hands. "Where are they?"

He nodded. "Ask your dog."

They all turned to see Cupcake sniffing around the door of the barn and whining. Jacob had been keeping an eye on the dog the whole time they'd been talking, ensuring he didn't wander or get into trouble. That dog was Annie's lifeline, and he was going to make sure the pup was safe.

"Cupcake!" Annie jumped to her feet and raced across the grass toward her puppy.

Jacob started to stand up to go after her, but Phoebe stopped him with her hand to his arm. "Jacob."

He turned to Phoebe, surprised by the softness in her face. "What's up?"

"The way you and your brother transformed her terror into confidence was incredible. Thank you for that."

He grinned and put his hand over hers. "Every Hart was Annie at one point in our lives. We understand that, and we're all hardwired to try to help kids through it."

Phoebe smiled. "Well, then, we're pretty freaking lucky that some sociopath chased us into your life." She leaned forward and gave him an impulsive kiss on the cheek, before hopping to her feet and jogging after her daughter.

Jacob didn't move for a long moment, stunned by her kiss.

It had been nothing more than a fleeting touch, but it had struck him in his gut. He couldn't remember the last time he'd let a woman touch him, let alone kiss him. He didn't trust anyone enough to let them that close, except his family.

But with Phoebe, it was different. He could still feel her lips on his cheek, her hand on his arm, and he loved it. He wanted more. He wanted more from Phoebe, from this family, from life.

But the moment he thought it, Jacob knew he had to let it go.

Phoebe and Annie deserved so much more than the broken fuck-up he was. He had to keep his distance. Keep them safe. From whoever was after them, but also from him.

CHAPTER SIX

THE MAN who Eliana had sent to rescue them might be an angel.

Phoebe stood in the doorway of the first stall with Annie, watching as Jacob greeted his horse, Freedom.

The horse was a massive animal. Pitch black. Scars across his chest and on his front legs. He was a little underweight, his coat still a little dull, but the light in the animal's eyes when Jacob had walked into his stall had been heart-melting.

The horse had practically run across the large, clean bed of shavings and buried his face in Jacob's chest. Jacob had stood there with the horse for a long moment, talking softly, while Annie clung to Phoebe's hand, watching the incredibly intimate moment.

Annie tugged on Phoebe's hand, bouncing in place as she waited for her turn.

She didn't say anything, and neither did Phoebe. She felt like they'd been given a secret glimpse into a private moment.

After a few minutes, Freedom pulled his head away from Jacob's chest and looked over at Phoebe and Annie.

Jacob set his hand on the horse's neck. "Those are my

friends, Annie and Phoebe," he said to the horse. "Would you like to meet them?"

Freedom lowered his head and blew out through his nose.

Jacob nodded. "Annie, come on over."

Annie dropped Phoebe's hand and eased toward him. Phoebe tensed slightly as her daughter neared the enormous animal and held her little hand to his nose. Freedom wasn't wearing a halter, and he could trample her daughter in a split second if he bolted.

A part of Phoebe wanted to grab her daughter and pluck her out of the stall to keep her safe, but she made herself do nothing. The best thing she could do for Annie was to allow her to become brave, to believe in herself, to believe in her power. Which meant Phoebe had to turn off her mama bear and trust Jacob.

Annie patted Freedom's massive nose. "Like velvet," she whispered in awe. "Mommy. His nose is like velvet."

Freedom snorted again, but Annie didn't flinch. "I can see his ribs," she whispered.

Jacob nodded. "Freedom was owned by a man who didn't take care of him, so I brought him here."

Annie looked at Jacob. "Did you kill the man?"

Oh, God.

Jacob didn't flinch at the question. "No. I didn't. That's not my job. I took Freedom and gave him a home and love."

"Is the man going to come after him?"

Again, questions that hit too close to home for the six-year-old. Phoebe hated that Annie still had those fears. She'd have to work harder to help her feel safe.

"No," Jacob said. "I made sure of that. Freedom is safe here. This is his forever home."

Annie suddenly burst into tears and flung her arms around Freedom's neck. Jacob immediately put his hands on Freedom as well, soothing the horse so he didn't panic.

Phoebe didn't know what to do. She wanted to go over and hug her daughter, but something inside her told her to wait. To let Annie have this moment with Freedom.

Freedom turned his head and rested his chin on Annie's lower back, and the two of them stayed like that.

Jacob looked over at Phoebe, and he smiled.

That smile. Her belly fluttered. His smile was so endearing. So warm. So honest. She'd trust this man with her life. With Annie's. Which was good, since that's literally what she was doing, but still.

She'd never met a man like Jacob before.

He was a big man. He was rough and definitely tough. A history that wasn't roses and butterflies. A past that made him not like being around people. And yet, he'd unlocked something in her daughter that Phoebe hadn't been able to unlock herself.

She suddenly hoped that they had to stay here for at least a few days. Every moment here would be healing for Annie. She didn't want to go home yet, even if his home was as barren as he'd claimed.

Annie finally turned around, her cheeks streaked with tears. "What if he comes for Freedom?" she asked Phoebe. "Mommy. What if the man comes for Freedom and tries to take him back? He doesn't want to go back. He told me he wants to stay here."

Were those her daughter's words about herself? She didn't want to leave here either? *Crap.* Phoebe had to keep some kind of boundary up so that leaving here didn't wreck Annie. "This is Freedom's home," she said. "He won't have to leave."

"But what if the man makes him?"

"He can't," Jacob said. "I made sure of it. Freedom is mine by law, and I also have a lot of protection for all the animals on the property."

"What protection? I want to see."

45

Jacob glanced at Phoebe, but didn't offer to show Annie all his security systems. "Lots and lots. It's a very safe place. No one can get in or out without me knowing it and allowing it."

"No one?"

"No one. Every person and every animal on this property is safe and protected at all times." He said it seriously, meeting her daughter's eyes when he said it.

And that, Phoebe realized, was why Eliana had sent her to Jacob's house. Because his need to keep himself and his animals safe had created a haven that would do the same for her baby girl.

Annie took a breath and nodded. "I want to brush him," she said, apparently satisfied with the safety discussion and moving on, as kids did. "Show me how," she demanded.

"Of course," Jacob said agreeably.

While Jacob got to work teaching Annie how to brush Freedom, Phoebe stepped away from the stall and looked around the barn. She could see red blinking lights at various intervals along the ceiling. Motion detectors? In the corners were cameras, carefully set to cover every inch, she was certain. Fire-suppressing sprinkler heads lined the ceiling, ready to come on at the first hint of smoke.

A big safe sat along the far wall, its digital dashboard blinking a green light.

The windows had bars on them. The big door was steel, moving on smooth rollers.

It was like they were inside a vault. A spacious, luxurious vault, but a vault nonetheless.

Safe yes, but a way to live? No. As much as she wanted Annie to get a chance to do whatever healing this place would offer her, Phoebe was restless to get away from alarms, bars on windows, and cameras.

She appreciated her little house more than she ever had

before. This place had a perfect lawn and almost perfect interiors, but it wasn't alive. She could see now what Jacob had been talking about, that people didn't like his home. It wasn't that it was sparse. It was that it was a prison, designed to keep the world out, but that also kept him trapped inside.

The place was sparkling clean. The hose was rolled neatly. The blankets were hung in almost perfect alignment. "Almost" was the key word. There was an energy to the place of trying to control it and make it safe, but enough things were slightly askew and not perfect that she knew that Jacob wasn't a master at making things this neat. He was trying, but a part of him needed to be freer than he was allowing himself to be.

The realization made her relax slightly. Jacob tried for rigid control in every nuance of his life, but in his heart, there was room for flexibility, disorder, and dirt.

Which was why he'd been able to adapt to them, because they weren't neat. They were pure chaos. Maybe he needed their chaos the way Annie needed his strength and his horses. Maybe they were there to help him break out of the prison he lived in, while Annie learned how to be strong and brave.

But what did Phoebe need?

She looked across the barn and saw Cupcake curled up on a pile of blankets in the corner, clearly tuckered out from all the excitement. Her heart filled with peace. All she needed was her daughter's well-being.

That was it.

Whatever it took. Whatever the cost. Whatever the sacrifice.

CHAPTER SEVEN

WHAT A DAY.

Jacob needed a ride badly, space, speed, and fresh air to process everything that had happened, including the threesome that was sleeping in his bedroom. But as he thought it, he realized he couldn't go for a ride.

He couldn't leave them unattended.

No more riding. Sudden panic closed around his chest, fast and tight, and he gripped the edge of the kitchen sink, suddenly oblivious to the stack of dirty dinner dishes he'd been loading in the dishwasher.

Riding was his sanity. It was Freedom's as well. The others would be all right with a few days off, but Freedom needed to run hard. And so did Jacob. He hadn't missed a daily ride in years.

Shit. Shit. Shit. He hadn't thought of that.

He stepped back from the sink and clasped his hands on his head, trying to catch his breath, but it was coming fast and hard. He felt trapped. He needed air. He needed space.

He tossed the dishtowel in the sink and bolted for the front door. He yanked it open and stepped out onto the front porch, breathing deep as the night air filled his lungs and whispered across his face.

The days were warm, but nights were cold in the high desert, and he breathed in the cool air.

He didn't dare take even a step away from the doorway, from those inside, even though the night called to him with all her force. Keeping his body as a barrier to the inside of the house, he stood still, his weight even on either foot, his hands loose by his sides, his hands flexing as he tried to work out the tension in his body.

"Sorry, Freedom," he said. "Tomorrow." But would he go tomorrow? Did he trust anyone else with this family's safety? Their presence trapped him, but at the same time, his gut recoiled at the idea of going more than a few feet from his new charges.

He heard his bedroom door open, but he didn't turn around. He just listened for the sound of trouble, while he continued to experience the Oregon night.

The door closed, and bare feet padded across the new carpet. Bella and Lucas had stopped by while they were all in the barn, so Jacob hadn't had to talk to them, which he was grateful for. He'd acquired food, dinner, furniture, and assorted towels and sheets without having to speak to anyone. Exactly what he'd needed today.

He loved his family, but the hours and hours spent helping Annie had been a lot for him. He hadn't wanted to deal with being social, and he hadn't had to.

Dinner had been quick, with Annie almost falling asleep at the table. He'd taken over cleaning up while his guests and Cupcake had gone off to bed.

His house felt weird. There were two new couches. Rugs. His gym had a mattress in it now that he was planning to sleep on. Extra towels. Daffodils. It had to have been Bella who'd left the vase of daffodils on the coffee table. It felt cluttered. Foreign. Not him.

But when he'd seen Annie curled up on the thick rug with Cupcake, he'd felt good.

It was all right.

He could handle it.

Or so he'd thought.

Right now? He wasn't so sure.

"Jacob?" Phoebe's soft voice brushed across his skin like a caress, and he closed his eyes, breathing in the sensation of her voice on his body.

"Yeah?" He didn't turn around, but this time, it was because he was riveted by her voice, wanting that more than he wanted the fresh air.

"Everything okay outside?"

"Yeah."

She came up beside him, stopping by his left side. She stood quietly beside him. "The night air is magical," she said. "I've always loved being outside at night."

He glanced over at her, surprised. "Really?"

"Yes. I used to climb onto the roof of our apartment building when I was a kid. I'd sleep up there sometimes, until it was safe to go back home."

He considered that. "What made your house unsafe?"

"My birth father," she said matter-of-factly.

Jacob flexed his hands. "Did he hit you?"

"No. He just yelled a lot and hit things. There were a lot of holes in the wall from his fists, and all our kitchen cabinets were broken. I hate men who yell now." She laughed softly. "It's funny, isn't it? Because some guy my mom was married to for a few years was a yeller, I still hate yelling. The brain holds onto all the wrong things sometimes."

"Yeah, it does." He waited for a minute. "What happened to Annie?"

Phoebe didn't answer.

Jacob swore. "Never mind. It's not my business. Sorry."

"No, it's okay." Her voice was quiet. "You need to know, I guess, since it's relevant to our situation. But don't tell anyone. I'm trying to help get her free of her past, and I want people to look at her as my daughter, and not see things she's trying to move beyond."

He looked over at her. "I'll never look at her differently."

Phoebe smiled. "I think I knew that." She paced away from him and sat down on the grass. "I was a client of Eliana's."

Jacob swore again, this time loud enough that Phoebe smiled. "Yes, agreed. It's never a good thing to be a client of hers, but it was fine. I got away, and it's fine."

He wanted to ask more questions, because things like that were never just "fine," but he decided to let her keep talking.

"When Eliana helps a mom, she makes them create a will and designate a guardian for the kids. If they don't have family they trust, she will connect them with a woman in her program, because we already know how to hide, right?"

Oh, hell. He didn't like this at all. "Yeah."

Phoebe laid down on her back, clasped her hands behind her head, and crossed her ankles as she stared up at the night sky. She looked utterly relaxed and at peace, even though she was speaking about tough stuff.

He respected that. A lot. Phoebe was a fighter.

"Well, Annie's mom was in the program, and she didn't have anyone to designate. Eliana asked me if I'd do it, and of course I said yes." She smiled. "I didn't realize that by saying yes, that one day, Eliana would show up at my door at three in the morning with a two-year-old girl and tell me I now had a daughter."

"No shit?"

"Best day of my life. I thought I'd never be a mom, but

then Annie was in my arms, scared, and traumatized, and I knew my life had a purpose." The peace and love in Phoebe's voice seemed to fill the whole night. She laughed softly. "My ex had just died, and I'd been just about to call my parents for the first time in five years, now that I could go back to my life, but then Annie arrived, and I had to choose."

"You chose her over your parents?"

"I had to. She's my daughter." There was a hint of sadness in her voice. "My mom and stepdad are amazing, but they knew when I left my husband that I'd have to disappear. They wanted me safe, so we said our good-byes, and that was it. I couldn't ask them to go with me and give up their whole life, so I just left."

Jacob sat down on the front step, absorbing that. He couldn't imagine walking away from the Harts, never seeing them again. "That takes a hell of a lot of guts." And she'd done it for a kid that wasn't biologically hers. He'd respected her before, but now? No words.

"Life takes guts," she said. "You either live, or you die while you're alive. I believe that someday I'll see my parents again. They'll meet Annie and fall in love with her. In the meantime —" She held her hands up to the sky. "I get a vacation in Oregon on a horse ranch. Does life get better than that?"

He smiled. He could tell she meant it. This woman had a hell of a dark past, and yet, somehow, she was lying on his lawn entirely at peace with the moment. He didn't understand it, but he was a little jealous. "Who is after Annie?"

"I'm guessing her bio dad. That's who her mom was hiding from. I don't have details, but I'm sure Eliana will be in touch when she has actionable info for us."

Jacob rested his forearms across his knees and leaned back against the house. The night was cool, but had enough warmth to feel good. "How dangerous is he?"

"I don't know. Bad, I think."

Jacob thought of the gun he had in his safe in the living room. He hadn't dared wear it on him with Annie around, but he wished he had it now. "And your ex?"

She laughed. "Definitely bad, but he's dead now, so it doesn't matter."

It doesn't matter. It did matter, but he respected her resilience. "What do you do for work?"

"I run the Confident Women's Queendom. It's an online membership program to help women find the confidence to get unstuck and change their lives. It's often focused on changing their personal situation, but it could be anything. Starting a new business, for example. Or just trying to experience their current life in a different way."

He stared at her. "No shit."

She laughed softly. "I'd never lie about my community. I treasure them. I do a Q&A every Monday for an hour, plus I record a new lesson each week. Then sometimes I do longer events. I'd love to do an in-person event, but obviously, that's on hold for now."

"I bet you're an amazing coach."

She laughed. "I like to think I am. I learn more every time I teach a new lesson, so I benefit too. We're all works in progress, you know?"

"Never thought about that. I am who I am. Nothing more complicated than that."

She laughed and rolled onto her side, propping herself up on her elbow to face him. "Jacob, you're so much more complicated than that. You're changing right now, while we're in your house causing chaos. We're always growing."

He could listen to her talk for hours. "I bet the women love your voice."

She paused. "My voice?"

"Yeah. It's like a hug or something. No judgment at all. You don't meet many folks who have zero judgment."

She smiled. "I don't have zero judgment, but it doesn't help my students if I judge them, so I do my best to see value in everything and everyone."

He thought about that. "I'm judgmental as hell."

Her laughter seemed to light up the night. "If people don't fit you, they don't fit. I get that."

The sound of her laughter faded into the echoes of the night. In the distance, he could hear coyotes barking, gathering their kin for their evening excursions. Frogs croaking from a nearby pond. The wind drifting through the trees. His home. His life.

"I like the coyotes," she said. "I can almost understand what they're saying. I think Mom is telling her teenagers that this is their first time on the hunt, and they better follow the rules and stay close. Uncle Bob is telling them to ignore her and have fun."

"And the dad?"

"He's gone ahead to make sure that everything is safe. He's clearing out the land mines, so to speak." Her voice was soft. "Some men are good. My stepdad is a great man. I miss him. I don't actually call him my stepdad. He's my dad. But I wanted to be clear for you."

"Dad, it is." Jacob loved her storytelling about the coyotes. He felt their presence on his rides, their friendship, their protection...and Phoebe felt it too.

The tension usually gripped him so tightly he almost couldn't breathe. Relief always came when he saddled up Freedom and they took off in the night. But tonight, he couldn't leave Phoebe and her daughter unprotected, so he sat on his front steps, breathing the night air into his lungs while Phoebe laid on the grass, staring up at the moon.

As he sat on his steps, scanning the woods for any threats

to the woman on his lawn, Jacob realized that he felt surprisingly relaxed. He knew it was because of the woman sharing the darkness with him.

The woman he hadn't wanted to bring home.

"You know what's weird?" he asked, his voice echoing in the dark outdoors that surrounded them.

"Many things are weird." Phoebe had her hands clasped under her head as a pillow. "What are you thinking of?"

"I want to kiss you."

The night fell silent again with his words, and he instantly regretted saying it. He was their protector, and his job didn't involve kissing her.

Then, she rolled over on the grass to face him again. "Why is that weird? I'm pretty amazing."

Relief rushed through him at the realization she wasn't mad. He relaxed slightly. "It's weird because I'm annoyed by most women. People, in general, as you know."

She flipped him a sassy grin. "If you stick around me long enough, you'll be annoyed. But you'll still want to kiss me. You can feel both ways."

He chuckled, loving her sass. "How would you feel if I kissed you right now?"

Her smile faded. "Oh, that's a super loaded question."

"Keep it simple."

For a long moment, she said nothing.

He waited.

Finally, she answered. "I think that if you got up, walked over here, and laid a hot, melty one on me, I'd probably be pretty pleased about it."

Desire coiled hard and fast in his gut. *She wanted him to kiss her.*

That was great news, because he couldn't stop thinking about it.

But he didn't move.

She didn't move either.

The words just sat in the air.

Because kissing her would be a mistake on a whole lot of levels.

"It's a bad idea," he said, testing the idea out loud. "We've got Annie around, a bad guy hunting you, and I'm about as messed up as a guy can be."

She nodded. "Plus, I haven't kissed a guy in a long time. My ex made me realize that life is better without a man in it."

"And I don't like physical contact with most people," he added.

"And yet, here we sit." She looked over at him, her blue eyes intense. "Together."

"Here we sit," he agreed.

Silence reigned again until she spoke. "How long has it been since you kissed a woman romantically?"

He let out a low whistle as he thought about it. "Years. Maybe ten? You?"

"Years. Maybe seven." She started laughing. "Dear heavens, Jacob. If someone could hear us right now, they'd think we're the biggest messes in the entire world. Between the two of us, we have seventeen years of no physical intimacy. Wow."

Heat simmered in his gut, and he met her gaze. When neither of them looked away, he spoke. "Maybe we should fix that."

She took a breath. "Gotta get back on the horse at some point, or you never ride again."

He slowly stood up. "Riding is life."

She scrambled to her feet. "Riding is adrenaline."

"You ride?" He walked across the porch toward her.

"I used to. Yes. I love to ride." She stood still in the grass, her bare feet hidden by the blades.

"My soul aches when I don't ride. You guys want to ride

with me tomorrow?" He neared her and stopped just in front of her.

"Yes," she whispered, her face raised to him. "I don't think Annie has ever ridden before."

"She'll ride with me. I'll keep her safe." His heart was racing now. Phoebe was so close. Not backing away. His need to kiss her was burning like wildfire through his veins. "I want to kiss you so fucking much."

"Do it."

"What if I do it, and it's hell?"

She burst out laughing so hard that she had to put her hand on his chest to keep her balance. "Oh, God, that's one of the funniest things I've ever heard. Thank you for that. All the tension is gone."

He didn't laugh. "I meant it."

"I know you did." She beamed up at him. "That's what was priceless. Kissing me won't be hell. There's literally no chance of it. Do you want me to kiss you, then? I feel confident that my soul won't be incinerated by demon fire if I do."

He was too tense to laugh at her joke.

Her smile faded, and her touch softened on his chest. "It's okay, Jacob. Will you trust me?"

He nodded.

"Close your eyes."

"Gotta watch for the enemy."

"For one moment. That's all."

He scanned their environment carefully, checking every sight and sound before returning his gaze to her. "Okay."

She smiled, then put her hands on his cheeks and rose onto her tiptoes. "Come to me, you big lug."

His heart was racing, but he let her bring him down to her. He kept his gaze on the twinkle in her eye, the sparkle in her smile, letting her delight chase away the tension trying to grip him.

Phoebe leaned in, and he closed his eyes, dropping his shields a split second before she kissed him.

The moment her mouth touched his, everything inside him shattered. All the noise. All the tension. A lifetime of pain and control and cold. It just exploded in a violent cascade of emotion and sensation.

She pulled back quickly, her hand still on his face, her gaze searching his. "You okay?"

He was wordless. His whole life, he'd thought there was something wrong with him because he didn't want to be touched, because he didn't like being intimate, because it made him feel trapped and restless and out of control.

But right now, with Phoebe's hands on his face and her kiss still lingering on his mouth, he knew that he'd found what he was meant to find.

With a low whisper of reverence, he slid his hand under her jaw and leaned in, taking her mouth in his, in the kiss that his soul had been waiting for him to find.

Phoebe slid her arms around his neck, her body leaning into his as she kissed him back. The kiss was surreal. Electric. Life. Desire awoke in him with a fierce howl, ripping through his control. He angled his head, deepening the kiss, sliding his hands over the curve of her ass.

Her body felt incredible beneath his hands. The curve of a woman. This woman. Her hips. Her lower back. Her ass. Her shoulder blades. He moved his hands all around, tracing the contours of her body, memorizing the curves, the lines, the softness.

Phoebe laughed quietly, breaking the kiss. "Your hands feel desperate on me."

He paused his hand on her hips, and took a breath. "Sorry."

"No." She touched his jaw. "Never apologize for who you are. If someone doesn't get it, it's on them, not you. But in this particular case, I get it, so that's even more reason not to apologize."

He closed his eyes and rested his forehead against hers. "I am completely out of my depth with you."

She rested her hands on his hips, mimicking how he was holding hers. "I feel that way as well," she said. "I fight for the independence of women. I taught myself to stand on my own, to never need a man or intimacy. I'm trying to teach Annie that strength. And yet, with you, I just want to abandon all of that and lose myself in you."

He kissed her forehead and pulled her against him. She came willingly, wrapping her arms around his waist as she rested her cheek against his chest. "You're not abandoning all that," he said. "Allowing yourself joy doesn't make you weak."

"And you know this how?"

"Because my horses are my joy. I live and breathe them. Riding them makes me feel like the greatest, luckiest man on this earth. I lean into that joy, because it makes me able to handle the rest of my life better. The horses make me able to lean into my family, who I love with all of my soul."

"Huh."

He laughed softly and rested his chin on Phoebe's head, continuing to scan their surroundings even as he held her and drank in the feel of her body against his. She was right. He had been desperate when he'd first touched her, but now he felt serenity. Calmness. Peace.

She wasn't going anywhere, and somehow, his soul understood that.

He had time. Which was good, because he needed it.

CHAPTER EIGHT

HOURS LATER, Jacob was dozing on a chair outside their door with his gun when his phone rang, jerking him awake. He answered it immediately. "Dylan. What's the deal with the threat against Phoebe and Annie? I need information. How immediate is the threat? What level?"

He hadn't been able to sleep in the gym.

He'd needed to be close to them, where he could be the final line of defense if someone got through everything he had set up.

Dylan didn't try for the small talk. "I just got off the phone with Eliana. The guy's name is Frank Robinson. He was in jail for almost killing Annie's mom. Big domestic violence situation. Eliana thinks that Annie's mom was killed in a hit that Frank called in from prison, but she has no proof."

Jacob leaned his head back against the wall. "Fuck."

"He got out yesterday, and she's pretty sure that he's coming for Annie. She thinks he somehow found out where Annie was, so I'm setting up a team at Phoebe's house to wait for him. We'll try to get him there."

Jacob banged his head against the wall lightly as tension slammed into his gut. It had been a long time since he'd needed to be on this level of alert. "Is there any way that he can track her here?"

"No. Unless he has Eliana's phone tapped, which is impossible. I check her systems constantly. All you need to do is keep them there. They're off the radar at your place, and as long as they stay there, he won't find them."

"But he found out where Annie was. I assume that info was also protected?"

"Yeah, we're working on finding that leak," Dylan said. "We'll find it. But no one knows Phoebe is there except Eliana, and the family. Nothing has been in writing on her computer or phone. Unless her phone is tapped, no one will know."

Jacob considered that. "How confident of that are you?"

Dylan sighed. "I wish I could say one hundred percent but until I figure out how he got Annie's location, I'm instructing you to stay alert. How sure are you that no one followed you?"

"Lucas was following me. We both watched. Saw no one."

"All right. Keep vigilant, but I think the threat is low at your place. Hopefully we'll find him soon."

"And do what? He's out of prison. He can keep looking until he finds them. Months. Years." He thought of Annie and Phoebe. "It's not good for them to have to live in hiding. That little girl needs to be normal."

Dylan paused, as if he were surprised by Jacob's comment. "Um, yeah. She does. You okay with her there or want me to get someone to grab them?"

"No. I have them." He snapped his response, quicker than he meant.

Dylan paused again. "It's like that, then, is it?"

"Like what?"

"They'll have to go home," Dylan said gently. "When this is over. They're going to leave."

Jacob didn't like that warning. "You don't know what they'll do," he retorted. "Why would they go back? Maybe they'll find something better. They like nice grass, and they don't have nice grass at their house."

"Grass?"

"My lawn. They made snow angels in it."

Another pause, then Dylan swore. "You sure about this?"

"About what?"

"Keeping them."

"I didn't say anything about keeping them."

"You feel it, though."

"I'm just keeping them safe. You asked me to do a job, and I'm doing it." The words felt like a lie. Because they were a lie. The little trio were already under his skin, and he liked them there.

Dylan sighed. "Jacob, I love the shit out of you. You know that. I think you're a fucking amazing human being. But not everyone will get you. I don't want you to be hurt."

"Hurt?" Jacob laughed softly. "*Hurt?* I'm not afraid of hurt, Dylan. You know that. I'm not afraid of anything."

"You're afraid of losing those you love," Dylan said softly. "You're terrified of dying before you feel whole again."

Jacob closed his eyes. "Fuck."

"We all feel that way," Dylan said. "I know you skate the edge, Jacob. If you get attached to them and they leave, it might put you over. Remember last time?"

"I remember." Last time. The time when he first found the Harts. He hadn't let himself be vulnerable since then. He remembered. Hell, he remembered. "It won't happen again."

"Are you sure?"

"Yeah." But as he said it, doubt cluttered his words. What

if he was wrong? What if it happened again? "I have my shit together now."

"I know, and we want it to stay that way, because we love you."

"I know." Jacob lightly banged his head against the door. "I'll stay focused on keeping them safe. That's it."

"All right. I'm going to text you a photo of Frank, so you'll know what he looks like. I'll call when I find out more. Heading to Phoebe's with a team now to wait for him. Eliana will call me if she finds out anything. She doesn't want to call you or Phoebe directly, just in case her phone is somehow being bugged."

"Got it." He hung up and leaned forward, bracing his arms on his thighs. Keeping Phoebe, Annie, and Cupcake? He wasn't trying to keep them...was he?

The answer popped into his head immediately.

Yeah. He was. He definitely wanted to keep them.

The thought made him smile. Damn, it felt good to care about someone, to be interested in someone, to want to share his space with another human being.

And if they left?

The thought made darkness surge toward him so fast that he couldn't breathe for a second. *Shit.*

He couldn't worry about that right now. Worrying was just a way of imagining a future he didn't want. His only job was to stay in the present. Keep them safe. Explore what it was like to have them in his space, in his life.

See if they still made him want to live after another day. And then another. And then another.

To see.

Nothing else.

At all.

Except keeping them all alive.

Shit. There was that.

CHAPTER NINE

HE'D SLEPT on the floor.

Phoebe smiled at the sight of the large, rough man sprawled on the floor in front of her door. Jacob was using a sweatshirt for a pillow, but his body was on the hardwood floor. There was a chair in the hall, and it looked like he'd tried to stay awake in the chair and then had finally dozed off.

She pulled the door shut and crouched next to him, studying him. His face was so much younger when he was asleep. The lines of tension were gone, and the muscles in his face were relaxed. She put her hand on his shoulder, feeling the heat from his body under her touch.

How incredibly sweet that he'd slept outside their door all night.

Yes, it also was a little concerning. Were they in so much danger that he needed to sleep that close? That his mattress down the hall wasn't close enough? Her smile faded at the thought, and fear slithered through her belly.

No.

She wouldn't live in fear. She couldn't go back to the emotional place that had nearly killed her. The absolute terror haunting her at every turn, certain that this time, when she walked around a corner, he'd be there, with a gun and a smile, ready to finally kill her.

That terror had died with her ex, and she didn't, couldn't go back to that way of living.

She had to be normal. Live normally. Let Annie grow up normally.

She patted Jacob's shoulder, and his eyes snapped open and he bolted upright. "What's wrong?"

Shoot. She hadn't meant to alarm him. "Nothing. Sorry. I didn't mean to wake you. You just looked so adorable sleeping there that I had to pat you. It's like when Cupcake is sleeping, and I just can't keep my hands off him."

Jacob's sleepy eyes regarded her as he ran his hand through his hair. "I'm like a puppy?"

"You're a complex man at night. A cute puppy the next morning. It's hard to keep up." His hair was mussed up, and her fingers itched to smooth it back. "Thanks for looking out for us."

He yawned. "Didn't mean to fall asleep."

"Heaven forbid you're human," she teased. "What good are you to us if you're too tired to fight for our honor when the moment comes?"

He cocked a brow. "You can defend your own honor. I'll just take care of your life."

She smiled. "This is true. We can take care of ourselves. I appreciate you noticing."

He smiled back, and before she realized what he was doing, he reached out and tucked a stray lock of hair behind her ear. "Morning."

And just like that, the heated, smushy tension of last night was back in her belly. "Hi."

They were so close to each other. All they had to do was lean in the tiniest bit and...

He leaned in.

And kissed her.

Yes.

She closed her eyes, basking in the feel of his mouth on hers. Last night, she'd been the initiator, and there was something so incredibly hot about the fact that he'd initiated this morning, when she still had bedhead and had barely managed to get dressed.

He slid his hand behind her neck, deepening the kiss, owning the kiss, seducing her with a kiss that was so full of emotion and need that it seemed to coil right through her belly and explode out through every cell in her body.

They were both on the floor, and he locked his hands around her hips, and pulled her toward him, right onto his lap. She sucked in her breath as she wrapped her legs around his hips, and her arms around his neck.

His hands were supporting her lower back, drawing her closer against him as he kissed her. In the bright light of morning, the desire was just as strong as it had been in the romantic darkness of the outdoors.

She couldn't believe how amazing it felt to be on Jacob's lap, to feel the warmth of his body heating her. He felt so strong, so present, so *human*. She searched his face, and he didn't look away. "What is this?" she whispered.

"It's called intimacy. Or making out. Or sexy times. Want me to get a Thesaurus? There are a lot of terms for it."

She laughed softly. "I meant, what's the deal with this attraction? We've both been doing just fine with the celibacy route for a long time, and suddenly, hours after we meet, we're making out on the hallway floor before we even manage to get breakfast."

"Making out on an empty stomach is considered very romantic in certain European countries."

She giggled and pushed at his chest. "Why do you need to be funny as well?"

"Because I'm that guy." His hands were still on her hips, his fingers tracing little circles on them.

"What guy is that?"

"The guy everyone wants to date, but no one can because I don't like people." As he said it, he pulled her in and kissed her again, a melty, swoon-worthy kiss that made him into a complete liar.

Being in Jacob's arms was amazing. It made her want him, more, so much more, so desperately. She'd been so happy being alone, but suddenly, that was gone, and all she wanted was *him*.

Which was a very dangerous place to be.

There was a whine behind her and a scratch at the door, and they both stopped. "Cupcake wants to go out," he said.

"I know." Relief rushed through her at the interruption. She was getting in too fast and too far with Jacob, and she needed to stop before she lost herself. Cupcake barked and scratched again, and she pulled back. "He's going to wake Annie. I need to let him out."

She scrambled off his lap and opened the door.

Cupcake slipped out and pounced on Jacob, while Phoebe peeked in on her daughter. Annie was sprawled on her back, her arms flung wide, her feet kicked free of the covers. It was the position of confidence, and her heart turned over. Despite having to go on the run, Annie wasn't scared. *Yes.* "We're making progress, baby," she whispered. "I love you."

She quietly pulled the door shut, then turned to see Cupcake sitting quietly at Jacob's feet, his tail wagging wildly while Jacob patted him. "How do you do that?"

"I'm good with animals. Horses. Dogs."

"I can see that." Her heart melted a little bit at the gentle tones Jacob was using with Cupcake. He was such a big man, but he had such a soft side.

Damn. She needed to stay focused. "What's a good place for me to set up for my calls?"

He looked up. "Calls?"

She nodded. "I have my Monday video coaching today with my community."

"You're not going online," he said flatly.

Phoebe raised her brows. "Of course I'm going online. I have women counting on me."

"No." He stood up. "It's not safe. You can be tracked."

She bristled a bit at his hardline stance. "I have great security. I'll be fine."

He narrowed his eyes. "You're willing to risk Annie?"

"What?" Sudden anger flooded her. "I would never risk her. How can you even say that? What's wrong with you?"

"There's no way to be online and be untraceable—"

"Yes, there is. I've been doing it for years. My ex never found me, and no one has found Annie. I paid a lot of money, more than I had at the time, to get set up so I could teach safely."

"What kind of security? A firewall? Because that's not enough. You can be tracked easily—"

"I have extensive security built into my computer and my entire set up at home. I was assuming you had security here as well, given what I saw in the barn. Am I wrong?"

"It hasn't been tested with the life of a six-year-old."

His words cut at her, right in her heart. "For your information," she snapped. "I've given up *everything* to be Annie's mom. She's my entire world, and I'd never risk her. But she deserves a life of financial security, and the example of a mom who can thrive in a career, make a difference in the world, and still be safe. I do her no favors if I cower and teach her that that's all women can do."

Jacob stared at her silently, clearly digesting what she'd said.

She poked him in his muscular chest. "I will keep my daughter safe, and I will continue my business. You can help or not help. It's your choice."

"I'm not putting you in danger."

"I'm not putting her in danger either."

He glared at her.

She pulled back her shoulders. "Do not stand in my way, Jacob. Until you've spent time crouched in a closet to hide from the man you're married to so that he can't find you to kill you, you don't get to judge me. Until you've been so broke that you can't afford to leave the bastard, you don't get to hold me back from earning money. I will *never* be trapped by a lack of money or power again, and I won't let Annie be trapped either."

Emotion flickered across his face. "I understand more than you would believe."

"You're not a woman, so it's not the same."

"I was a boy. A boy without power or money. I do understand."

His words took all the anger out of her with a whoosh. She didn't know what to say. "Jacob. I didn't know."

"I didn't tell you, so that makes sense. Unless you're psychic?"

"Not psychic."

"Then you're off the hook. I have money. What do you want? How much do you need? I can set her up for life."

Phoebe stared at him, stunned by the offer. "I don't want your money." Of course, a part of her wanted to cheer and give him her account number to wire whatever he wanted into it. But she knew better.

"Why not? It's great money. Works as well as anyone else's money."

"No, it's not that. It's just that charity doesn't empower me or her. It doesn't teach her that she can carve her own path, no matter what happens. It doesn't teach her that she doesn't need to rely on anyone, ever, for anything."

"It's not charity. It's giving you both the freedom to live how you want."

"How I want to live is to have a career that changes women's lives and empowers me. Not to hide in fear in a prison, even one as beautiful as the prison you've made for yourself."

He frowned. "I don't live in a prison."

Phoebe sighed. "You do, Jacob. Look around you. You've used the excuse of needing to be safe to trap yourself. It's not living, Jacob."

His jaw flexed. "It's keeping you safe."

"It is," she agreed, "And I appreciate that. But never at the cost of living." She could see from his expression that he didn't understand. "Never mind. But I do need to do my class today. What can we do to make that happen?"

He looked like he wanted to throttle her. "It's not safe."

The man was intractable, but she was used to negotiating with an intractable six-year-old, so the odds were in her favor. "Isn't Dylan a security guy?" She knew he was. He'd helped set her up originally, through Eliana.

He narrowed his eyes. "Yes."

"Let's ask him. See what he says." She paused. "This is really important to me, Jacob. It matters."

He stared at her, then swore. "I'll call him. But if he says no, then you need to let it go. You would hate yourself for life if you made a choice that resulted in harm to Annie." His voice was rough. "Trust me on that one, Phoebe. Nothing is worth that. Not even your soul."

Her heart turned over for his pain. He'd made that mistake. She could feel it in every word he spoke. Who had he lost? Who did he blame himself for? "Not your fault," she said softly. "Whatever it was, it wasn't your fault."

His eyes became haunted. "It was. And I will always have to live with that. Don't make that mistake, Phoebe. Just don't."

"I won't." He was right. She knew that. But she also knew that hiding wasn't the answer. Hiding made the danger get bigger and bigger, as if it could feed on her fear. "I will keep her safe," she said. "I will. We will," she added, because she could sense he needed it. "Together, we will keep Annie safe... and thriving. Brave. Capable. Able to take care of herself if we aren't here every minute of her life."

Jacob stared at her, and she could feel the tension radiating through his body. For a man who claimed not to like people, his need to keep her and Annie safe belied his claims. He pulled out his phone and put it on speaker.

His brother answered immediately. "Everything okay?"

"Yeah. Phoebe needs to get online to teach a class to her remote students. Assuming Annie's dad has access to the highest level and best technology available to track her, which we have to assume, can she do it safely from my house?"

"Yep. No problem. It's good."

Phoebe grinned as Jacob's eyes narrowed. "You'd risk a six-year-old's life on that answer?" he asked.

"Jacob. I'd risk *your* life on that answer. I set up your place to protect you from the same threat level. Everyone in the family is set up to that level of protection. Phoebe? You there?"

Jacob handed her the phone. "Yep."

"Eliana gave you the computer you have now, right?"

"Yes, she did."

"Then it has all the software I created for her to make sure her clients are safe. Between the two of you, you guys are good to go." He paused. "What kind of class do you teach, Phoebe?"

"I have an online community in which I coach women to develop the confidence they need to make whatever changes in their lives they want to make."

"Damn. Do you work with Eliana on that? Most of her clients could benefit from that."

Wow. The idea made electricity leap through her. "I don't think Eliana knows what I do. I started the community after I went into hiding the first time."

"She would love that."

"I would love that, too. Helping women like me? That would be amazing."

"I'll run it by her next time I talk to her. Maybe after this is over, you guys can connect. Right now, she doesn't want to talk to you directly in case someone has tapped her phone, but I'll pass the word on."

"Sounds great! Thanks." Phoebe hung up the phone and handed it back to Jacob. "That would be so fulfilling! I mean, I help women like that a lot, but to actually work directly with Eliana's clients would be fantastic. I know what they're dealing with. I've been there."

Jacob was frowning at her.

She put her hands on her hips. "What? You can't still be worried? Dylan said he'd trust your life with what he set up."

"I know." Jacob took a breath and ran his hand through his hair. "I would still prefer you not do it."

His tension was palpable, and it was making her anxious. "Jacob," she said softly. "I don't know what happened in your past, but I need you to believe in your ability to keep us safe. I need to do this. Dylan chose you for a reason. Can you keep us safe? If I were to go online and this guy finds us, can you keep us safe?"

His jaw flexed, and for a long time, he didn't answer. Then finally, he nodded. "I can. Yeah."

She felt his hesitation. "But...?"

"I need to carry a gun. I don't want to do that with Annie around. I don't want to scare her or endanger her."

"I have four guns at home. I have a safe under my bed, one in my office, and one in the kitchen. I also have one in the car. Eliana made me learn how to shoot and made me have the guns. Because no relocation can be completely secure, she makes sure all her clients can defend themselves if they have to."

Regret flickered through Jacob's eyes. "I don't like that you and Annie have to live like that."

She sighed. "Honestly, I don't either. I got rid of all my guns after my ex died, but when Eliana showed up on my doorstep with Annie, she had more guns for me. But my point is that if you need to carry a gun to keep us safe, then please, carry a gun. I didn't bring any with me when you picked us up."

He stared at her for a long time, then turned and silently walked across the living room to a safe in the corner. He opened it with his handprint, then pulled out a shoulder holster and a gun. He put them on, then put a jacket on before turning to face her.

His jaw was hard, his eyes like flint. Putting on that gun had flipped a switch in Jacob.

CHAPTER TEN

SHE COULD FEEL his energy had shifted. His nerves were strung taut, and he was on edge. Absolutely focused on safety and defense.

She sighed. "We're not good for you, are we? We're making you go to a place you don't want to be."

Jacob held up his hand to silence her, then walked across the living room. He slipped his hand under her chin. "You make me go to a place I fucking love." Then he kissed her.

The kiss was pure intensity, as if he were channeling all the fierceness echoing through him into the kiss. Not at her, but with her. Into her. His muscles were taut and hard, his body looming over her like a human shield. He had flipped a switch, but she could tell now it was raw, untamed, unapologetic power. The man she'd first met had been contained and controlled, but the man kissing her was pure fire and heat, and power.

She might not want to get tangled up with him, or any man, but there was no chance of her summoning any resistance to the intensity pouring through him. But before she could wrap her arms around his neck and lean into him, he released her and stepped back.

She narrowed her eyes as she watched him. "You're so much more on edge than you were," she said. "How is that good for you?"

He just shook his head. "It's complicated. What time is your class?"

Not the most subtle change of subject she'd ever experienced, but she decided to let him redirect her. What made a man as strong and tough as Jacob be so tense? What made a man like him lock himself in a prison of his own making? Whatever his past was, it still held him in a very tight grip, and she and Annie had made his past come alive for him again, somehow.

She didn't like that they'd done that to him. Not at all. "Five o'clock."

He nodded. "We'll be sure to be back in plenty of time."

"From what?"

"You and Annie want to go for a ride today?" he asked. "Freedom needs a run. Annie can ride with me. I'll keep her safe."

The idea of a horse ride sounded like a dream. "I'd love that. And I'd love for her to have that experience."

He flashed her a grin. "Great." He stretched his shoulders. "I need to go feed the horses, so as soon as Annie's up, we need to head over there so I can take care of them."

"We'll be okay in the house. You can go to the barn."

"Can't. Not when we're on high alert. We're sticking together." At that moment, Cupcake barked at the front door and wagged his tail. "Even you, puppy." He strode to the door and opened it for Cupcake, but stood in the open door, so he could watch the dog and the inside at the same time.

His attention to Phoebe and Annie was absolute. It felt

good, but at the same time, Phoebe craved her freedom and her independence. She didn't want to be under lockdown.

Jacob was watching her. "What's wrong?"

She stretched her arms over her head. "Just feeling restless here. I'm used to my independence and freedom."

"Me, too."

She felt the truth of his words and sighed. This wasn't her home. It was his, and she knew they were intruding. But they were doing the best...

"Hey."

She looked over at him as she walked toward the kitchen to start breakfast. "What?"

"I meant it when I said I like what you make me become."

"And what is that?"

"More."

She raised her eyebrows as she opened the fridge. "More what?"

He shrugged. "It's complicated. And it's not easy for me. But it's good."

She leaned on the door of the fridge, watching him as he stood in the doorway, guarding her dog and her kid at the same time. He was tall and muscled. A raw, untapped force of male power. "Since about two weeks after I married my ex-husband, I've been uncomfortable around men. I see all of them as a possible threat. I'm good with a gun now, and I work out, but pound for pound, I know I'd be in trouble if any man decided to come after me."

Jacob turned toward her, listening. His jaw was hard.

"I was scared I was going to teach Annie to be afraid of all men. I want her to be able to live a normal life, but I live in such fear that it's been difficult. That's why I started teaching the confidence class. Because I needed to learn it as well."

He propped his shoulder against the doorframe, giving

her his full attention, with the exception of the frequent glances to check on Cupcake's safety. "I'd never hurt you."

She smiled. "That was my point. I believe I am safe with you. I believe Annie is safe with you. And that is a feeling I haven't had around a man in a very long time. I don't know that it will translate to other men, but it's a huge, welcome step for me. Thank you."

"Thanks for saying that." He smiled, the most adorable, charming, and honest smile she'd seen in a long time. It kind of melted her heart a little bit, this tough guy smiling like that. "I'm pretty fucked up," he admitted, "but there's one thing I'd never, ever do is hurt someone or something."

"Unless they were trying to kill me."

"Yes." He flashed her a resigned grin. "There are exceptions to every rule," he agreed. "But you need to know that every person in my family can be trusted as well." He paused. "You and Annie need to meet them. If anything ever happened to me, you need to feel comfortable going to them for help."

Sudden panic hit her. "What's going to happen to you?" She felt safe for the first time in forever. She wasn't ready to give that up. She wasn't ready to give *him* up.

"Nothing." He held up his hand. "It's theoretical. Just good to have a backup plan. I want you to meet more people in my family."

Panic nagged in her belly. "I'm very proud of the fact I ran out that door of my house with you," she admitted. "But I'm not really feeling a burning need to meet more people. I have trouble trusting people now. I don't want to meet a bunch of people."

"I know. That's why you need to. I'm going to ask Bella and Lucas to go on the ride with us today. I want the extra protection," he added, before she could argue. "It'll be good for you."

She narrowed her eyes. "You're very bossy."

He laughed softly. "I'm good for you, Phoebe. Roll with it." He gestured at the suitcases in the corner, and the stuffed animals and dog toys strewn about his living room. "Like you're good for me."

"Because you don't like people, so we're forcing you to be social and messy?"

"Among other reasons, yeah." He paused, an undertone to his words that made heat pool in her belly.

"Again," she said. "You did it again. You made that little comment that made me think of nakedness and kisses with you."

He flashed her a grin. "I did it on purpose that time. You just look so darned appealing leaning on the fridge door like that. I want to go over there, haul you into my arms, and kiss you until we both forget why we should stop."

"Why should we stop?" Her question was a little breathier than she meant.

His eyes darkened. "Lot of reasons."

"Like what?" She couldn't think of a single one right now, other than the obvious one that Annie could walk out at any moment.

"I'm a fuck up."

"So?"

His eyes became darker. "That's it," he said. "That's the only reason I have. If it's not enough..." he shrugged. "Then we're going to have to get naked as soon as Annie's asleep tonight."

Her heart started racing. "No."

"Why not? Because I couldn't come up with a reason."

She let out her breath. "Because it scares me."

He didn't release his gaze. "All the more reason," he said softly. "It scares the hell out of me, too."

"Really?"

He nodded.

"Why?"

He glanced outside at the dog again, and she knew he wanted to come to her. But he didn't. He stayed where he was needed to keep everyone safe. "It scares me because I have worked hard to isolate myself, aside from my family. I don't want to want or need anyone."

"Right? I completely agree. It's a good way to live."

"That's what I always thought. But it feels so damn good to want you. I fucking love that you make me want you, that you make me scared, that you make me softer, and, at the same time, make me so tense I feel like my neck's going to snap."

Oh, Lordy. "That's a lot."

"It's only the start." He paused. "I hope."

There was so much tension between them that she felt like she would get her hand stuck in it if she reached out to the air in front of her. "What does that mean?"

He paused, his gaze surveying her. "I think I'll save the explanation for later."

"How about now?" The start of what? What was he thinking? "You aren't looking past this time are you? That we could keep going, even though we haven't even started yet?"

He glanced outside to look at the dog, then slowly returned his gaze to her.

He said nothing.

"Jacob? What did you mean?"

"Not sure you want to know."

"I do." Did she? Her heart was racing so fast that maybe she didn't want to know. But she did. If she fell for him, she wanted to know if it would be safe. Was he thinking of more? Would he be there with his hands out to catch her if she let herself go? If her heart took her to places she didn't want to go?

"I think," he said slowly, clearly weighing his words, "that you and I—"

At that moment, Annie opened the bedroom door, rubbing her eyes. "Mommy. I'm hungry."

Disappointment flooded Phoebe, and she felt like screaming. Seriously? Jacob flashed her a grin, looking irritatingly satisfied with the interruption.

Men. So annoying.

Phoebe made a face at him then turned to her daughter, who was shuffling down the hall. "Hey, baby. How about waffles for breakfast?"

She nodded. "Waffles are good---" Then she saw Jacob in the doorway, and she brightened. "Uncle Jacob! You're still here!"

He gave Annie his full attention. "I'm always here. I live here."

"Yay!" She bounded across the living room, rushed right past him, and ran outside, shrieking with delight as she ran into the yard and called her dog.

Jacob moved away from the door and onto the porch, his attention fully outside now, watching Annie. "You can make breakfast," he said to Phoebe. "I've got watch duty."

As Phoebe watched Jacob move off the porch and into the yard, she could see Annie running around with Cupcake, laughing and delighting in the morning. She suddenly felt a huge weight slither off her shoulders, a shadow she hadn't even noticed until it dissolved. Suddenly, she felt overwhelmed. Tears filled her eyes and she sat down on the kitchen floor, hugging her knees.

Ever since Annie had arrived, Phoebe had needed to be one hundred percent "on" at all times, always the only line of defense and stability Annie had. She was a single mom of a traumatized, endangered kid, which meant *everything* was always on her shoulders.

But suddenly, for the first time in years, she could sit on the floor in the kitchen and let go. She could hear Annie and Jacob shouting outside, laughter in their voices.

Annie was safe and happy, and Phoebe didn't have to be the one to make it happen. Even when Annie was at school, Phoebe was always ready for the call that she needed to pick her daughter up. But right now, in this moment, Jacob was handling it.

She bowed her head, resting her forehead on her knees, letting the tears slide down her cheeks. Tears of relief. Of exhaustion. Of gratitude. *Thank you, Jacob*, she whispered.

For this moment. This one little moment of not having to be the one holding the entire world together. Of simply sitting on the floor, taking care of no one but herself.

A gift. One she hadn't even realized she needed. She leaned her head back and took a shuddering breath. "God, this feels good," she whispered.

The moment she did, guilt shot through her. Was she a bad mom to cherish a moment to herself? Probably, but she was all Annie had, so she would have to be enough. And was it so wrong to bask in a few minutes of help?

No, she realized. Because Annie needed a bigger world than just her mom. Being outside with different adults was good for her. It would help make her bolder and braver, and that was what Annie wanted for her.

That thought made her smile ironically. Jacob would be laughing at her, because it was exactly what he'd said to her moments ago, that it would be good for Phoebe to be outside with different people.

She supposed he was correct that they needed to meet Lucas and Bella. If he trusted them, she could, too. Theoretically at least, but convincing her brain of that fact might be a little bit more of a challenge.

She grabbed the counter and pulled herself to her feet,

peeking out the window. The trio had several tennis balls, and Annie and Jacob were playing catch, while Cupcake raced after every dropped ball. Annie was fully focused on Jacob, laughing with delight at his antics. Her daughter's trust of Jacob was absolute, and it made Phoebe want to cry with joy.

Their joyful bond was real and visceral, and anyone watching would probably assume that Jacob was Annie's dad.

Annie's dad. With a whole family of siblings that Jacob said were as trustworthy as he was.

An idea popped into Phoebe's mind as she watched them play, an idea that was brilliant and ridiculous at the same time. Jacob seemed to feel her attention, and he looked over at her. He pointed to her, and Annie spun around and waved at Phoebe.

Phoebe waved, leaning on the window as Jacob jogged after Annie as she raced across the grass. Never letting her get far. Always watching Annie, but his gaze also continuously scanned their surroundings, always watching and aware of all possible threats at all times.

They were safe with Jacob, Phoebe realized. Truly safe, both physically and emotionally. She was right to trust him, and it felt amazing.

"Mom!" Annie put her hands on her hips. "I'm hungry! Is breakfast ready?"

Right. Food. Normal things that felt good to be able to focus on. "I'm working on it!" She waved at them both, then went back to the kitchen, humming cheerfully to herself as she got breakfast together.

When she was a little girl in her messed-up home life, this was how she'd always imagined life would be when she grew up. A little family with laughter, puppies, and safety, in a beautiful home with a gorgeous lawn, freedom, and love.

Ironic that the first time she experienced it was when

they were in hiding from a sociopath, but she'd take what she could get, and appreciate every moment.

Because she knew all too well that it could end at any second.

But right now, she had it, and she was going to do her best to let Annie and herself experience it fully, for whatever it was, or whatever it could be.

CHAPTER ELEVEN

"IT'S SO great to have another woman around!" Bella Hart rode up next to Phoebe a few hours later. Bella was wearing a pink cowboy hat, and her horse was a gray, dappled mare who was energetic and a little crazy. "You're doing great!"

Phoebe smiled at Jacob's sister. The friendly woman had already broken down Phoebe's defenses in the hour they'd all been out riding. Bella was warm, funny, and there was a wisdom and understanding in her eyes that made Phoebe pretty certain that Bella had some shadows in her past that weren't too dissimilar from her own. "Thanks." She patted the neck of her horse, Ghost. "He's being nice and calm."

"Of course he is. Jacob would never let you on a horse that wouldn't take care of you." Bella reined in her horse to keep pace with Phoebe. Ahead of them were Jacob and Lucas. Annie was riding with Jacob, sitting in front of him in the saddle, and Cupcake was taking a break on a little dog sidecar that Jacob had rigged up on Lucas's horse. The two men were chatting easily, making Annie giggle, but Phoebe could see the way they both continued to scan their surroundings.

"He's a good man, isn't he?" Phoebe said.

Bella raised her brows. "Jacob? Yeah."

Phoebe heard the undertone in Bella's voice and looked over at her. "Why did you hesitate?"

Bella was quiet for a moment. Finally, she spoke. "Jacob had a rough childhood. It still affects him."

Phoebe nodded. "I gathered that."

"He's the toughest man you'll ever meet, but also, he's fragile in some ways. So fragile." Bella's voice was filled with such love and affection that Phoebe's throat tightened.

To have someone speak about her with that kind of love would be incredible. Jacob was so lucky. "I keep checking in with him to make sure we're not too much for him."

Bella smiled. "You are too much for him, I think, but in a beautiful way. In a way that none of us have been able to be."

Phoebe watched Annie look up at Jacob, hero worship on her face. "What do you mean? He says he doesn't like people, but he doesn't mean you guys."

"No, he loves us, but he still has to work sometimes to calibrate himself when he's around us. But looking at him with Annie and you..." Bella smiled. "I've known him for a long time, and I've never seen him relaxed like this before, not even with his horses. And it's making him more relaxed about me and Lucas being in his space."

A warm feeling settled around Phoebe. "That makes me happy," she admitted. "I was worried that we were bad for him."

"Bad? No, that's not the word I'd use." Bella cocked her head. "Can I ask you something?"

Phoebe nodded. "Of course."

"What do you think of Jacob?"

Her heart started to race. "He's a good man."

Bella burst out laughing. "Oh, come on, Phoebe. Seriously? What kind of answer is that? You know what I'm asking."

Her heart beat faster. "He's a treasure with Annie," she admitted. "My daughter needed him, and every moment she has with him is a gift."

Bella smiled. "That's so crazy. I know Jacob's amazing with traumatized horses, but I don't think any of us besides Dylan would have guessed how he is with Annie. But it makes sense. He's got the biggest, most beautiful soul of anyone I know."

Phoebe smiled, watching him lean forward and whisper something to Annie. "I can see that."

"What about you? What do *you* think of him? Do you think he's hot?"

Oh, Lordy. "I don't want to date anyone."

"Not what I asked."

She glanced at Bella. "I'm not used to having girlfriends to talk about men with."

"Well, then you need me, clearly." Bella rode closer and lowered her voice. "Here's my real question, what I really need to know. And I want as honest an answer as you can give me. Okay?"

Phoebe nodded. How could she deny anything to this family that was taking such care of her and her daughter? "Okay."

"I love Jacob with all my heart, and we've all been protecting him his whole life. But I see the way he is with you and Annie, and I know that something about you guys has touched his heart despite all his efforts to isolate himself. I need to know: if he falls for you, is there a chance that you would meet him half-way? Is there a chance that you feel anything for him?"

Phoebe felt her cheeks heat up. "We just met him yesterday."

"Yep. But magic is magic when it's there." Bella waited.

Phoebe bit her lip. "I don't want to date anyone."

"I know. You already said that. Be brave, Phoebe. Feel whatever it is you're feeling and tell me what it is. That's what the Harts do. It's a rule we live by. We're always honest with each other, no matter what. We don't keep secrets from each other, no matter what. That's what kept us alive as kids, and we still live that way."

"I'm not a Hart."

"You are for now."

Bella's words made sudden tears fill Phoebe's eyes. *You are for now.* She'd been separated from her parents for so long. Been alone for so long. And now, suddenly, she had this temporary family. "I already don't want to leave him," she whispered. "When he kisses me, there's no other place I want to be."

A huge grin spread across Bella's face. "He's kissed you?"

"More than once, yes."

"Yay!" Bella clapped her hands, startling her horse, who danced sideways. "Holy cow, Phoebe, that is awesome."

"I'm scared," Phoebe admitted. It felt so good to admit it, to have someone to talk about it with. "It's been a long time. It's not what I was looking for. I don't know how it would work."

"You don't need to know. We never know the ending of anything," Bella said, moving her horse closer again. "Just take it one day at a time. All you need to know is that you can trust Jacob. He'll take care of you and Annie no matter what, and he doesn't mess around with women. If he's choosing to kiss you, it's because he means it."

Bella's words felt good, so crazy good. "Okay," Phoebe said with a smile.

"Okay indeed." Bella grinned. "The only way to find out what's going to happen and if it's going to work out, is if you go all in and see what happens. So, we're going to give you some space."

"What? No." Her heart started hammering. "I'm not ready—"

"No one ever is." Bella winked, then raised her voice. "Lucas! Let's take a loop and make sure we're not being followed!"

And with that, she kicked her horse into a gallop and headed toward the men. Lucas looked back over his shoulder, then nodded. He gave Annie a high five, carefully lowered Cupcake to the ground, where the puppy started racing around and barking with joy, then he kicked his horse into a canter, meeting up with Bella as she neared. The two Harts peeled off, circling back behind them.

Jacob looked back over his shoulder and slowed his mount so that Phoebe could catch up. "You doing all right?"

Damn. That smile. He was too freaking handsome. "Absolutely." After her conversation with Bella, Phoebe couldn't look at Jacob the same way. The walls she'd worked so hard to hold together had dissolved, and suddenly, all she could think about was that Jacob would never have kissed her if he didn't mean it.

Was he thinking he wanted them to stick around? Was she thinking that she wanted to?

It was too soon. Much too soon.

"Mama!" Annie held out her arms as she neared. "Can I get on with you?"

Jacob nodded. "Ghost is solid. He won't bolt. You guys will be okay. I'll make sure you stay safe."

"All right, then."

Jacob rode close, so close that his leg brushed against hers as they both came to a stop. He reached over and held onto Ghost with one hand, while he helped Annie scramble off

Freedom and onto Phoebe's lap. He was so careful with Annie's safety that it made Phoebe's heart turn over.

Her little girl deserved to feel safe and secure, and she could tell that Jacob's huge bulk and energy gave Annie a feeling of safety that Phoebe had never been able to provide on her own. She was all about female empowering and energy, and they were fine without Jacob, truly fine, but he brought something to their lives that was unique to him.

Something that felt good to both her and Annie.

Annie settled back against Phoebe's chest, and she wrapped her arms around Annie, breathing in the warmth of her daughter. She kissed the top of her baby's head. "I love you, my little munchkin."

"I love you, Mama." Annie took a deep breath, sighing with contentment as she relaxed against Phoebe. "I love horses. I love being outside. Can we do this every day?"

Phoebe looked over at Jacob, and he nodded.

"Yes, we can, sweetie. Every day that we're here, we can go ride."

That we're here. The minute she put that limit on it, she met Jacob's gaze. He frowned, studying her. She could see him thinking, but his face was inscrutable. The conversation with Bella made her wonder if he was thinking about keeping them around, but she truly couldn't believe he was actually thinking that. Yes, maybe he liked having them around, but long term?

It was too soon. He wouldn't be thinking that. She couldn't be thinking that.

"I was thinking of lunch by a river up ahead," Jacob said. "There's a waterfall that's beautiful."

She nodded. "Sounds great."

"All right then." He fell silent as he rode beside them, but it was a comfortable, happy silence. She felt at peace in his presence. He didn't feel like an effort. He just felt like peace.

They rode for a few minutes, then Jacob peered at Annie. "She's asleep," he said quietly. "Big day for her."

Phoebe nodded. "Yep. I don't think she'll ever want to go back to school after being here."

"I get that." He looked around, scanning their surroundings, reminding Phoebe of their reality. "I didn't like school. Dropped out when I was twelve. Made my own way."

That didn't surprise her at all. "Was that when you met Brody and the others?"

He shook his head. "I was on my own for about three years before I hooked up with them. I think I was fifteen when I first met Brody."

"You were homeless and alone from when you were *twelve?*"

"Yeah. It was better than the alternative. But when I met Brody, I knew I had a chance to make it. Until then, I wasn't sure."

Phoebe thought about that. "What was the alternative?"

Jacob glanced at Annie, then shook his head. "Later."

Later. He wanted to tell her. That made her feel so good. But also, wow. Whatever he'd experienced was bad enough that he didn't want to take the chance that Annie would overhear it. Because he was a protector.

"I'd like to hear about your history," he said. "What makes you the way you are. Later, of course."

Again, a warm feeling inside her. She didn't like talking about her past, but it made her feel good that he wanted to know. That he cared enough to know. "Okay."

He smiled at her. "Okay, then."

She smiled back, her heart feeling lighter than it had in a long time. She was definitely feeling things about Jacob, for Jacob, things that scared her much less after the conversation with Bella. Of course, she wasn't ready to admit or commit to *anything*, but knowing a little more about Jacob made her more willing to experience what she was feeling, instead of trying desperately to hide it from herself.

A shadow passed over him, and they both looked up. A huge bird was flying overhead, and she saw a flash of a white head. "Is that a bald eagle?"

He grinned. "Yeah. I was hoping they'd be out. The spot we're going to is a place they love to go fishing. I was hoping we'd see some."

Excitement rushed through her. "Really? That is amazing! How far away are we?"

"A few minutes." He grinned. "Want to go faster?"

"Yes!" She locked her arm tightly around her sleeping daughter, then urged her horse into a slow lope. Cupcake ran alongside them, his tail up and his ears flapping, clearly in absolute doggie joy. Jacob stayed right beside her, close enough to grab Annie or her reins if anything happened, but giving her the freedom to do it on her own.

And when she thought the day couldn't get any more perfect, the river came into sight. She gasped in stunned surprise to see all the majestic, elegant birds soaring high above the wide river. "How many eagles are there?"

He paused, then said. "I counted eleven. You?"

She nodded her agreement. "Magic. It's literally magical." She nudged Annie awake as they reined to a stop. "Annie. Eagles! Watch—"

As she spoke, an eagle swooped out of the air, dove straight toward the river, and hit the water with a big splash, then came right back up into the air with a fish in its talons.

Magical. Literally magical. "I never want to leave," she whispered in awe. "I could stay here forever."

"Good," Jacob said.

She looked quickly at him, but he was watching the eagles, not her.

But he was smiling.

CHAPTER TWELVE

PHOEBE DIDN'T WANT to go teach her class.

She wanted to continue sitting on Jacob's couch and watch Annie and Bella playing Go Fish, while Lucas and Jacob moved in more furniture that Lucas had brought. Another bed, so she didn't have to sleep with Annie. A kitchen table. An adorable pink dresser and an art table for Annie, along with a whole bunch of art supplies.

"You all are treasures," she said as she watched Lucas set the table down and arrange the small, matching chairs around it. The day had been amazing. So much laughter and fun. Eagles. Coyotes. A herd of elk, even! Cupcake had slept in his portable bed on Lucas's horse the whole way home, but Annie had been too excited to sleep. She'd ridden with Jacob, Phoebe, Bella, and Lucas in rotation, wanting to meet all their horses. Phoebe had never seen Annie so outgoing and free, and she loved every minute of it.

Jacob was magical, but so were his siblings. Such good people who cared. Protectors, it was obvious, but not at the expense of a depth of soul, which was freely shared.

Lucas grinned as he moved the little art table against the

wall. "We've never had a little girl around here. It's fun." He set several huge pads of paper, markers, and watercolor paint on the table. "Annie? You like art?"

She looked over, and her face lit up. "Is that for me?"

"Sure is, kid. What do you think?"

"Mama! Look!" She abandoned the game and nearly hurtled herself over to the table. "Glitter markers!" She pulled them out and started coloring immediately, immersed in her craft, humming under her breath to the upbeat music playing on Jacob's home theatre system.

Bella grinned at Phoebe. "She's a great kid."

"I know." Phoebe was so used to the school calling her all the time, telling her how Annie wasn't measuring up to their expectations, how she wasn't following the rules, or behaving the way they wanted her to behave. She couldn't believe how good it felt to be around other people who saw the same beauty in her little girl that she did. "Thanks."

Maybe Annie was in the wrong school. Maybe there was a school out there that could see her daughter's gifts instead of trying to mold her into something she could never be. Because in one afternoon, the Harts had taught Phoebe that there were others out there who could support Annie in the way she needed it. To accept her. To nourish her.

Jacob set down a stack of fleecy, brightly colored blankets that Phoebe suspected were destined for Annie's bed. "You go online in twenty minutes. Don't you need to set up?"

"Yes. I do." But she didn't move. "I feel like I'm going to break the vibe here. No one will be able to talk while I'm on the class."

Lucas rubbed his jaw. "Jacob has an office in the barn. You can teach there."

"The barn?" she echoed. "I can't teach my class in a barn."

Jacob was frowning. "When I have a new horse, I often

93

sleep there until they're comfortable. I have a whole set up in there."

"That's a great idea," Bella said. "Lucas and I will stay here with Annie and Cupcake. I'll make dinner, and we'll keep her safe and entertained."

"No, no," Phoebe shook her head. "I need to stay with Annie—"

"Annie," Bella said, "how do you feel if your mom goes to the barn to teach her class? I'll stay here and cook."

Annie looked up at Bella. "Can we bake brownies?"

"You bet."

"Yay!" Annie abandoned her art and ran to the kitchen. "Where are the chips? Jacob, where are the chips? I want chocolate chips."

Phoebe laughed as Annie started pulling open cabinets. "You won her over with the baking. It's her favorite thing in the world."

"Well, I'm a professional chef, so our bond is real." Bella winked at Phoebe. "We have it covered, Phoebe. Go do your thing. Your job is important."

"I know—" She glanced at Jacob. "You'll stay here with her?"

"No," Lucas said, walking over to her and Jacob. "Phoebe, you need protection as well. Jacob has to go with you and stay there."

She shook her head, alarm shooting through her. "No. He needs to be with Annie."

Lucas's face was understanding, but unrelenting. "How do you think Annie would handle it if something happened to her mom? You both need to be safe. Annie's got me and Bella, and we're absolute fucking badasses. And you have Jacob, who is halfway decent as well."

Phoebe didn't like being separated from Annie, but the house was small and Annie was so happy. She didn't want to make everyone be silent for an hour and a half. She looked at Jacob. "What do you think?"

He glanced at her, then met Lucas's gaze. "They matter to me," he said softly to Lucas. "It's everything."

Phoebe's heart tightened at his words.

Lucas nodded. "I know that. Top level alert. We're as good as you are, plus there's two of us."

Jacob looked at Annie, and then back at Phoebe, then swore.

"You can't be in two places at once," Lucas said. "And your horses need you, too."

All her bravado from earlier about her need to teach her class was gone, stripped away by the thought of leaving her daughter in danger. Nothing else mattered, except her baby. She needed to make sure she was safe, and ensure she wasn't scared. "Look," Phoebe said, "I'll skip my class—"

"No." Jacob interrupted her. "It's important." He paused. "I do trust Bella and Lucas. And they're right that you can't be alone."

"I'll do it in the gym—"

At that moment, Bella started blasting the new *Little Mermaid* soundtrack, and she and Annie started belting out the lyrics.

Pure joy and relaxation for Annie, who always had to be quiet when Mama taught a class. Why would Phoebe hold her back? She'd literally told Jacob again and again how important it was not to live in fear, to show Annie that she could embrace life and be strong and safe, but still free.

She had to do this. "Okay, Jacob. The barn it is."

Lucas met her gaze. "I promise you she'll be safe."

"I know. I know." She took a breath, her heart pounding. She felt like she was being torn apart right now. She needed so many things in this moment, and she had to prioritize.

She had to trust.

Oh, she wasn't good at that.

Jacob picked up her computer bag. "Do you need anything besides this?"

"No. Everything I need is in there." She gave Annie a quick hug, which her daughter barely even noticed, took reassurance from Bella and Lucas, and then followed Jacob out the front door.

She was tense as they walked, her stomach churning. "I don't think I can do this. I don't even know them. How can I trust her with them?"

Jacob stopped, took her hand, and turned her toward him. "Eliana has entrusted her women with our family on multiple occasions. Would she do that if there were any chance we weren't good enough to keep her clients safe?"

Phoebe tried to focus. To think logically. "No, but you never know—"

"Annie's happy and safe. If you go back in there in a panic and don't do your regularly scheduled call, how does that affect her?"

She swallowed. "It teaches her to be scared. To not trust anyone except me. To hide. I also lose integrity with my community, which could undermine our financial well-being."

He nodded.

"Damn you for listening to me earlier." She spun away and stalked toward the barn. "I'm freaking out here. How can I teach my class?"

"Because you're a professional." He reached past her and used his palm print to open the door. The door slid open, and she stepped inside, turning to look at his house. The door slid shut, cutting her daughter off from her view. Panic hit her hard. "I can't do this—"

Jacob held his phone out to her. "FaceTime is magical."

She looked and saw her daughter and Bella dancing in the kitchen. She unmuted it, and her heart seemed to inhale with relief when she heard her daughter's laughter. "Oh, God. Thank you. Can we keep this on?"

Lucas popped his head in the frame. "I'll keep it on them the whole time you're gone."

Bella and Annie waved at the camera. "Hi, Mama!"

"We'll move the phone if we leave the kitchen," Bella promised. "Have fun!"

Phoebe clutched the phone as Bella and Annie went back to baking. Lucas wandered into the frame, peering out the window behind them before moving on. Phoebe pressed mute on the phone and took a breath. "Okay," she said, her voice shaky. "Okay, it's all good."

"Check this out."

Phoebe turned and saw that across the wall were a number of screens. Each one showed a high-resolution video of his property, including each room in his house. "I have thirty-six cameras," he said. "I can see every inch of my property. No one could get close without me knowing."

"Wow." She walked over and stood beside him. She could see Annie and Bella baking, and many shots of nature. "This is a lot."

"It's more than the others have, but it's what I need."

She slanted a glance at him. "Why do you need more?"

"Later. You need to do your class." He walked over to the side and opened a door. "In here."

She peered past him, and she saw the room had a bed, a dresser, and a desk. Not much else, but it was enough. "Perfect."

"Can you keep the door open? I'll be quiet. I just want to be able to keep an eye on you."

She nodded. "You bet." She set the phone on the desk, propping it up so she could see Annie, then she set her computer bag on the desk. The moment she pulled out her computer, she felt everything inside her settle and focus.

This was her life's work: helping other women have the confidence they needed to do whatever they needed or wanted to do.

She needed to do this not just for the money, but because it made her soul whole.

Jacob helped her log into his network, then slipped away as she got ready.

By the time she started the call, she was wholly immersed in her world. And when she saw the faces of the women in her community, she knew she'd done the right thing to make the call.

This was her mark to leave on the world, and what she did mattered.

CHAPTER THIRTEEN

JACOB HUMMED SOFTLY to himself as he leaned on Freedom's stall door, watching the horse munch as Phoebe finished up the Q&A portion of her class.

The hour and a half he'd been in the barn, working with his horses, and listening to Phoebe had been an extraordinary gift for him.

His horses were always peace, but the addition of Phoebe had raised it to a new level.

He'd been willing to have Phoebe run her class while he was in the barn with his animals, because his job was to take care of Phoebe and Annie.

He'd expected that having Phoebe present and teaching would be a distraction, a break in the equilibrium he needed so badly in his barn.

But he'd been wrong.

He loved listening to her teach. She spoke to her students with such warmth and humor that he knew why they stuck around. Her advice was innovative and insightful, and her absolute lack of judgment of anyone was stunning.

He judged the hell out of people, most of it bad.

But Phoebe gave credit to every single woman, saw them as worth being loved, both by her and by themselves.

Shit. After listening to her, he was ready to fall in love with her, too.

She was a gift to the fucking world.

He patted the stall door, then walked across the main floor to Phoebe's doorway. He folded his arms and leaned against the doorjamb so he could watch her coach.

She glanced over at him. He expected her to wave him off, but she just gave him a little smile and kept talking.

Right. He could stay.

Her voice was different when she spoke to her clients. She had more confidence. More authority. More electricity. He could tell she was completely absorbed in her coaching. She'd set aside her problems and her fears, and she'd given herself over completely to empowering others.

Fucking riveting.

He gave himself over to peace when he was out riding Freedom, or sitting alone in the barn listening to the sounds of his animals. But even then, the past nagged at him, whispered through his mind, always present, always stalking him, never leaving him.

But while Phoebe was teaching, she let go of everything else. The only sign that she had any other life besides the call was the periodic shift of her gaze to the phone she'd propped on the table, just to check on her daughter.

He was jealous. And impressed. And just in awe.

She took two more questions, gave a few housekeeping instructions about when the replay would be available and clarification about their assignment, and then she disconnected.

She leaned back in the seat, stretching her arms above her head. "That was a great call," she said. Her eyes were sparkling, and there was so much energy pouring off her. "Thanks for making me do it."

He didn't move from the doorway. "After listening to you help all those women, I'll never let you skip a call again. You're fucking magic."

She smiled at him. "Why thank you, kind sir. I do my best."

He could tell she felt relaxed and peaceful. "No wonder you coach these women. It lights you up."

Her smile widened. "It does," she agreed. "I think it's because I spent so much of my life being afraid and feeling powerless. Anything I can do to help other women move past those emotions and into a place of strength and hope feels so good. Plus, when I teach them, it makes me be better at choosing more helpful thoughts for myself."

He sat down on the bed and braced his forearms on his thighs. "Listening to you makes me feel like people can change."

She spun the chair so she was facing him. "People can change."

He searched her face. "How did you do it? How did you get from whatever darkness you were under, to being able to coach like that? You're pure light."

Phoebe sighed. "I'm not pure light."

He raised his brows.

"I'm not." She got up from the chair and flopped down on the bed on her back. She stretched her arms out above her head and stared at the ceiling. "My dad was a terrible man. I was scared all the time growing up. Scared he was going to kill me."

Jacob swore under his breath, then stretched out beside her, propping his head on his hand so he could watch her. "Is he dead now?" If he wasn't, Jacob was going to have to go after him.

"Yes. My mom eventually divorced him, and she married an amazing man who became the dad I never had."

Jacob could hear the genuine affection in her voice, and he was glad. She deserved love.

"But I wanted to follow my own path. I still resented my mom for staying with my dad as long as she had, for the trauma of my childhood. I rebelled by marrying the first handsome, rich, powerful guy who would have me, thinking that marrying a powerful man would make me powerful."

"But it doesn't. Because it's his power."

"Exactly. He turned out to be the same as my father."

"Shit."

"Yeah, right?" Her voice was matter of fact, but he could hear the years of weight as she spoke. "A friend of mine referred me to Eliana, and she helped me disappear. But every minute I was in my new life, I waited to turn around and find him standing in my doorway. Hunting me."

Jacob ground his jaw. "I know that feeling."

She turned her head to look at him. "Your ex-husband?"

He laughed softly. "No, my dad. And his friends. I was a pawn for them."

She rolled onto her side so she was facing him. "I'm sorry."

He shrugged. "It was a long time ago, but he's not dead. He just got out of prison a couple days ago."

Phoebe's eyes widened. "Is he going to come here?"

"I don't know. I mean, we're in the celebrity rags a lot, but I don't know that he would ever think that Jacob Hart, billionaire rancher, is the scrawny little Jacob that he bullied. But I still wait for him to come." The words were hard for him to admit. He was a grown fucking man, but his dad still haunted him. His family knew, because the Harts didn't keep secrets, but he hadn't had to tell them. They just seemed to know why he'd had to put so many safeguards in his home.

Admitting to Phoebe was different. Unexpected. Tense.

But she didn't judge him. She simply nodded. "I get it."

I get it.

Three simple words, but they seemed to take a thousand pounds off his shoulders. "I've always considered myself a complete fuck up because I can't get over it."

She smiled and took his hand, tucking it against her chest. "There's no such thing as getting over it. We grow, we heal, we expand, but it's all still a part of us." She smiled. "I think you've done great."

He shrugged. "As you said, I live in a prison."

"Yes, that is true. But your empathy enabled you to reach Annie, and all your horses..." she paused. "And me," she said softly. "You make me feel safe again."

He laughed. "You made me feel like a hero. I appreciate that."

"You are a hero. To Annie. To the horses. Just like I'm a hero to the women I help. And to Annie. We have to remember to see the hero in ourselves. It's so easy to forget to do that."

As she spoke, Jacob let her voice soothe him. Her voice was light and soft, filled with warmth and peace. "How did you get to where you are?" he asked. "When I'm with you, I feel different. Like...hope." Yeah, that was it. "No, like I can see a light in the distance that I never saw before. I wasn't looking for the light, but now I can see it."

Phoebe smiled and snuggled a little closer to him. "When my ex died, I felt the most glorious sense of freedom for the first time in my life. While I'd been hiding, I'd started doing a lot of research on self-empowerment and how to change your life. It was either that, or crawl under the bed and never come out."

He smiled. "And you're not the type to hide."

She laughed softly. "You figured that out, did you?"

"I did." A lock of hair had fallen across her cheek, and he wanted to brush it away, but he didn't want to scare her, or to cross boundaries she didn't want crossed. "When did you start coaching?"

"I actually started coaching right away, as soon as Eliana relocated me. I needed to earn money, and I didn't want other women to go through what I went through, feeling too powerless to make changes in their lives. So I started coaching others, not realizing that by learning what to teach them, I saved myself."

He smiled. "Best person to save."

"I know." She reached up and smoothed his hair, and his whole body settled at her touch. "I called my parents, told them everything that had happened, and then booked a flight home to see them. After not being able to talk to them for years, it made all my resentment vanish. All I wanted was to be home."

His heart ached for her. He couldn't imagine having to walk away from his family. They were everything to him. "And then Eliana showed up at your door with Annie."

She nodded, tracing her fingers along his jaw. Her touch was almost absentminded, a movement that she was simply doing because it felt right. "Someday, I'm going to be sitting on my parents' couch again. Annie's going to be on my mom's lap, while her grandma reads to her. I keep the vision in my head. It will happen."

She was so fucking resilient and hopeful. "I admire the hell out of you."

Phoebe smiled at him. "That feels good to hear. I feel like I'm running on empty so often. You've helped a lot. Even Cupcake is calmer around you."

"He's a good dog." Jacob paused, then reached up and moved that lock of hair he'd been eyeing. Phoebe met his gaze as he touched it, and her eyes were soft and trusting. He smiled. "The way you look at me is surreal."

"How do I look at you?"

"Like I'm a gift."

"Perfect. Then I'm sending the right message."

He ran his finger lightly along her jaw. "That's what I'm thinking about you."

"It's been a long time since I've trusted a man," she said softly. "It feels good. It makes me feel safe."

He loved that. He absolutely loved that he could make her feel safe. "I want to kiss you," he said, his voice lower and rougher than he intended.

His heart melted a little at her answering smile. "Yes," she said.

"All right." He inched a little closer to her, then leaned in and kissed her.

The first time he'd kissed her had been unexpected. This time, he'd known it was going to be good, but it was even more than he'd anticipated. Even in the short time he'd known Phoebe, emotions had become more tangled with her, and that added a glorious complexity to the kiss.

Phoebe leaned into him, sliding her arms around his neck. He immediately encircled her waist and pulled her flush against him. Her leg went over his hip, his knee went between her thighs, and suddenly the kiss took on energy that sizzled through his body.

He couldn't remember the last time he'd been wrapped around a woman. And he knew he'd never been in a bed with a woman who called to him like she did. He wanted to be here. He wanted to kiss her forever. His entire soul was attuned to her every breath, to the heat of her body, to the way her fingers drifted through his hair.

He angled his head, deepening the kiss, and she responded

with the same intensity coursing through him. Her breasts were against his chest, a glorious connection. He slid his hand over her hip, and along her thigh as he kissed down the side of her neck. He wanted to consume her, but at the same time, he needed to take it luxuriously slow, experiencing every kiss. Every moment. Every first touch of each part of her body.

There'd never be another first intimacy with Phoebe, and he needed to immerse himself in it. Her scent. The curve of her hip. The taste of her lips. The warmth of her breath.

Phoebe flattened her hand on his chest, over his heart, and he paused to put his hand over hers, holding her close. "Yes," he whispered.

"I never want to leave your arms," she said softly. "I can't believe how good it feels to be tangled up with you."

He smiled. "I feel the same way."

She searched his face. "Really?"

"Yeah." He tightened his grip on her waist, then kissed her again. A kiss that was more intense. Less safe. Less contained.

Phoebe pulled him close, pressing her body against his as she kissed him back. She slid her hand under his shirt, and he sucked in his breath at the feel of her palm on his bare skin. Incredible. Fire. Emotions rushed through him, and he tugged her shirt up, palming her ribs—

His phone rang, startling them both.

He swore. "That's my family's ring. I have to answer it."

Phoebe bolted upright, checking the phone propped up on the desk. "They're still baking. They're okay."

She collapsed back onto Jacob's chest as he dug his phone out of his pocket and answered. It was Lucas. "What's up?"

"You guys gotta make a choice."

Jacob frowned. "What choice?" He put the phone on speaker so Phoebe could hear. "What's up?"

"I know that neither of you like phones, but just wanted

to give you a heads up that FaceTime goes both ways. Which means everyone can see what you two are doing over there. Either you guys need to stop, or we're turning off FaceTime. No one needs to see that."

Oh, crap.

Phoebe threw her arms over her face and started laughing, which made the tension dissolve from Jacob's body. "Tell me that Annie didn't see that," she said, still laughing.

"She's obsessed with chocolate at the moment, but I can't promise anything." Lucas was chuckling. "Look, Phoebe, my brother has been depressingly solo for a long time, so I'm all about you guys having a little fun over there. We have Annie covered. Stay as long as you want, but I need to turn off the FaceTime."

"I've been thriving as a lone captain of my ship," Jacob said, still laughing. "Nothing depressing about it."

"What about that time when—"

"All right," Jacob cut him off as Phoebe started laughing again. "I'm trying to win this woman over. Don't be telling all my secrets before I have her secured. Just say great things about me."

Lucas chuckled. "Phoebe, all kidding aside, Jacob's a fantastic human being. If your weird matches his weird, and it seems like it does, then you couldn't find a better person to let into your life." He paused. "But if you don't get him, because he's different, then get off that bed right now and don't mess with him. He can't take it."

Phoebe's eyes widened, and her gaze shot to Jacob's face.

Jacob's amusement faded. "Didn't need that last bit, Lucas. Hanging up now."

"Right. Dinner will be in an hour. We won't expect to see you before then." Lucas hung up the phone, and then a moment later, the FaceTime call ended.

Jacob set the phone on the bed beside him. "You want to

head back to the house?" He figured she did. Losing eye contact with Annie would give her reason to get up, as would Lucas's little speech.

But she didn't get up right away. "You're trying to win me over? Or was that just you teasing Lucas?"

He swore under his breath. "I'm not as fucked up as he made it sound."

"You're not fucked up at all," she said. "But you are...different."

A darkness settled in his gut. "I know." He knew that Annie and Phoebe had made life come at him from a different angle, one that he was learning to lean into, but he'd never defend himself to her.

He'd learned long, long ago that trying to win over someone who didn't get him was hell. "You want to go? Let's go." He rolled to the edge of the bed, but just as he was about to swing his feet over the side, she stopped him with a light touch to his shoulder.

"Jacob."

He closed his eyes, his body going into high alert at the sensation of her fingers on him. "What?"

"I'm not ready to declare I can handle a relationship."

"That's fine."

"And living here is only temporary. It could end tomorrow or the next day."

Or never. "Yeah."

"And even if I was ready and wanted a relationship, I'd have to choose Annie over my own happiness, if it came down to that."

He thought he was pretty great for Annie, but whatever. "Sure."

"So, I can't promise anything beyond this moment."

Something in her tone made him turn to look at her. "What are you saying?"

She gave him a tiny smile. "Right now," she whispered, "all I want is to spend the next hour with you, in your arms, feeling safe, beautiful, sexy, and wanted. My daughter is safe, so I can relax. I want this, you, for myself. But beyond this moment, when this hour is over, I don't know. I can't make the promise Lucas said you needed."

Energy came alive inside Jacob that he'd never experienced before. A fierce, pulsating desire for intimacy, a need to protect, a peace that told him he was exactly where he needed to be.

He moved over to her and cupped her jaw with his hand. "I'm not the fragile puppy my family thinks I am," he said. "I just like my space."

"Except with me?" It was a genuine, worried question.

"Except with you, Annie, and Cupcake," he confirmed. Then he leaned in and kissed her, a kiss that meant more than he was willing to say in words.

CHAPTER FOURTEEN

JACOB'S KISS melted Phoebe's heart the moment his mouth took hers.

This kiss was different. It was intentional. Committed. Male.

And she loved it.

With a sigh of more happiness than she ever thought she'd feel in the arms of a man, she pulled him close and kissed him back, raising the heat level.

Delight leapt through her when he responded by rolling her onto her back and descending on top of her, his hands tunneling through her hair, his body warm and heavy on hers, pinning her to the bed in the most delicious way.

She loved the feel of his weight on her. It felt steamy and hot. Safe, as if he were protecting her with his body at the same moment he poured fire into every one of her cells.

As the kiss grew hotter, she grasped his biceps. They were hard and sculpted, ridiculously sexy. "Will you take your shirt off?" The request tumbled out before she realized it, but he didn't hesitate.

He just sat up and grinned at her. "I'd love to." He ripped

110

it over his head, revealing a washboard stomach that was pure insanity.

"Are you kidding me with that?" She spread her palms over his stomach. "I wait all this time for a guy, and this is what I get? I feel like all the self-worth mantras about what I deserve are totally paying off right now."

He laughed. "Been keeping myself in shape for you, baby. I knew you were coming. Just didn't know when. What if I finally found you, and then you bolted because I had a beer belly, poor hygiene, and a saggy ass? I couldn't take that chance."

She put her hands on his butt and squeezed. As she did, he flexed his glutes, and she started laughing. "They're literally like steel."

"Buns of steel. That's me. I ride horses, hide in my prison, and work out. Simple but effective life. And now..." He slid his hands along her arms and raised them over her head. "And now I add sweaty, twisted-pretzel time with a gorgeous single mom to my workout plans."

She laughed, even as heat seemed to rise from her skin. "I love pretzels."

"Me, too. Let's be pretzels." As he said it, he dropped to her side, then dragged her into his arms. Their feet tangled up with each other, and then he stopped. "Shoes. We're still wearing shoes. This is never going to work out for me. I exercise barefoot, and I definitely want to get this sexy-times workout correct."

She held up her foot. "I concur. De-boot me, my prince."

"That's so hot." He rose to his knees, grinning when she put her feet on his chest. "I've been dreaming of freeing your cute little feet since I first met you. Dreams do come true, even for men like me."

Her heart started to pound as he untied her shoes, taking

time to slide his hands down her calves as he worked on the laces. "It feels like a boot seduction," she said.

"I'm a cowboy. I'm all about the boots." He slipped one off her foot and set it on the bed. "I'd toss it across the room in a show of untamed lust, but I like to have my boots nearby. Just in case we need to run."

The reminder of their situation, and the danger that was still hunting them, grounded her in a hurry. How long did they have until life changed for them? She knew from her own life that everything could change in an instant. This might be her last moment with Jacob, her last chance to feel what she was feeling. At any second, Lucas might call with news that would strip away this moment with Jacob.

She didn't want to miss out. She needed him. She needed this chance to be with a man who made her feel whole, not scared or less than.

She sat up and pulled her shirt over her head. "Now," she said.

Heat flickered in Jacob's eyes. "You call the shots, sweetheart." He made quick work of her other shoe, then he finished disrobing while she did the same. When he turned back to her, and his gaze traveled along her body, sudden nervousness pulsed at her.

Was she enough for this amazing man?

"Hell, yes," he whispered, his voice filled with awe. "Being with you makes me realize that it was worth all the battles I fought to get to this moment. You're worth *everything*."

Tears filled her eyes at the genuine honesty in his voice, and she held out her arms to him. "Come to me, Jacob."

He moved across her, settling on top of her, allowing her to pull her to him. He kissed her tenderly, almost reverently, as if she were a fragile illusion that would shatter if he pushed too hard.

He wasn't wrong. She felt like that moment was exactly

that. A glimmer in time that would be gone before they both knew it.

She placed her hands on either side of his face. "Jacob."

He pulled back, searching her face. "What?"

Words filled her, words that were so much more than what she was ready to say. Declarations. Emotions. Dreams of forever. She couldn't even let herself dream them, think them, let alone admit them to him.

"Nothing," she said. "Kiss me."

He didn't move. "If you're having second thoughts—"

She smiled. "Exactly the opposite. And the thoughts I'm having are a little much."

His beautiful face softened. "Oh. Got it. Me, too." He didn't say more, and she didn't ask.

Instead, they both allowed the moment to fill them, the magic of kisses and touches that neither of them had experienced for so long. Their laughter, their teasing, the fun mixed with their need and desire.

After what felt like hours of the silliest, most intimate, most heated explorations and kissing, she ran her fingers through his hair. "This is fun, with you. I didn't know it could be fun."

He looked up, his arms wrapped around her thighs. "So much fun," he agreed. "You're sexy as hell. I could spend all day here with you."

"All night?"

"All month."

"All year?"

He scooched up her body and settled his hips between her thighs. "All forever, Phoebe." Then he kissed her at the same time he sheathed himself inside her, finally surrendering to what they had been wanting and building with all their laughter and explorations, not giving her a chance to express a reaction to his declaration.

All forever, Phoebe.

His words seemed to settle in her heart, filling it to bursting as her body welcomed him. In that bed, in his arms, consumed by his body and his wonderfulness, Phoebe didn't feel panicked or trapped or unsure. She just felt...perfection.

Jacob kissed her as he moved, driving deeper and deeper in a rhythm that was pure tantalizing sensation, until need and desire was coiled so tightly inside Phoebe's body that she felt like she was going to explode.

"Phoebe." One final thrust and the orgasm took over her, gripping so tightly that a little scream tore from her throat. She didn't try to hold it back. She surrendered to the moment, to the sensations coursing through her, to him.

He did the same, and the moment was more than a moment could be. It felt like her body had become peace. Her cells inhaling deep breaths of space and room in a way they never had before. Her heart felt like dancing and giggling.

Jacob laughed softly, and rested his face in the crook of her neck. "That was..."

She wrapped her arms around his head and smiled. "It was what?"

"Mmm..."

"It was, wasn't it?"

"It's amazing what happens when two weirdos get together." He kissed her lightly, making her smile.

"I had no idea."

"Me, either." He settled beside her and pulled her into his arms, tucking himself up against her back. "I'd really like to fall asleep wrapped around you, but dinner's almost ready. We gotta go."

"I know." She didn't want to move either, but she was glad she had to. Her life wasn't one that could afford for her to take a few hours off to indulge herself. She had stolen an hour.

That was all she got. She'd make it be enough. "Is there a shower in here?"

"Of course. I actually built the barn first, and I lived here with the horses while my house was being constructed. I needed to be able to stay here all the time if I had a horse who needed it, so I have a full bathroom and even a mini-kitchen.

Phoebe smiled. "Of course you stay with the horses whenever they need you. You're a protector."

"Maybe." He reached past her and picked up his phone. "Dinner in fifteen minutes. You can shower first. I'd offer to shower with you and make sure you really get your back clean, but if I do, we'll miss dinner, and then we'd have to explain to Annie, and it'll get all sorts of awkward."

She laughed, lightness in her heart. "All right. Show me the way."

"I need to make sure there are clean towels." He kissed her once more, then rolled off the bed. Phoebe took a moment to watch him walk across the floor.

He had no shame in his body. Completely comfortable being naked. He might be a little antisocial and "unusual," but he was comfortable in his own skin. He was who he was, and somehow, he'd learned to fully accept himself.

He glanced over at her. "What's that look for?"

"I was admiring your self-worth."

He burst out laughing. "Only a life coach would admire my self-worth when I'm parading around her naked, flexing my abs as hard as I can to show off." He turned to face her, held up both arms and flexed his biceps. "What about these?"

She grinned. "Impressive, but those aren't what got me into your bed."

"I know, but still..." He wiggled his brows. "Nice bonus?"

She burst out laughing and climbed out of bed. "You're so silly."

"But hot?"

She walked up to him and slipped her arms around his waist. "Absolutely gorgeous," she whispered.

When she saw the flash of relief in his eyes, she realized that despite his bravado, there was still a part of him that worried he wasn't enough for her. Was Lucas right? Was this strong protector actually endangered by her? "I don't want to hurt you," she whispered.

"Life is full of opportunities to be hurt," he said, leaning down to kiss her. "I'm tired of hiding from them, because when you protect yourself, you also don't live. So don't worry about me. I'm okay."

She searched his face, and then nodded. "All right."

"Shower?"

She took a breath. "Yes." Once she showered, they'd be back with the others, and this moment would be over. Would there be another one? Maybe, maybe not. "It was perfect," she said. "Thank you."

Understanding flickered in his eyes. "It was worth it, no matter what happens."

She nodded. "I agree."

But as she turned away, a part of her wondered if it really had been worth it. He'd awoken a part of her that felt good when she was with him, but what about when she wasn't? When she went back to her life, alone, could she still live her old way, or had he broken that part of her forever? What if he'd opened her heart to dreams that would refuse to be ignored again?

What if he'd made it impossible for her to tolerate her life anymore?

She stood there in sudden shock, envisioning going back to her house with Annie and Cupcake. Emptiness flooded her.

Holy crap. She was in trouble.

"There are towels," Jacob called out from the bathroom. He walked back in. "You're all set—" He frowned. "What's wrong?"

Phoebe lifted her chin. "Nothing. It's perfect."

His face darkened. "I said it was okay if you couldn't promise anything past this moment in terms of us, and I meant it. But one thing I can't ever tolerate are lies. It's not how my family does things. No matter how dark your thoughts are, no matter how badly you screwed up, you never hide it. You never lie about it."

She stiffened. "I'm not your family." She knew she wasn't his family, and she had to remember it. She'd lost her family, and these lovely people who had spent the day with her and Annie weren't her family. She had to remember that. She was still on her own, her and Annie.

"You're family for the moment." He walked over. "And you're inside my heart forever. So, no lies, Phoebe. What the hell is going on inside your head right now that's making you look like I just ripped your heart out and incinerated it?"

"You didn't do anything."

He narrowed his eyes. "What's going on?"

What was she supposed to do? Admit to him how hard she was falling for him, how scared it made her, and how scared she was that being with him had made her too weak to stand on her own?

No. She didn't talk about things like that, and not to him, an almost stranger, who was vulnerable himself and the cause of her distress.

"Phoebe. Talk to me. It's how we do things here. Emotional walls get us killed."

"No." Phoebe put her hands on her hips. "You grew up in this circle of trust, which is great for you, but I haven't been able to trust anyone for a long time! The only people I can trust are my parents, and I haven't seen them in almost ten years, and I've spoken to them only once during that time. I don't know how to trust! I don't know how to pour out my feelings and dance with joy for making myself vulnerable. And I don't want to, because it's scary and makes me feel unsafe. I don't like feeling unsafe, so I can't just stand here and pour everything out to you!" She threw up her hands. "See? This is why it's just too soon to start talking about forever, Jacob! Because we have fundamental incompatibilities that won't ever work together. What we had was a great hot minute, but we can't build a forever on that!"

She pushed past him before he could answer, stalked into the bathroom, and shut the door. There was a lock, so she used it, then sat down on the toilet and covered her face and the tears on her cheeks.

What the fudge had just happened? She'd literally yelled at Jacob. She hadn't yelled at anyone in years. Maybe ever. She wasn't a yeller. She never lost her temper. But when he'd told her she had to be all open and sharing in order to be a part of his family and his world...she'd snapped. She'd felt so inadequate. Not enough. That she could never be enough, simply because she didn't want to talk about how she felt. About what scared her. About how hard she was falling for this man she barely knew.

There was a light knock at the door. "Phoebe. Can I come in?"

"No." She sat up and wiped her cheeks. "We don't have time to talk. Dinner's in ten minutes." She turned on the shower, drowning out any more conversation between them. She went to take off her clothes, then remembered she was naked.

Because she'd just been naked with Jacob.

Oh, God. What had she done?

CHAPTER FIFTEEN

PHOEBE'S TENSION was palpable the rest of the night.

Jacob saw Bella and Lucas frowning at the two of them, but they were all working too hard to keep Annie happy and laughing that no one brought it up.

But everyone noticed that anytime Annie came over to Jacob and tried to climb on his lap, Phoebe called her daughter away with some excuse that was invisible to a six-year-old, but glaringly obvious to the adults in the room.

Did Phoebe think he was bad for her daughter? The thought twisted something ugly in Jacob, a darkness that he'd fought long and hard to overcome. And why was Phoebe putting up such a wall? He knew she'd been into it when they'd been together. She'd still been on board afterwards until something had snapped and she'd shut him out.

He didn't know what had happened, but it was triggering all sorts of shit in him that he didn't want to be reliving.

By the time Phoebe and Annie headed off to his bedroom to get Annie to bed, he felt like he was going to snap. He was so tense that his muscles hurt, and he was on such edge that every fast movement or unexpected sound triggered his startle reflex.

"Good night, Jacob!" Annie ran over to him and leapt into his arms.

He grinned and swept up the little girl in a hug. "Good night, pumpkin."

She beamed at him. "You'll be here in the morning when I get up?"

"I'll be here."

"And then Bella and Lucas will come over, and we'll ride again?"

He looked over at his siblings, and they both nodded. "Yep."

"Tomorrow I'm going to name the new pony. I'll know then what to call her. Can I pet her tomorrow?"

Jacob had let Annie only peek at the new pony today, because the animal was still settling and nervous. "Maybe tomorrow. We'll see how she feels."

"Okay!" She beamed at him, and then wiggled to get down. He released her, and something inside him turned over as she sprinted down the hall, raced into his room, and catapulted herself onto the bed. Cupcake ran after her and did the same, and then Phoebe followed and shut the door, pausing to look at him before she closed it.

"Fuck." He clasped his hands on his head and turned away, looking at his siblings. "What the hell?"

Bella and Lucas looked at each other, then Bella patted the kitchen counter. "Come in the kitchen," she said quietly. "So they won't hear us."

He swore under his breath again and walked into the kitchen. He leaned against the stove and folded his arms over his chest while his siblings joined him.

"First question," Bella asked. "What were you thinking

when Annie and Cupcake ran into your room just now? You had a weird expression on your face."

He closed his eyes. "That the room was meant for them. That I fucking loved seeing them in there."

"You weren't annoyed?" Her voice was softer now.

"No." He opened his eyes to look at his siblings. "What the fuck, you guys? Why don't I want to go on a ride and get out of here?"

"What do you want to do?" Lucas asked.

"I want to stay here. I want to sit outside the door and make sure they're safe."

Bella pressed her lips together. "What do you *really* want?"

He didn't need to think about it before he answered. "I want to be in that room with them. I want to be reading to that little girl. And then I want more time with Phoebe."

His siblings exchanged looks, and he didn't miss the worry on their faces. "What?"

Bella turned to him. "I know you don't always get people, but Phoebe was giving you super bad vibes tonight—"

"I know that. I'm not an idiot." He clasped his hands over his head. "It was great. We had a great time in the barn. I've never experienced that before. And then she got up to shower, and she was still laughing and teasing, and then, suddenly, there was a chasm between us."

Bella burst out with laughter. "Oh, God, you had me totally freaked out. It's fine."

"What's fine? It's not fine."

"She freaked out because she's falling for you," Bella said. "She's not ready, and she's scared, but she's realizing how amazing you are. She's trying to put distance between you so she doesn't have to admit to herself how she's feeling."

Hope settled in Jacob's chest, a painful, unfamiliar emotion. "You think?"

Lucas grimaced. "Maybe she just doesn't want more, and you came on a little strong."

"Strong?" Jacob thought about what he'd said. "I might have mentioned forever."

Both his siblings groaned, and Bella sighed. "Jacob, you can't do that. It's too soon."

Lucas nodded. "Bella's right. You can see how skittish Phoebe is. You can't scare her like that."

"Scare her? By being nice? By making her feel safe?"

"No," Bella said gently. "By making her realize that she could have it all with you."

Jacob looked at his sister. "That's wrong?"

"It is when she's not ready." Bella smiled. "Women are skittish like that, Jacob. We'll run like hell if we start to fall for a guy and we're not ready. Especially if he's saying all the right things that break through our walls."

Jacob rubbed his forehead, suddenly tired. He'd started to feel normal around Phoebe. Not lost. Like he could feel the ground under his feet. And he'd been wrong? Doing everything wrong? "Whatever."

"No," Bella said. "Not whatever. If you like her, don't give up on her. You have time."

Lucas nodded. "Don't scare her, but just be yourself. Just be you. It'll be okay."

"Okay?" Jacob echoed. "What does that even mean? What the hell is 'okay?' I don't want okay."

Bella sighed. "Jacob, this is the way it is. You guys just met, and you're using words like 'forever' to a woman who had to run for her life. There is no way on earth she will believe that you actually mean forever, and if you do, she doesn't believe that you know her well enough to make that promise. So, she can't trust you, and she can't trust herself around you, because you make her yearn for something she gave up on."

Lucas raised his brows. "Or, she just isn't into him."

Bella snorted. "It's Jacob. What woman wouldn't fall for him?"

"Any woman who isn't right for him," Lucas shot back. "He's not a regular guy, and a lot of women won't get who he is or see how amazing he is."

Jacob smiled as he listened to his siblings argue about Phoebe. He felt their support and their love in a way he didn't usually experience. Usually, they were treading so carefully around him that he just interacted with them as he needed to. But tonight, some of the walls he kept up between them weren't there. "Thanks," he said.

They both looked over at him. "For what?" Lucas asked.

"For all of it. I don't think I ever thanked you. So thanks."

Lucas grinned and put his hand on Jacob's shoulder. "No thanks is ever necessary, bro. Family forever."

"Family forever!" Bella flung her arms around both of them and dragged her brothers in for a hug.

Jacob tensed, expecting to recoil when he felt their arms go around him, but for some reason, tonight it didn't bug him. Felt all right, in fact.

Bella pulled back, staring at Jacob. "You let me hug you."

"Yeah. Weird, right?"

Tears filled her eyes. "It's Annie and Phoebe. They're changing you."

He nodded. "I can feel that. Yeah."

Lucas swore. "Don't get too attached, bro. You don't know what'll happen."

"I know." Shit. He knew.

"Keep your walls up," Lucas said. "Remember the last time?"

Worry filled Bella's face. "Oh...please be careful. I mean, I love that you let me hug you, but not at the cost of—"

"I know." Jacob's familiar tension was back, when he'd had

too much of people, too much in his space. "I'm good." He felt restless, like the walls were closing in on him.

Lucas sighed, reading Jacob's tension. "Time for us to jet, Bella. We'll be back tomorrow, if you want us."

"I'll text in the morning. Let you know." Jacob clenched his hands, trying to release the tension building inside him.

"Remember," Lucas said, "don't get so caught up in how you feel about Phoebe and forget that there's a real threat to their safety." He paused. "And to yours, too. Dylan told us that your dad's out of prison."

"I know." *His dad.* Jacob shook out his hands. "You guys need to go. I need space."

His siblings exchanged glances, but they both grabbed their phones off the counter. "How about if we watch from outside?" Lucas suggested. "We won't be in your way."

"No. I have my cameras. They'll alert me. You guys gotta go." He could feel sweat on his forehead, and he saw Bella's gaze go to it.

"How about we stay here to watch the house, and you go for a ride?" she offered.

"No. I want to stay here." He didn't bother to walk them to the door. He just stayed where he was.

"All right. Call if you need us." Lucas put his hand on Bella's back and began urging her toward the door. "Come on, Bella. He's fine."

Bella shot a worried look back at him. "Text later and let us know you're okay."

"I'm fine. Just need you to go."

They didn't argue. They'd been through this so many times with him before, they never took it personally, and he appreciated that. He never had to explain, never had to feel guilty. They accepted him in the way he needed to be accepted.

He closed his eyes as he heard the front door shut and lock.

For a long moment, he didn't move. He just breathed in the space. The quiet of the house. The freedom to simply be, where he didn't have to talk or listen or explain.

It took several minutes for him to recalibrate sufficiently to pull out his phone and arm his system. He checked all the video feeds, which showed his siblings leaving, but no other activity. All was secure.

He tossed the phone on the counter, then walked across the room and sank down on his couch, his original couch, not the soft one they'd brought in for his guests.

He rested his forearms on his knees and bowed his head, resting it on his fingertips. He was still sweating, and tension felt like it was choking him. He could hear sounds and voices from his childhood, ones he hadn't heard in years. They were suddenly back, loud and acrid, eating away at him just as they had so long ago. Sounds brought back by his father's reappearance.

He won't come.

He won't come.

He won't come.

Jacob wasn't scared of his father anymore. He knew the man had no power over him. But the memories were brutal, and he didn't want to have to drag his mind into the places that seeing his father would take him.

His mind shifted to Annie, to Phoebe, to Cupcake. What kind of man was after them? A man like his father? A man without a soul?

Tension wrapped tighter around Jacob, squeezing his lungs so tightly that it was difficult to breathe. This was the moment when he always ran for the barn, grabbed a horse, and bolted out into the night.

But he didn't want to go.

He didn't want to leave his house.

No...it wasn't his house that was calling to him. It was the trio in his bedroom. He needed to stay near them. To keep them safe.

To keep himself safe.

Behind that closed door, they weren't in his space. They weren't talking to him, asking him for what he couldn't give. But they were a presence. He wasn't alone, and he felt it.

He needed them. He didn't need much from them. Their presence was enough.

As soon as he thought it, real fear shot through him.

He *needed* them?

Shit. He was in trouble.

CHAPTER SIXTEEN

Phoebe waited as long as she could.

She waited until the house had been quiet for a while, and she was sure Jacob had fallen asleep.

Careful not to wake Cupcake or Annie, she cracked the door of the bedroom and peered out into the hall. She didn't see Jacob anywhere, so she stepped out and scurried to the bathroom.

As she got ready for bed, guilt ate away at her.

She knew how she'd acted tonight. She'd seen the looks that the Harts had shared. No one had said anything, and she'd appreciated that they'd all focused on making Annie laugh and feel relaxed.

But she knew they'd noticed.

She hadn't missed the way that Lucas had looked at his brother with concern. Why? Because she'd been distant and cold.

She braced her hands on the sink and stared at her reflection in the mirror. She looked tired. Her mouth was pinched. There were bags under her eyes. She intentionally lowered her shoulders, surprised by how much she had pulled them up from tension.

"This isn't how you want to be, Phoebe," she said to herself, to her reflection. "You can't let fear turn you into a woman you don't want to be."

She'd fought so hard to find joy. To learn to let herself be happy. To live fully.

And yet, the first moment someone had shown her kindness, she'd shut down. She'd hurt him. She'd used fear to poison the gift that life had given her.

"What do you want?" she asked herself.

She waited, but there was no answer from inside. Just a void. She sighed, recognizing that feeling. When she'd first gone on the run, she'd been numb inside after being trapped in her marriage for so long. It had taken her a long time to let herself come back to life, to hear the voice of her heart.

And now...silence again.

What would she tell one of her students right now?

Phoebe would tell her to slow down, to ask what good things were trying to get through, that she was blocking. To listen for the answer. It might be faint. It might be distant. But to listen.

She closed her eyes and took a deep breath, focusing on finding that little spot of feeling good inside her heart. That little spot of happiness, deep inside. The unconditional happiness. The happiness that simply existed for no reason.

After a moment, she felt it. She felt that energy rise through her. She let herself smile, still carefully keeping her mind blank, except for the feeling of well-being.

"What thought fits that emotion?" she asked herself.

The image of Annie throwing herself into Jacob's arms popped into her head.

The feel of the wind whipping across her face as she rode earlier in the day.

The sounds of Jacob's laughter while they'd been playing in bed.

The feel of his arms around her, holding her like he was her guardian, there to keep her safe, and to let her grow at the same time.

She opened her eyes and looked at herself in the mirror. This time, there was a sparkle in her eye. The tension around her mouth had vanished, replaced by a half smile. Even her skin looked less pale. "Thank you," she whispered, to herself, to the universe, to whatever greater power had guided her from fear into this moment of feeling better.

Everything that had matched her good feeling centered around Jacob, and being here, in his home.

Which was why she'd freaked out. Because all of that was temporary.

But as she stood there, she realized that that was a poor reason to pull back. Protecting herself? From what? From feeling valued? Protected? Safe? Protected from remembering what it felt like to have a family around her? Protected from Annie getting a glimpse of what a family could be like?

So what if they had to go back to their life? Wouldn't it be better to go back, knowing that there was more out there they could hope for? Wouldn't it be better to have a sparkle of life and hope in their hearts, than to go back and fall into their routine without realizing they *could* have more?

"If I let myself go all in with Jacob, it will hurt to leave here," she said to her reflection. Her reflection stared back at her, and she heard the little voice inside her say, "So what? You've survived so much. You can handle whatever comes, but go *live*."

Right. Go live. She deserved it, and so did Annie.

She took a deep breath. She needed to talk to Jacob. Was it too late? Had she blown it?

Maybe.

But maybe not.

She wasn't even sure what she would say to him. But she knew she had to try.

Summoning her courage, her heart racing, she opened the bathroom door and stepped into the hall. She peeked in the gym, but he wasn't in bed, or anywhere in there. She walked down the hall and stood in the doorway to the great room. For a minute, she didn't see him anywhere, and panic started to hammer at her.

Then she saw him sitting on the couch. His forearms were braced on his thighs, and his head was down, resting in his palms. His shoulders were taut, and the energy rolling off him was tense and haunted. Her heart tightened. "Jacob?"

He didn't move.

She walked into the room. "Jacob? Are you all right?"

He jerked and sat up, his gaze shooting to hers. His eyes were wild and unfocused. "What? What's wrong?"

She held up her hands. "Nothing's wrong. Everything's okay."

He stared at her for a second, as if trying to process her presence, then understanding seemed to come into his face. He swore. "Sorry. I was thinking about something."

"I can see that." She could feel his pain, and she wondered what thoughts had had such a grip on him. "Can we talk for a minute?"

His face was stark, his eyes weary. "I'm not at my best right now. Tomorrow would be better."

She started to say "okay," to remember that he needed his space, but then something inside her told her not to walk away. "If I sit with you, would that feel okay to you?"

He looked at her for a long moment, saying nothing, but she could see he was thinking about it, genuinely considering her question. "It would," he said finally. He pointed to the chair across from him. "Have a seat."

"Can I sit on the couch? With you?"

He closed his eyes, and she felt his tension ratchet up. "Phoebe," he said, his voice rough. "You are free to be how you need to be. It's important that you understand I'll never ask you to be what you're not."

She kept standing, not wanting to sit on the couch without his permission, but unwilling to give up and sit across the room. "Thank you."

He opened his eyes to look at her, his face haunted. "But tonight didn't work for me," he said. "I can't play that game. Make love to you. Laugh with you. Bond with you. And then have you shut down like that. It's fine that you need to be like that, but it doesn't work for me."

Regret filled her, and she sat next to him. "I'm sorry about that."

"It's fine." He stiffened and started to get up to move away from her, but she caught his arm.

"Are you scared?" she asked. "Scared of what happens when I leave?"

He paused, halfway to his feet. He didn't answer.

"I'm scared," she said. "I'm scared I won't be able to go back to my life now that I know what it's like to be here with you and your family. So I shut you out. But then I realized that life is short. We both know that good things can end at any moment, no matter how careful you are." She paused. "I don't want to be careful anymore, Jacob. I want to feel alive, the way I feel when I'm with you."

He took a breath, then sat back down. He put his hand over hers, lightly holding her hand against his arm. "I feel better around you than I feel alone," he said, his voice raw. "I don't remember that ever happening before. People sometimes make my soul hurt. You don't. Even tonight. Lucas offered to stay here so I could go ride, because he could tell I was a mess, but I wanted to be here in the house. Where you were."

Her throat tightened. "To protect us?"

"Maybe. Part of it, for sure." He rubbed his thumb over the back of her hand. "But I also simply wanted to be near you. When we were in the barn together, I didn't have to talk or pretend I was okay. I could simply breathe in the peace that your nearness gives me."

His words brought tears to her heart. They were the sweetest words a man had ever spoken to her, and she could tell he meant them. "What now?" she asked. "What do we do now? About us?"

He shook his head as he flattened his hand over hers. "I don't know. I haven't been in this position before."

"You've never been close with a woman?"

He smiled faintly. "Did I tell you I don't like people?"

She laughed softly. "You did, actually. That includes women who think you're handsome and charming?"

He raised his brows. "I don't know. I've never met a woman who considers me handsome and charming."

She smiled. "That's a very unsubtle way of fishing for compliments."

He grinned. "Did it work?"

"Yes." She turned so she was fully facing him. "Jacob Hart, I find you both handsome and charming. And an amazing lover. Does that make you want to run away?"

He paused, and she knew he was actually considering the question. Looking inside to see how he felt. Then he shook his head. "Nope. Don't want to be anywhere but here."

Her smile seemed to bubble up inside her. "It's where I want to be as well."

His answering smile held a tenderness that was heart-meltingly sweet. He reached up and tangled his fingers in a lock of her hair, and then leaned in to kiss her.

CHAPTER SEVENTEEN

IT WAS A SLOW, tender kiss of so much more than sex, and it made her insides turn to smushy jelly.

He kissed her for a long time, sitting there on the couch with her, one hand holding hers to his arm, the other in her hair.

It was intimate and tender, unlike anything she'd ever experienced, almost more intimate than making love, or at least in a different way.

After a long time, Jacob broke the kiss, but before she could miss him, he leaned back on the couch, and drew her down with him, nestling her against his body while he stretched out on his side, tucking her against him.

She wiggled around so that she was facing him, then laughed when she saw his frown. "What?"

"I had spooning plans. You can't be staring at me if we're going to spoon."

She wrinkled her nose at him. "We can spoon in a minute, but first I wanted to talk."

"Am I in trouble?" But his voice was teasing.

"I just want to tell you that you make me feel treasured, and I really appreciate it."

His smile faded. "You deserve to feel that way."

"Thank you." She took a breath, summoning courage, courage that might shatter the moment. "But there are still shadows in your eyes. I want to help those shadows fade. Is there a way I can help you?"

He was quiet for a moment. "When my family says something like that, I just want to get up and walk away. And I do. But when you say it..." He paused. "I feel hope. It's a flicker. Fleeting. But it's there."

She smiled. "Hope matters."

"Yeah." He leaned in and kissed her again.

She kissed him for a moment, then put her hand on his chest. "Talk to me, Jacob. How can I help you?"

"Mmm..." He wrapped his arms around her and tucked her against him.

She laughed and let him draw her against him. "You're not very subtle with your conversation avoidance."

"Was I avoiding your question? I didn't notice." He pressed a kiss to her hair and then rested his chin on her head.

"Jacob."

"What?"

"Tell me one thing."

"About what?"

If it were any other man, she'd be getting frustrated by his refusal to answer, but Jacob was different. She understood him, which meant, she didn't take offense, and didn't find him frustrating. But she did want to help him. "One beautiful memory from your childhood."

"Beautiful? From my childhood? There aren't any."

Her heart tightened. "There must be something."

He was quiet for a moment, and then he spoke. "I

remember one day, one really bad day, I was on my way home. I saw a woman carrying a puppy. It was light brown, floppy ears, black nose. She was whispering to the puppy, and the puppy was wagging his tail, staring up at her. He was so tiny, but the trust on his face was absolute. I knew he believed that woman would keep him safe. It was the first time I understood that some people protected others, instead of hurting them."

Oh, Lordy. That one story spoke volumes about his childhood. It helped explain his need to keep people at a distance, his dislike of most people. It wasn't dislike. It was self-preservation, and she understood that all too well. Phoebe nestled more snugly against him. "I forgot that fact, too," she said. "Until I met you."

His arms tightened around her. "We're a couple of rays of sunshine, aren't we?"

"The sun always shines, even when it's hidden by clouds."

He laughed softly. "You never stop, do you?"

"Stop what?"

"Trying to be positive. See the best in situations. Have hope."

"I do the best I can," she agreed. "Even at the worst of times, if you can find something to be grateful for, it helps. Even a tiny little bit of hope can be enough to get you through the next minute, and the one after that."

"On your worst night, what were you grateful for?" His question wasn't a challenge. It was genuine.

She knew the night immediately. "I was hiding in the bathroom. My ex was kicking the door, trying to break in. I knew if he got in, I was going to die. As I sat there and watched the cracks starting to form in the door, I decided I was lucky that I'd had my mom and stepdad. I was grateful that I'd known kindness in my life. I was grateful that my stepdad had taken care of us. Then I looked up and saw the moon through the window. I decided to be grateful that the moon was beautiful, and I could see it before I died...and then I realized I was looking through a window! It was a tiny window that didn't open, so I threw the toilet lid through the window, squeezed out, and then ran. Met up with Eliana that night and never went back."

"Hell. I'm sorry."

She shrugged. "It is what it is. I just don't want Annie to ever experience anything like that." She paused, suddenly remembering the idea she'd had the night before. "Can I ask you a crazy question?"

"Of course."

"I often worry what will happen to Annie if something happens to me. She needs someone who will protect her and that she'll feel safe with."

Jacob didn't say anything, but his arms tightened slightly.

Phoebe pulled back and sat up, needing to look at Jacob as she spoke. "Eliana makes us all designate a guardian, as you know. I have some woman designated who I don't even know, but she's in Eliana's program."

Jacob's eyes were dark and hooded, riveted on her face. Waiting for her to finish. She had a feeling he knew what she was going to ask.

"The bond between you and Annie is already strong, and she loves Bella and Lucas. Would you be Annie's guardian? No, wait, not guardian. Will you be her dad if something happens to me? Eliana will do all the paperwork to make it legal. I know it's a lot, and hopefully, I'll never need it but—"

"Yes."

Sudden, unexpected tears filled her eyes at his absolute, immediate answer. "Really?"

"Yes," he said again. "Absolutely. I'll sign whatever I need to sign. And I'll update my will to make her my heir, regardless, and to put Bella and Lucas as her guardians if anything happens to me. That way, if you and I are together and a dragon takes us out, she's still covered."

Phoebe stared at him in surprise, stunned by the extent of his response. "You're serious."

"Yeah." He sat up, energy rushing through him. "I'll be honest. I was thinking about doing it anyway. I don't have any heirs. My siblings have everything they need and more. What's my legacy when I go? I have everything set up in assorted charities, except for the land, which stays in my family, but I'll switch it over to take care of Annie. Do you think she'd want the house? She can have my house."

Phoebe stared at him, stunned. "We just met you."

He raised his brows. "And yet, you just asked me to be Annie's dad. How can it be okay for you to be sure about me, but not for me to be sure about you and Annie?"

"I...I...I'm just not used to anyone taking care of me. Or having someone to help make sure Annie's safe and loved."

Jacob nodded. "I get that, but when I look at the shadows in Annie's eyes, I know what it's like to be six years old and living like that. It's like looking into my own eyes again, talking to myself as a kid again. I want to help her in a way that no one helped me."

Phoebe felt the absolute truth in his words, and she knew he meant them. No matter what, Annie would forever be on his radar to take care of. "Thank you!" She threw her arms around his neck, and he caught her, wrapping his arms around her.

"No need to thank me," he said, gruffly. "It means...a lot... that you would trust me with her."

Phoebe pulled back to look at him. "Of course I would. You're an amazing person."

He shook his head. "I'll be honest. I know I'm a great guy. I know I'm a protector. I know that anyone who matters to me can count on me, no matter what. But people don't see that because I'm different. You see it, and that...I just...yeah. It means a lot."

She smiled through her tears. "Well, it means a lot to me to know that Annie will be okay no matter what."

"She will. I promise. She'll be a Hart now, for life."

Phoebe suddenly felt like she couldn't talk. She felt so overwhelmed. To know that her daughter was safe. That Annie had the protection of Jacob and his siblings. That Annie had the financial resources. And most importantly, that this family that was so full of love would give that to her. "Great." *Great.* Such an understatement. But there were no words to express the enormity of emotions consuming her.

Jacob laughed softly. "If you keep crying, I'm going to cry."

"No, don't. If you cry, I'm going to completely lose it."

"I'd love to promise that," he agreed. "But we both know that I am a total failure at playing whatever game I'm supposed to play."

"Not a failure," she whispered. "You just play the game that's right for you."

"I don't play any games. I just survive." He paused to run his hand along her hair. "You need to know that whatever happens between us won't change what we just discussed. If you go all cold turkey on me again tomorrow, I'll still call my attorney and get Annie set up financially and legally as my heir, and my siblings as her guardians. My promise is to Annie, not to you, and you don't need to fall in love with me to protect her. Got it?"

"Fall in love?" she echoed, her heart almost stopping. "With you?"

"Yeah, you don't need to do that to protect her. It's not conditional. I want you to understand that. Do you understand that?"

She nodded silently, his words still overwhelming her. Fall

in love with him? That was so much. She didn't deserve that. Not with him. Not with this amazing man.

"But I am going to be honest with you," he said.

"Okay."

"I never thought that there was a human being alive that I would want to be with in my darkest moments. But then I found you." He paused. "I wasn't prepared for you. So, I'm having to play catch up to being able to handle it. But I like it. I want to pursue it. I'm not going to give up because it's tricky, or because it sometimes rocks me on my ass."

She swallowed. "What are you saying?"

He laughed softly. "I'm that bad at communicating, am I? Shit. I'll lay it out. I'm falling hard for you. Maybe in love. Still trying to understand it. But I want to keep going, and I'm going to keep pushing at both of us to see what can happen between us. I'm not going to stop just because one of us freaks out, unless, of course, you tell me to stop. If you don't, then, I'm going to try to romance the hell out of you, and us, and see what can happen."

"I wasn't prepared for you, either." Her heart started racing. "I'm going to freak out," she said. "I can promise you that."

"Yeah, I will too. That's part of why we fit."

"If we fit. We don't know."

"We know we fit so far, that's as far as we need to know." He grinned suddenly. "You didn't tell me to stop."

"No," she agreed. "I didn't. Not yet, at least."

"It's not because you feel obligated about Annie, right?"

She swallowed hard. "I will never sacrifice my well-being to a man for any reason," she said. "I learned my lesson. I accept your support of Annie, because I also see that she is a treasure, and that we both feel called to love her. So, yes, I get that, I accept that, and I'll never kiss you for her."

He smiled. "But you'll kiss me for me?"

"Right now I will. I don't know about tomorrow. But you have my permission to pursue me for the moment."

"Fantastic." Jacob's smile was radiant, lighting her up with his joy. "I'm going to kiss you now."

She sucked in her breath in anticipation. "All right."

"'All right?' That's your response?" He chuckled as he grabbed her by the hips and pulled her onto his lap. "How about something like, 'holy smokes, that's the best offer I've ever had. Kiss me, cowboy, and make me fall in love with you like no woman has ever fallen in love with a man before.' How about that? That sounds like a good response."

Anticipation raced through her, along with fear that she ignored. "Will you settle for 'kiss, me, cowboy?'"

He feigned a grumpy face, but his eyes were dancing. "For now, I guess, but I'm going to get the rest of that sentence out of you someday." He then kissed her, sparing her the need for a response.

Which was good, because a part of her had really wanted to say that last part. But she didn't have to say it now, because this amazing man wasn't going to give up on her, no matter how difficult it was for her to let him in.

CHAPTER EIGHTEEN

JACOB AWOKE INSTANTLY at the sound of the bedroom door opening. He peered over Phoebe's head and saw Annie wander out in the hall, rubbing her eyes, clutching a soft, pink blanket. It was deep night, and the house was dark, except for the two soft lights he'd kept on for her.

"Annie," he whispered. "Your mommy's over here."

She turned, saw them on the couch together, and then ran over, her bare feet barely making a noise as she ran. She dove on top of them, and he caught her before her knee hit him in the crotch.

"Mama," she whispered sleepily.

Phoebe woke up with a start. "Annie? What's wrong?"

"I want to sleep with you and Jacob." She nestled herself between the two of them, tucked her hands under her chin, and then immediately closed her eyes with a contented sigh.

Phoebe met Jacob's gaze over her daughter's head, and he gave a quick nod, to tell her it was fine with him. The couch was deep, and there was enough space for the three of them, as long as he stayed on his side.

Phoebe smiled sleepily at him, wrapped her arms around

Annie, and then closed her eyes. Within moments, the room was filled with the deep breathing of mother and daughter sleeping soundly on the couch with him. Phoebe's feet were tucked with his, and Annie's back was against his chest, using him as a backrest.

He lifted his head so he could watch the two of them sleep. Both of them were completely relaxed in his arms, trusting him to keep them safe while they were at their most vulnerable.

Both of them had many reasons not to trust a man, and yet they had both surrendered fully to sleep while with him.

The deepest sense of satisfaction settled in Jacob, and he smiled. This was perfection, he realized. Or at least, perfection for him. It was the peace and the place he'd been missing his whole life, and suddenly, it had dropped into his life without any warning.

And, miraculously, he had let them in.

The floor creaked, and he raised his head to look. Cupcake was standing in the doorway, looking confused.

He laughed softly. "Cupcake. Come." He snapped his fingers. "Come on, boy."

The dog wagged his tail, then trotted across the floor. He hopped onto the couch, did a little circle, and then lay down in a tight little ball across Jacob and Phoebe's feet. The dog was warm, like a little foot furnace, and Jacob smiled. "No chaos tonight," he said softly. "Just peace."

He'd found he didn't mind the chaos of the day, but the peace of the nighttime? It had taken on a whole new meaning. All those frantic, desperate rides with Freedom in the darkest hours of the night, trying to outrun the noise and the shadows and the voices in his head? They'd been a reprieve, but never permanent. No healing, just a respite.

Right now, he felt like healing was possible. That there

could be a time when he didn't have to guard against memories and demons, when the only thing in his head was peace.

He looked down at the three sleeping figures. They had an entire house to roam, and yet they were all on the couch with him.

And in the most unexpected of discoveries, that was exactly where he wanted them.

CHAPTER NINETEEN

PHOEBE AWOKE to the sound of Jacob talking on the phone. She opened her eyes, saw she was on the couch, and then remembered spending the night on the couch with him and Annie.

Annie was still asleep, sprawled across the couch, her arms around Cupcake.

Phoebe kissed her daughter's head and then slid off the couch. Jacob was in the kitchen, and she could smell the coffee he was brewing.

He looked over as she neared, and the smile he gave her made her whole insides melt. It was so warm, so inviting, so tender. "Hi," she whispered.

Jacob held out his arm, and she walked into his embrace, letting him pull her against his side. "I'm going to put you on speakerphone," he said into the phone. "Phoebe's with me now."

She rested her head on Jacob's chest. His tone and body language were relaxed, so she wasn't worried about whoever he was speaking with. Bella maybe? "Hi," she said into the phone.

"Hi Phoebe. My name is Ryan Wilson. I'm working on redoing Jacob's will right now. I have a couple questions for you, if you have a moment."

Phoebe looked at Jacob in surprise. "It's five in the morning."

He nodded. "Yeah, I didn't want to waste time. What if I got run over by a bunny on the way to the barn this morning? Things need to be in order."

Emotions clogged her throat as she took the phone. This amazing man she'd just met was making sure her daughter would always be taken care of. "You're like a guardian angel."

He grinned. "I'm no saint, and I think you know that. This feels right. That's all."

"Thank you," she said earnestly.

He nodded. "Talk to Ryan. Get it figured out. Ryan, whatever she wants is fine with me."

"Right on. Ready, Phoebe?"

"Yes, of course." She stepped away from the kitchen to talk to Ryan. As she worked out the details with Ryan, she saw Annie wake up. Her daughter saw Phoebe was on the phone, so she wandered into the kitchen with Jacob. He hoisted her up on a stool, and they began to mix blueberry muffin batter together.

The man was a natural with Annie. His kindness and patience were off the charts, which she never would have expected based on his description of himself that first night. Last night had been amazing. She'd kept waking up during the night, realized she was tucked in with Jacob, Annie, and Cupcake, and then fallen back to sleep with the most wonderful sense of happiness radiating through her.

Ryan asked her another question, and she realized she was so caught up in Jacob and Annie that she hadn't been listening at all.

She turned to the window so she could focus, looking out at Jacob's beautiful lawn. "Can you repeat that?"

"Yes, indeed. Jacob would like to leave forty million dollars to Annie and you. It will be in a trust, but you can take out whatever you want."

She gripped the phone. "Forty *million* dollars?"

"Do you want more? He said more is fine if you want it."

"No, God, no." She glanced back at the kitchen. Jacob was wearing an old, faded tee shirt, jeans, and no shoes. His whiskers were the effect of more than a day or two without shaving. His hair was just a little too long to be fashionable. He looked like a ridiculously handsome hermit, not a man who tossed forty million dollars at strangers in his will. "That's too much. She doesn't need that."

"He said that's the minimum. You can start a foundation if you want. Whatever you want. Just so you know, I'm adding in a clause that says if you are found guilty of killing him, you and Annie forfeit your inheritance."

Phoebe started laughing. "Killing him?"

"Money is a powerful motivator. I've advised him against doing this, seeing as how he just met you, but he's adamant."

Phoebe paused. "Is the forty million a large part of his estate?"

"No."

Wow.

Ryan continued on to describe the trust, and that Jacob's will would list Bella and Lucas as Annie's guardians if he were her parent at that time. By the time he finished, Phoebe was in tears again.

"Mama? What's wrong?"

"Nothing, sweetie. I'm just happy." Phoebe looked over at the kitchen, at the man upending her world. "That's too much," she said.

"It's my money. I want it to go to the two of you. I don't have anyone else. It feels good to me."

She felt the truth of his words. That he didn't have anyone. That it mattered to him.

"Take it," Jacob said. "You won't ever get it, because we're both going to be rocking and rolling well into triple digits, so really, it's theoretical only."

"Well, in that case, okay." She turned back to Ryan. "Sounds good."

"Great. I'll have the paperwork over to you shortly. We'll use a remote notary until you can sign in person. It will stand up in court."

"Today?"

"As Jacob said, bunnies are everywhere." He was chuckling when he said it. "I'll call back when I'm sending the files." He said his good-bye, then hung up.

Phoebe leaned the phone against her chin, watching her daughter descend into giggles as Jacob put batter on her nose. There was absolute connection between them, and it let her know it was the right choice to pick Jacob, not some woman she didn't know who was in hiding somewhere else. "Can I use your phone to call Eliana?"

He shook his head. "Call Dylan. He'll call Eliana. She doesn't want to speak to us directly."

"Right. Okay. I'm going to make the call in the bedroom." The last thing she needed was Annie hearing her make plans for when she died. Annie made Phoebe promise that she'd be right back, and then she hurried into the bedroom.

She shut the door and then sat on the bed. The room had been so sparse when they'd first walked in, but now it was filled with everything a six-year-old could want. The Harts had jumped into action to make her and Annie feel safe, and they had the heart and financial resources to make it happen.

She hadn't known families like this existed, even though

they weren't biological, they were still everything to each other.

With a wistful sigh, she pulled up Dylan's name and hit send.

He answered immediately. "Everything okay?"

His concern was genuine, and it made her smile. "This is Phoebe. Everything's good."

"Phoebe! Hey! It's great to hear from you. How's it going with my brother? I know he's unusual, but he's a good man."

She smiled as she picked up a sweatshirt of Jacob's that was folded neatly on the dresser. "He's amazing. Thanks for sending him to get us."

"Amazing?" Dylan paused, surprise evident in his voice. "Jacob's *amazing?*"

"He is." She took a deep breath. "I'm calling because Eliana makes all her clients have a will in which they identify who will raise their kids if something happens to them."

Dylan pivoted with practiced ease, making her wonder how many of Eliana's clients he'd worked with over the years. "Yes, I've heard her talk about that."

"Well, right now, I have a woman designated that Eliana recommended, but I don't know her. Annie's never met her."

Dylan hesitated, clearly trying to figure out where the conversation was going. "Annie won't ever need her, but it's good to have an option."

"I want to change my will from that woman to Jacob."

There was absolute silence.

"Dylan?"

"Did you just say you wanted to designate Jacob to be Annie's guardian if anything happens to you?"

"Yes, exactly."

"Does he know this?"

She smiled. "He does."

"And he's all right with it? He understands what that

means? Were you clear? You really need to lay things out for him sometimes."

She frowned. "Jacob isn't as fragile or broken as you guys think he is. He needs his space sometimes, but that doesn't mean he doesn't understand things."

"Sometimes, yes, but not always. I need to know exactly how you explained it to him."

Phoebe rolled her eyes and walked to the door. She opened it. "Jacob! Dylan wants to talk to you. He doesn't believe me that you understand what you agreed to. Can you clarify and then give him the green light to call Eliana and get the paperwork going?"

Jacob's face lit up, and he whispered to Annie. "You stay here. I'll be right back."

"I'll go to the kitchen." Phoebe met Jacob in the hallway, and then giggled when he locked his arms around her waist and pulled her in for a kiss.

"I'm not gonna lie," he whispered to her as he wrapped her up. "I was a little worried you were going to change your mind in the light of day."

She pulled back to look at him. "Did you want me to change my mind?"

He met her gaze. "Absolutely fucking no."

His response made everything inside her relax. "All right then. Convince your brother that you have the brain capacity to comprehend what you agreed to, and then come eat breakfast."

He laughed as he took the phone. "My family sees me in a certain way, and that will never change. He won't see what you see, or see how I am with you."

Phoebe was pleased by his statement, happy that she saw Jacob for all that he was. "Well, then just tell him to take orders from you and call it a day."

"Will do," he grinned as he took the phone. "Hey, Dylan."

He paused. "Yeah, you could say that." He laughed, happiness in his voice. "I didn't either, but I decided to just go with it." The door shut behind him, cutting off the conversation.

Phoebe wanted to stay and listen, but Annie held up her hands. "The blueberries made my fingers purple!"

"I see that." Phoebe laughed as she headed for the kitchen. She heard Jacob's deep laugh from the bedroom, which made her smile even more. She wanted so much to stand here, in this experience, and not run away. She wanted to be brave enough to see if she could fall in love with him, and to see if he was the man worth her forever.

He was the man worth Annie's forever, so that was a good start.

CHAPTER TWENTY

"ARE BELLA AND LUCAS COMING TODAY?" Annie clutched Jacob's hand as the three of them, plus Cupcake, headed down the path toward the barn.

Jacob glanced over at Annie. "No, not today. I told them we didn't need their help today." He'd actually called them and told them not to come. After last night, he wanted to take the day and give the relationship with Phoebe a chance. Just them. No one else. To see how it went. Lucas had been resistant, but Bella had cheered him on.

It meant that Jacob couldn't take them on a ride away from the house, because he wanted extra eyes when he was away from the house, but he'd decided it was worth it.

He needed to try this, and he needed it now, before either he or Phoebe could freak out and put on the brakes.

"I like them! I want them to come!" Annie glared at him then pulled her hand free and ran ahead toward the barn, Cupcake barking and dancing around her.

Phoebe moved closer to him and slid her hand in his now free one. "Are you sure we're safe enough not to have them?"

"Yeah. We'll stay around the house. I have all the security

systems turned on. If anyone breaches the perimeter, I'll know." Her hand felt so good in his. It felt right to be connected to her that way, casual, intimate, relaxed. "I never thought I'd be a hand holder. I don't like it when most people touch me."

Phoebe squeezed his hand. "Everyone needs to be touched."

"Everyone needs to feel safe, and being touched generally doesn't make me feel safe."

She glanced at him, understanding in her eyes, and he stiffened. "Your dad?" she asked.

He watched as Annie put her hand on the security panel, and it opened for her. He'd programmed both Annie and Phoebe into his system, like his siblings, so that if they ever needed to get into the barn in a hurry, they could.

The barn was fully secure, even more than his house. He'd built it that way because that had been his home at first. The windows were laced with steel wire, and they locked automatically when he triggered the panic button. The building was fireproof, bullet proof, and had enough generator power to last for six months.

It was a little much, he could admit now, but when he'd built it, he'd needed that sense of security it gave him.

"My dad used to beat the shit out of me," he said quietly as they followed Annie inside. She ran across the barn floor, calling to the horses, but heading straight for the smallest one in the last stall. "Even as a kid, I had amazing tech skills. He would rent me out to anyone who wanted my skills, no matter what they wanted it for. Sometimes they'd come in the middle of the night, wake me up, and toss me in their van to go break into a vault somewhere." He paused. "They weren't good people."

Understatement of the century, but he didn't need to

relive it anymore. He'd wanted to move forward, let go of the power his past had over him.

Phoebe's hand tightened in his. "So, as a kid, you never had the chance to feel safe, or to control who was in your life."

"Correct." Habit made him pause to close the door behind them and set the alarm as he always did, but then he stopped. It was a beautiful day out, and the sunlight was streaming into the barn. There was a light breeze that filled the air of the barn with the scent of freedom.

He turned toward the wide-open doors and stood there, facing the outdoors.

"Jacob?"

"Every single time I walk into the barn, I close the doors behind me and set the alarm, even if I am headed right back out. I never think about it. I just do it." He stood there, not moving. "For the first time since I built this place, I want to leave the doors open."

Phoebe leaned into his side. "Do we need them closed to be safe today?"

"No. I'll get notified if anyone comes close."

"You know I believe in living a normal life whenever possible, and teaching Annie to feel safe. Letting her be normal."

He glanced at her, surprised by the emotion in his chest. "So, leave them open?"

She smiled. "Leave them open."

"All right." He put his phone in his pocket, leaving the doors open. "I can hear the birds," he said. "I can't hear them when all the doors and windows are closed."

She grinned. "Let's open the windows, then."

He glanced back into the interior of the barn, which suddenly felt so dark. "Yeah, let's." He pulled out his phone, opened the app for the barn again, then went to the windows.

His finger hovered over the button. "I've never opened the windows before."

"If your techie thing doesn't work, I know how to open windows by hand," she teased. "I'll be willing to show you."

He slung his arm over her shoulder and laughed, pulling her against him. "You're so sassy."

"I am," she agreed. "Give it a try. See what magic happens when you let the outside in."

"Magic indeed," he mused as he touched the button.

The windows began to slide open almost instantly, as if they'd been ready and waiting for him to finally set them free. He took in a breath as he watched them open. "I never thought of it before," he said. "I like it."

"Jacob," Annie shouted. "Can I go into the stall?"

"No," he called back. "Wait for me!"

"Then hurry up!" she shouted impatiently.

"Coming!" Jacob gave Phoebe a quick kiss, then strode across the barn floor toward her daughter, who was bouncing restlessly on her tip toes, her hand on the stall door, as she urged him to hurry.

When Jacob opened the door, Annie peered inside, crooning to the little pony.

Phoebe caught up, leaning over the door to watch.

The pony was in the corner, her face turned away.

Jacob went down on one knee and put his arm around Annie's waist to keep her back from the pony. "I just got her a couple days ago," he told Annie. "She's still scared. Do you see how she's not looking at us?"

Annie nodded, leaning against him in full trust.

"We need to let her know she's safe now. It will take time, but we'll do it."

"How do we tell her?" Annie whispered.

"First we give her a name." He'd a few in mind, but as

soon as he'd met Annie, he'd known she needed to name her. This pony needed to be Annie's project.

"Rosa."

Behind him, Phoebe sucked in her breath.

He raised his brows. "Why Rosa?'

"Because that's my grandma's name. Grandma Rosa. She loves me, and someday I'm going to meet her. She loves to knit, read, and tell silly stories about growing up on a farm. She loves horses so much. So, it's the perfect name."

Ah...Annie must be talking about Phoebe's mom. His heart tightened at the realization that Phoebe must talk a lot about her mom to Annie, trying to give her a sense of family and normalcy even if it wasn't safe for her to meet her grandparents. "Well, Rosa it is. Your grandma will be so happy when she finds out you named the pony after her."

Annie nodded. "Rosa," she said to the pony. "My grandma is brave and strong, just like you."

Rosa turned her head toward them and snorted softly.

Jacob put a piece of carrot in Annie's hand. "Hold your hand flat, with your palm up," he said. "Don't go to Rosa. Just hold it out for her for as long as you can, to see if she decides to come over. It has to be her choice. We never force our horses into discomfort. They always get to choose what they want to experience."

Annie nodded and held out her hand, the carrot on her palm.

Rosa looked back into the corner, and Annie sighed and lowered her hand.

"No," he said, using his index finger to raise her arm again. "It takes time to build trust. We'll wait longer, and maybe she'll come over."

"What if she doesn't?"

"We'll try again another time. And then another time. And

as many times as it takes. It might not seem like we're making progress, but we are. We're teaching her that we're safe to be around, that we're not going to hurt her or scare her."

Annie nodded. "Okay." She held out her hand again. "Can I talk to her?"

"Talking is a gift to her," he said. "It's like a Band-Aid for the heart."

Annie looked over at him. "Is that why I like it when my mom talks to me when I'm in bed at night and scared? Because it's a Band-Aid for my heart?"

"That's exactly why."

She smiled, then looked over her shoulder at Phoebe. "I love you, Mama."

"I love you too, Annie." Phoebe's voice was thick with emotion, and Jacob looked back at her as Annie held out her hand and began talking to Rosa, telling her she was safe.

Phoebe's hand was over her heart, and her eyes were shining with tears as she watched Annie. Her gaze flicked to Jacob, and she smiled. "You're a treasure, Mr. Hart."

He grinned. "Glad you think so." He couldn't believe he'd landed in this little trio that fit him like this. Yeah, he knew he was great with horses, especially traumatized ones. He knew he was a good guy. But he'd been around a lot of people in his life who made him feel like he was the one who was wrong.

These two made him feel like he was all right.

He hoped he did the same for them.

"She's still not coming," Annie said, frustration evident in her voice.

Jacob lowered her hand. "You're getting mad," he said.

"She won't come!"

"Okay." He scooped Annie up and carried her right out of the stall before she could say anything else. "Phoebe, can you close the door?"

She nodded as he carried Annie right to the other side of the barn and set her on a hay bale.

The six-year-old put her hands on her hips and glared at him. Standing on the hay bale, she was almost eye level with him, and the little firecracker was taking advantage of her elevated position "I wasn't finished!"

"Yes, you were."

She stomped her foot. "No, I wasn't!"

"You think that the way you're yelling right now is going to make Rosa feel safe and trust you?"

Annie opened her mouth to shout, and then looked over at the stall. She folded her arms over her chest and glared at him with the full fury of a six-year-old unleashed.

Jacob shrugged. "You can be as mad as you want out here, but you can't ever be around my horses when you're mad. They can feel it, and they will get scared and never trust you. When you're mad or frustrated, you quietly walk away from whatever animal you're with. You can go back when you're feeling ready to love them."

Annie narrowed her eyes and glared at the wall behind him.

He almost laughed at the full amount of rage she was directing at him, but he managed to keep a straight face.

"Annie. I will never take my anger out on my horses, and you won't either. That's the way it is. Got it?"

She refused to answer.

"You can stand on that hay bale until you're ready to say yes. Taking care of living creatures is a gift from the angels, and we always have to honor it." He paused. "I'm not mad at you, Annie. I still love you. You can be as mad as you want. Being mad is completely fine. I just need to know that you will always put the horses first. That's all. When you're ready, let me know. I'll be working with Freedom while I'm waiting."

He glanced at Phoebe as he turned away. She was watching with a frown on her face. He swore under his breath. He'd totally parented Annie just then, without consulting Phoebe first on how to handle her kid. Shit. He hoped she wasn't mad, or he hadn't undone work she'd done with the girl.

Phoebe glanced at him as he walked past, and she smiled and gave him a little nod.

Relief rushed through him. *He'd done all right.* He'd never handled a kid in a situation like that before, especially not one he cared about. He'd reacted on instincts, not even thinking, but he'd had two little ones to protect in that moment: Annie and Rosa. He'd had to come up with a solution that protected and empowered them both. Maybe he'd done all right.

Whistling softly under his breath, he walked into Freedom's stall, taking a moment to bond with the horse before snapping the halter on and leading him out. He used the remote on his phone to close the bottom half of the exterior door, so that the air could still come in, but Freedom couldn't bolt, since he didn't ever tie the horses.

Annie was still standing on the hay bale, her arms folded over her chest.

Phoebe hadn't gone over to her daughter. Instead, she walked over to Jacob. "Can I have that carrot? I'd like to sit with Rosa for a while."

He grinned and dug the carrot out of his pocket. "You bet. Remember, if you get frustrated that she won't come, then leave the stall. Take a break. It can be a long process working with these horses. Leave the door open. I like her to feel like she's not trapped."

"Got it." She smiled at Jacob, patted Freedom's neck, and then walked over to Rosa's stall. She slipped inside and sat down in the clean shavings and held out her hand. She began singing to Rosa, and the moment she did, Annie whirled around to look.

"That's my song," she said.

Phoebe ignored her and continued to sing.

Jacob looked at Annie. "Does the song make you feel safe?"

She nodded, watching her mom. "Mama sings it to me when I have nightmares. She pulls me onto her lap and sings until I fall asleep. It's not for Rosa. It's mine."

He smiled. "What if you sang it to Rosa? Maybe if you know how much it helps you, Rosa will feel that and it will help her." He paused. "Rosa has nightmares."

Annie looked at him. "She does?"

He nodded. "Yep. That's why she's scared during the day. They're always with her."

Annie pressed her lips together. She watched her mom singing to Rosa for a few minutes, while Jacob started brushing Freedom. He kept one eye on her, and he could see the longing on her face.

He waited a few more minutes, and then walked over to Annie. He held up another carrot. "I have an extra if you want to go help your mom."

"Yes!" She snatched it from his hand, but before she could jump down, he stopped her.

"I still need your promise."

She looked at him. "I promise not to be mad with the horses," she said. "I'll leave if I'm mad."

He smiled. "Perfect. And make sure to go slow, because fast movements sometimes scare them. Can you go slow?"

She nodded.

"All right, then." He lifted her down, and she walked as quick-slow as she could. She kneeled next to Phoebe and then held out her hand as she joined her mom in the song.

Jacob leaned on Freedom, his chest tightening as he

listened to the beautiful song about faith and hope, watching as his two visitors held out their hands with the carrots. Rosa kept her face in the corner, but the two never faltered. They continued to sing, and Annie climbed onto her mom's lap while they waited.

Fuck. He never thought he'd share his horses with anyone, and he never thought that anyone would care like he did.

But the way they were sitting there singing to Rosa was healing every tear in his heart.

Yeah, this was going to work for him. He knew that now, all the way to the depths of his heart. The pieces of his soul that had always been missing were sitting on the floor of Rosa's stall right now.

He knew it for sure.

But did he fit them? Would they stay here with him? Because he knew he would never leave. He could never leave. This was his home. His family. His horses. Would Phoebe and Annie stay?

He didn't know.

But he was willing to take the chance. He was willing to risk breaking in half forever for this chance to have them in his life.

CHAPTER TWENTY-ONE

PHOEBE SMILED as she walked into the living room that evening. *Frozen* was playing on Jacob's computer, since he didn't have a television. Annie was sound asleep on his lap, and Cupcake was sprawled on the floor. Jacob's head was back, and he was snoring.

She sat down on the armchair across from the sleeping bunch and looked at them, really looked at them. Annie, her beautiful daughter, with her brown skin and dozens of braids. Jacob, with his whiskers and his dimples, which she could see even in sleep.

She'd noticed scars on his forearms when he'd been working in the barn, making her wonder where he'd gotten them. He'd had hard times. Very hard. A man with no reason to trust had let himself find an amazing family. A man who needed his space and things his way had let her, Annie, and Cupcake into his life, and allowed them all to thrive.

The man had a gift for protecting. For nurturing. He'd spent the whole day in the barn with her and Annie, teaching them how to build trust with Rosa, including teaching them patience. Phoebe thought she was good at being resilient and positive, but the level to which Jacob took it was extraordinary.

They'd turned the horses out in the pasture, and stayed outside with them to keep an eye on them. It was Rosa's first time out in the field, because he'd wanted her to build confidence in her stall first. Watching Rosa gain her confidence as she followed Freedom around the beautiful pasture had been so rewarding. Jacob had created a funnel by which he could turn the horses out without ever touching them, which was needed for his new arrivals like Rosa, who didn't yet want to be touched.

Everything about his barn was for the benefit of his animals. He'd thought of everything, as only someone who had personal experience with trauma would think of.

Phoebe could see that the horses were his peace. They forced him to go to a place of serenity and patience, because he practiced the lesson he'd taught Annie, to walk away from the horses the moment that he felt any negative energy that they could pick up. To heal them, he had to become a healer and encompass his healing, soothing energy.

He needed to help the animals, which meant he'd needed to become the man who could. And he was doing the same for Annie...and for Phoebe. Even Cupcake had calmed down since their arrival. Maybe it was because he was getting more exercise and activity, but Phoebe suspected it was also Jacob's energy that seemed to wrap around everyone in his presence.

Phoebe leaned forward, resting her arms on her knees, breathing in the moment. She looked around his house. She knew that if anything lasting were to happen with Jacob, she and Annie would have to come to his world. As amazing as Jacob was, she understood that he was rooted here, and he needed to be here to thrive.

Could she thrive here?

She could work anywhere, so that wasn't an issue.

But what was the town like? What would it be like to have his family around? What were the schools like? Her gaze settled on sleeping Jacob. Most importantly, could she thrive being with him? She'd planned on being a single mom. She didn't need anyone's money. She had her daughter. Her home. Her independence. The freedom to make her own choices every minute of the day.

Could she be happy sharing her life with Jacob? Giving up some of that independence? Freedom? In exchange for love, co-parenting, support?

Her heart tightened, and she realized she wanted it, that shared life, but she didn't know if she was built for it anymore.

"What's that look for?" Jacob asked sleepily.

Her gaze shot to his, and she saw he was watching her through half-mast eyes. "I was thinking that I don't know if I can give up independence and freedom to be here with you."

He blinked, and she saw him summon his energy to wake up enough for the discussion.

"Never mind," she said. "Go back to sleep. We'll talk later."

"No. I want to talk now." He reached over Annie for his water bottle and took a drink. "All right," he said. "I'm ready. What's going on?"

She sighed. "I think I'm falling in love with you, but—"

"Hang on." He gently set Annie to the side, and then sat up. "You're falling in love with me?"

"I said I think I might be—"

"Falling in love with me."

She shifted restlessly. "Well, yes, but—"

"I'm already hook, line, and sinker for you, so that's great news."

Some of her tension faded, and she smiled. "Hook, line, and sinker?"

"Yeah. I think it's a fishing reference, but I don't fish, so I can't stake my life on that." He leaned forward, his eyes intense. "Look, Phoebe, I spent today really looking to see if I could do this with you, Annie, and Cupcake. I brought you guys all the way into my world, into the space that is wholly and solely mine. I needed to see if I could share that with you, or if your presence took away what I need to experience with it."

Her heart started to race. She hadn't thought about the fact that he was also testing to see if they fit. It wasn't only up to her. It was a team decision, obviously. "And?"

"And—" His phone beeped suddenly, and he held up his hand. "Hold that thought."

"Really?"

"Yeah. Safety first." He pulled out his phone and looked at the screen. His brow furrowed, and he swiped his phone. He touched the screen a few times, then his face drained of all color. "Holy fuck."

He bolted to his feet. "You and Annie and Cupcake get into the bathroom. Lock the door. There are no windows in there and the door is reinforced. It's built as a safe room."

"What?" Alarm shot through her. "What's going on?"

"Get Annie." He hit send on his phone. "Lucas. My security system just picked up a truck at my gate. It's my fucking father, and two men are with him." He paused. "Yeah, I'll get them in the bathroom. I'm not going outside until you guys are here. Come around and let yourself in the back door. Once you're here, I'll go out and meet him." He paused. "I have to face him. He won't ever stop. Yeah, call everyone."

He hung up. "Into the bathroom."

"Your dad?" Her heart broke for him. There was so much tension bleeding off Jacob that she felt like it was strangling him. There was even fear, born of a childhood that had never let him go. "Jacob—"

"He just got out of prison." He reached down and scooped up a sleepy Annie. "We're going to go camping in the bathroom," he whispered.

She didn't wake up. She just wrapped her arms around his neck and kept sleeping. "Grab the pillows off the couch," he said to Phoebe. "My driveway's not that long. They'll be here in a minute."

Alarm coursing through her, Phoebe grabbed a few cushions. "What do you think he's going to do?"

"Try to force me to give him money. Whatever it takes." He swore under his breath as his knee hit a coffee table. "Come on, Cupcake, let's go." The tension was coiled so tightly, but he kept his voice calm and reassuring for Annie and Cupcake.

The man was a master at controlling his emotions around vulnerable beings. No wonder he was magical with the horses and her daughter.

His urgency was evident to Phoebe, however, so she worked fast to set up a makeshift bed on the floor of the bathroom, bringing in blankets and pillows from the bedroom. Within moments, Annie and Cupcake were snoozing happily on the floor of the bathroom.

"Get inside," Jacob said as he strode across the room to his safe and put his palm on the security panel. "Don't come out until I tell you that Rosa let me touch her. That's our code."

He opened the safe and pulled out two handguns.

She stared at the guns. 'You think he's going to shoot you?"

"If he can't get my money, yeah. He'll do whatever it takes." Jacob looked over at her. "Including hurting you three. So get inside now."

They both heard the crunch of tires outside, and Jacob's face tightened. "Get in the bathroom."

She didn't move from the doorway of the bathroom. "Give me a gun."

"You good with it?"

"Yes."

He strode across the room and gave her one of his guns. As he handed it over, they heard the sound of car doors slamming. Multiple doors. "Son of a bitch." He turned to Phoebe. "I'm staying inside until my siblings get here. Once they're here, I'm going outside to deal with him. You stay in that bathroom. Got it?"

She nodded, then put her hand on his arm. "Jacob."

"What?"

"You're not a little boy anymore. You're a powerful, wealthy man with a big, badass family at his back. He can't do anything to you anymore. Do you hear me?"

He stared at her for a long moment, then he took a deep breath. "I hear you. Thanks." He leaned in and kissed her, quick and hard, but with so much emotion. He pulled back. "You fucking stay safe," he said, his voice rough.

"Of course." She waved her gun. "I'm a badass. It's all good."

"All right." He gestured for her to step into the bathroom. This time, she did. He didn't move away until she locked the door.

Then he lightly bumped his fist against the door. "You got your phone?"

"Yep."

"Call or text me if you need me, but don't trust any texts from me. Only my voice, only that one phrase."

She leaned her head against the door. "Got it. Be safe out there, Jacob."

But he didn't answer.

He'd already moved away from the door.

All she could do was wait.

She looked at her precious babies laying on the floor, and then at the gun in her hand. Suddenly, she knew she couldn't stay with Jacob. She had enough danger stalking her and Annie. No matter how much she fell for Jacob, there was no way she could bring more danger into Annie's life. She owed her daughter a better life than that.

Sudden tears surged into Phoebe's eyes, and she blinked them away.

There would be time for tears later. Right now, she was back where she'd been long ago, ready for someone to try to kill her.

She sat on the edge of the tub, between the door and her babies, held the gun at the ready, and waited.

And tried not to think of the man she definitely was falling in love with out there, alone, with a man who had terrorized him so long ago.

CHAPTER TWENTY-TWO

JACOB STOOD in his living room, facing his front door, his body between the front door and the bathroom. He could see the back door from where he was, so he was at the center.

His doorbell rang, and he tensed.

His fucking *father*. He'd been out of prison for hours, which meant he'd known all along who Jacob Hart was, and he'd had a plan in place to come after him.

Jacob didn't move toward the door. Right now, he was in a defensive position only until he got backup.

He waited, the seconds ticking by excruciatingly slowly.

The doorbell rang again.

He didn't move.

"Jacob! It's Dad! Open up!"

The sound of his father's voice brought Jacob to his knees. His legs literally gave out, and he went down to the floor. What the fuck? How could his old man still have that effect on him?

His head started buzzing, and he suddenly couldn't breathe. He felt like the darkness was closing in on him. He wanted to run. To find Freedom. To race as fast and far as he could, to escape into the darkness, into the silence, into the night.

If he didn't have the trio in his bathroom, he would sneak out his door to the barn and leave, get Freedom, and ride until he had no strength left to ride anymore.

But he couldn't.

He had to stay.

His head started hurting. So much.

"Jacob!" His father bellowed. "Open the fucking door!"

Jacob braced his hands on his thighs, trying to breathe. His vision was dotting, spinning, and—

"Jacob." Phoebe was suddenly there, her hands on his shoulders. "You're okay."

He closed his eyes, sweat beading on his brow. He couldn't even breathe. The panic was closing in on him—

"Jacob, honey, I'm here. You're not alone with this anymore."

He still couldn't think—

"Jacob!" Phoebe stood in front of him, wrapped her arms around his head, and pulled his face into her belly. "Put your arms around me. Now."

He was failing her. Danger was all around, and he couldn't protect her, like he couldn't protect Sienna before. He saw his little sister in his mind again, his baby sister, her face, the last time he saw her, when he was taken away that night and then she was gone when he got back and he never saw her again—

"Jacob."

He dragged himself out of her grasp and staggered to his feet. "Run," he whispered, his voice raw. "Run. Run while you can. I'll stall them. He can't get Annie like he got Sienna. He can't." He grabbed her shoulders. "Run!"

Phoebe put her hands on his wrists. "He can't get to Annie. He can't get to me. He can't get to you."

"Jacob!" His dad's shout echoed through the house. "Open the fucking door!"

"No!" The word tore from Jacob's throat. "No!" The "no" he'd never been able to say before ripped from him, straight from his gutted soul.

"Jacob." Phoebe was still there, still holding onto him, still talking. "Come here." She grabbed his wrist, and dragged him across the floor, right to the bathroom. "Look. Look at the floor. They need you now. This minute. They're yours to protect. You have to come back."

He stared at the floor, at the puppy and the little girl snuggling on the cushions. But for a second, he saw Sienna, with her red hair, and her freckles. "Sienna?"

"No," Phoebe said firmly. "It's Annie. She's alive, and happy and well, and she needs you right now. This minute. She loves you, Jacob. Cupcake loves you." She paused. "I love you."

Love. *Love.* The word seemed to drive a wedge into the past trying to consume him, and he looked over at Phoebe, standing there, still holding his wrist. "You love me?"

She smiled, but her brow was knitted with worry. "I do." She put his hand on her chest, over her heart. "Can you feel that? Right there? That's unconditional love. You're enough for me, for Annie, for Cupcake. Exactly as you are."

He stared at her, and suddenly, the past seemed to dissolve around him. He saw Annie sleeping on the bathroom floor, clear as day. He saw Cupcake snuggled up next to her. Sienna faded into his past, and he saw only the three who were in his life now. He reached out, and Phoebe came into his arms as he reached for her.

He buried her in his arms, and she melted into him.

His dad continued to shout for him, but Jacob didn't move. He just stood there in the doorway to the bathroom, holding Phoebe tight, feeling her arms around his waist, holding him, hugging him, trusting him.

He pressed a kiss to the top of her head and took a long, deep breath that seemed to let go of a lifetime of weight.

There was a rattle at the back door, and he looked up to see Lucas and Bella walk in. As soon as he saw them, he closed his eyes and surrendered himself completely to Phoebe, trusting his siblings to keep watch for a moment. Lucas and Bella could be his eyes and his guardians while he grounded himself in the angel that he'd allowed into his life.

His siblings didn't say anything, but he felt them standing nearby, waiting until he was ready. Always, they gave him the space he needed. Always, they accepted him for what he needed and who he was.

Jacob suddenly felt the enormity of his life. Of the people he had in it. Of the family who were his real family. Of the way they had protected him all these years, his shield against the world when it became too much to handle.

Silently, he held out one of his arms, then almost laughed when Bella and Lucas exchanged surprised glances.

"This might be a one-time thing," Jacob said. "You better take advantage."

Bella burst out in delighted laughter and threw herself into his arms, putting her arms around him and Phoebe. It took Lucas only a moment to pivot, and then he too walked over and slung his arms around the crew.

They stood there like that for a long moment. Jacob had never been in the middle of one of his family's group hugs before, and it felt...stunningly good.

There was a loud thud on the front door, and then his father shouted, "I'm going to shoot out the lock. I know you're in there!"

Jacob stepped back, and the three others dropped their

arms. He gave his siblings a smile, Phoebe a quick kiss, and then said, "I'm going out the back door. I'll circle around and come at him from the side." There was no way he was opening the front door, and giving the man a clear shot at his family.

"I'll go with you," Lucas said.

"No. I want you here with Phoebe, Annie, and Bella."

Bella and Phoebe held up their guns. "We got this," they said at the same moment, then looked at each other and burst out laughing.

Laughing. There was laughter in his hallway when the monster from his childhood was literally beating at the door. Jacob never would have believed it possible. "I want to go alone."

Lucas and Bella looked at each other. "The man is a monster," Lucas said. "You don't get to go alone."

"I need to go alone." He set his boundaries, as he always did with his family, and then headed toward the back door. As he stepped outside, Lucas walked out behind him and shut the door.

Jacob stopped. "No."

Lucas faced him. "Since we've known you, we've all respected your boundaries, Jacob. Because we love you, and we do our best to understand you. But the reason you have those boundaries is because of the guy banging on your front door. There's no fucking way you're walking out there alone, and I frankly don't give a shit what your boundaries are right now. Family is family, we claim the right to protect each other. I'm claiming that right now, so deal with it, and let's go talk to him before he breaks down that front door and gets to the girls."

Jacob stared at his brother in surprise. It was the first time any of his siblings had ever refused to respect his boundaries. He waited for the instinct to get angry and push him away, but it didn't come. All he could think about was his sister, and the trio in the bathroom. He couldn't do it alone, and he didn't want to. "Okay, let's go. You armed?"

"Hell, yeah." Lucas put his hand on Jacob's shoulder, then the two brothers headed around the side of the house.

Jacob paused at the corner of his house, listening to his father talk with the men who had accompanied him. The men's voices didn't sound familiar, but it didn't matter. It was the same men from his childhood, maybe in a different body, but the men were the same.

He looked at Lucas, and his brother nodded. "We got this, Jacob. It's time."

Jacob took a breath, shook out his shoulders, then walked around the corner.

CHAPTER TWENTY-THREE

HIS DAD WAS STANDING with his back to Jacob, so he didn't notice when Jacob walked around the corner.

Jacob felt a jolt jar through him when he laid eyes upon his father for the first time since he'd run away when he was twelve. This was the man who'd haunted him for so long, who had lived in the shadows of his mind and soul all this time. The monster who had loomed so big that the shadow cast Jacob's whole world into shades of gray.

But as his dad stood there talking with the other two, Jacob suddenly, startlingly saw that his father was simply...a man.

A man who was shorter, leaner, and less-muscled than Jacob was.

A man whose name was no longer Dad. It was Ivan Denman, criminal, convict, and loser.

Ivan's buddy looked over and saw Jacob and Lucas. He leaned in and spoke to Ivan, who turned around. His eyes were still blue, but they were like ice. Cold. Heartless. Nothing human in them at all. Nothing like Jacob's family, or Phoebe.

Jacob put his hands on his hips as Lucas came to stand behind him, mirroring his offensive stance. "What do you want?"

"Jacob." Ivan held out his arms like he was going to hug Jacob and started walking toward him.

"Don't come near me." Jacob's gun was at his hip, within easy reach, but he didn't feel compelled to grab it. He suddenly realized he didn't need a gun to deal with this old man. He didn't need anything. Ivan Denman could not hurt him, not anymore.

Ivan stopped, and his eyes narrowed. "Got all rich and famous, did you?"

"What do you want?" he repeated. His voice was low and calm, reflecting the calmness that had surprisingly settled over him.

Ivan settled his weight back, eyeing Jacob speculatively. Jacob could see the wheels turning in his head, assessing Jacob, and trying to figure out the best approach. "You got your money for your security software when you sold it. Billions."

Jacob said nothing. He just watched him unflinchingly, meeting his father's gaze for the first time in his life.

"Yeah, well, I gave you those skills," Ivan said. "I taught you everything you used to make that software. I deserve half."

Lucas snorted, but Jacob didn't react. "Do you?"

Ivan pulled his shoulders back. "Yeah, I fucking do."

"What happened to Sienna?"

Ivan's face flickered in surprise. "That girl who lived with us?"

"My sister. Yeah."

"She wasn't your fucking sister. She was a leftover from my old girlfriend."

Anger coiled in Jacob's chest. "She was my sister," he reiterated firmly. "What happened to her?" She'd been sleeping in her bed when Jacob had been dragged out of his and tossed into a van to help one of his father's associates. When he'd come back, she'd been gone. He'd looked everywhere for her, raged at his father, threatened everyone he knew, and never found a clue. "Did you kill her?"

"I sold her."

Jacob felt his knees start to buckle, but then Lucas put his hand on Jacob's shoulder. The feel of his brother's hand sent strength shooting through Jacob, and suddenly, the little, scared, helpless boy that had lived inside him for so many years was gone.

All that was left was a protector. A man who had strength, resources, and a family to protect. Movement behind Ivan caught Jacob's eyes, and he saw two more of his brothers, Colin and Tristan, walking silently up behind his father.

Hell, yeah.

Jacob strode across his grass, the grass Annie loved, right toward his father. His dad's pals moved in close to Ivan, but they didn't pull their guns. Because they still didn't understand the man Jacob had become.

He walked right up to Ivan as Colin and Tristan neared. He pulled out his gun before his dad or his henchman could react, and he held the gun under Ivan's chin. As he did so, Colin and Tristan put guns to the heads of the other two men, who immediately held up their hands.

Lucas just folded his arms over his chest and grinned.

"Tell me who you sold her to," Jacob demanded.

Ivan met Jacob's gaze with unflinching remorseless. "You'll never shoot me. You're soft. You always were soft."

Of course, on some levels, Ivan was right. None of the Harts would ever shoot anyone in cold blood. But Ivan didn't know that. Jacob narrowed his eyes. "Your blood runs in my veins," he said, letting a chill etch into every word. "I have enough money to make anything happen that I want. Anything. Including a long private visit for you and your friends in a windowless cement shack, where you all get to experience all the pain that Sienna and I experienced, again and again, until all you want to do is die, and even that won't come for you. No one to save you. No one to hear your screams. Just like the two little kids who you betrayed like the demon you are."

Out of the corner of his eye, Jacob saw his brothers fight to suppress their grins, because they knew he was completely bullshitting Ivan. As fucked up as the Harts were, there wasn't a single sociopath among the bunch. But Ivan didn't know that. Jacob had to look away to keep from laughing in Ivan's face.

God, it felt good to be able to laugh in the monster's face, instead of cowering from his reign of terror.

Ivan's eyes widened, and real fear crept into his eyes.

Tristan coughed to cover his laughter, and suddenly Jacob couldn't keep it in. It just felt so fucking surreal to not be scared. He burst out laughing, and the look of absolute horror on his dad's face made him laugh even harder.

"You're fucking insane," Ivan gasped.

"I am," Jacob agreed, as his brothers all broke into grins. "I'm a crazy-as-shit, billionaire with more resources than you can ever imagine. I'm untouchable, as are all my siblings, and anyone we care about." He leaned in. "I can pay for the very, very best hunters in the entire world to come after you, and there's nowhere you can hide to stay safe. Do you understand? You'll never be safe again. You can never feel safe again. Because you never know when I'm going to make that call to make you a target. But I can promise you one thing: I will have you watched at all times, and if you *ever* do anything to hurt anyone, especially anyone I care about, I will make that call. One strike and you're out. And I might make the call anyway. Because I can, and we both know you deserve it."

Ivan looked frantically at Jacob, and then at his brothers, who were all sporting the biggest shit-eating grins.

Finally, Ivan shook his head. "You wouldn't. I'm your old man."

"Nope. You're just an asshole."

At that moment, two big black SUVs rolled down the driveway. Dylan's security team from his detective business. Jacob grinned as four huge, heavily armed men in suits got out of the trucks. Jacob pointed at Ivan. "This is the guy. Escort him out and follow him closely until the shadow team arrives. Once they're there, you can pull out."

His brothers started laughing again, because they knew there was no shadow team, but Ivan looked sick. "You bastard," he snapped.

"Who did you sell Sienna to?"

"Fuck you."

Jacob nodded at the security team, and they all pulled their guns out and pointed them at Ivan. His brothers grinned, then they all did the same, so that there were seven guns pointed at Ivan.

It was a lot.

Not really Jacob's style.

But it also felt damned good, and he had a sister to protect. "I want a name."

Ivan lifted his jaw, and sweat beaded down his temple. "Big Billy."

Big Billy. The name wasn't familiar. But it still made chills run down Jacob's spine. "Full name."

Ivan paused for a moment, and Jacob could tell he was trying to remember, not stalling. Finally Ivan said, "Billy Sampson. Only met him a couple times. Don't know if that was his real name or not."

"Tell me everything you remember about him."

"I don't know. He brokered a couple shipments for me. A middleman. Never heard from him again after I sold Sienna to him."

Jacob ground his jaw. "Did he deal in women? Did he traffic women?" The thought made him sick, but he had to know what his sister had faced, where she might have gone.

"All I saw was drugs."

"Why did he want her?"

More sweat was pouring down Ivan's face. "I don't know. He didn't say. What did I care? Didn't matter."

Jacob stared at the man who had once ruled his life. "It did matter, and it does now. Sienna matters. I matter. You are *nothing*. Remember that. And remember that I have all the control now."

Ivan lifted his jaw. "Oh, yeah? If you want me tortured, then why you going to let me go?"

Jacob smiled. "Because I want you scared and looking over your shoulder every single minute of every day for the rest of your life, just like the two kids you were supposed to keep safe."

Jacob took a breath, but realized he had nothing else to say. He was done. Done with this man who had haunted him for so long. He looked around at his brothers, who were all standing there, guns out, having his back. "I love you guys."

They all grinned. "Back at ya, Jacob."

Satisfaction settled deep in Jacob, a freedom he'd been seeking his whole life, a freedom from his past. He looked down at the old man who had been so scary for so long. Now? He was just a powerless old man. "That's all. Leave."

Then Jacob turned away and walked back around the house. He knew the security team would make sure Ivan and his pals got off the property. Jacob also knew he'd laid out a significant enough threat that Ivan would never come after him or his family again. Jacob was safe, and he hadn't had to stoop to the level of his dad and hurt anyone.

He'd won, and it felt incredible.

Jacob didn't look back as he walked away. He wasn't even tempted.

He simply let him go.

And when he heard footsteps behind him, he knew it was his brothers following him back into his house.

His family. His world.

CHAPTER TWENTY-FOUR

BELLA TURNED off the security video of Jacob and his dad that she and Phoebe had been watching, since Bella had access to his security system. "Holy crap," Bella said. "That was amazing."

Phoebe was stunned by what she'd seen. What she'd heard. This man had sold Jacob's sister? Now she had a glimpse into what Jacob had endured as a child. She'd known it must have been bad to have created the response in Jacob, but...wow...

Her heart broke for him...and for what it meant for them.

The back door opened, and Jacob walked in, followed by two men she didn't know, plus Lucas.

"Jacob!" Bella raced down the hall and flung herself into Jacob's arms. "I'm so proud of you."

Jacob hugged his sister, but his attention was on Phoebe. He kept walking, walking straight toward Phoebe.

She could see the need on his face, and she knew now wasn't the time to tell him that there could be no future with them. Tomorrow would be time enough. Tonight, Jacob needed her, and she wanted to be there for him.

So, she held up her arms and swept him up in a hug when he reached her. He locked his arms around her waist and lifted her off the ground, crushing her against his chest, burying his face in her hair. He held her that way for a long moment, until his family consumed them with hugs and cheers.

Jacob laughed. "Annie's asleep. Keep it down." He waved them all to the kitchen, keeping his arm around Phoebe.

As they walked away, Phoebe heard her daughter's sleepy voice calling to her from the bathroom. "You guys do your thing," she said. "I need to do Mom stuff."

Jacob frowned. "I'll help with Annie."

"No." She touched his arm. "Go with your family. We'll be here when they leave."

He smiled and nodded. "All right." He kissed her quickly, then released her.

Phoebe paused to watch his family surround him with support and love. There was triumph, but there was also a depth of weariness and pain, making her realize that every one of them had a similar past, and they all had gone through that moment with Jacob, experiencing it from their own places of trauma.

And yet, they were in that kitchen, laughing, supporting each other, always there together as a family. Loving each other. She had a sudden desire to walk over there, introduce herself and meet these other members of the Hart family. To feel their love directed at her.

"Mama!"

Sudden tears filled Phoebe's eyes, and she turned away, slipping into the bathroom. Annie was propped up on her elbows, frowning sleepily at the door, while Cupcake thumped his tail happily. "Why am I in the bathroom?"

"Because Jacob was watching a loud movie and I thought the bathroom was quieter." Yep, she was going to lie to her daughter. Any good mom knew that strategic lies were the stuff of masterful parenting techniques.

Annie held up her arms. "Bed, mama."

"You got it, honey." Phoebe picked up her daughter, then used one hand to open the door. Cupcake ran out into the kitchen to greet the guests, while Phoebe slipped into Jacob's bedroom with Annie. She tucked her daughter into the big bed, retrieved the fuzzy blankets and stuffed animals from the bathroom, then snuggled her daughter, who needed her or Cupcake in order to fall asleep.

Annie fell asleep quickly, but Phoebe didn't. She kept replaying the scene from outside. The sociopathic depravity of Jacob's dad. *He'd sold Jacob's sister.* All the guns that the Harts had pointed at his head. Jacob's face when he'd turned to walk away: triumph, empowerment, and a peace she'd never seen in him before.

How had Jacob become so full of love and nurturing when that was his past? It showed the strength of his character, the power of his soul, the healing effect of finding his family.

He was such a good man. It was no wonder he could connect with animals with a tough past, with Annie, and even with her. He understood those shadows, but he also knew how to find peace and goodness in himself despite those tentacles.

She didn't want to leave, she realized.

She wanted to stay with him. In this house. In this life. With him, his horses, and his family. Annie would thrive. She would thrive. And she suspected Jacob would thrive.

But the little girl in her arms didn't give her that choice.

As soon as Annie's biological father was found, they had to leave...and quickly, before it became impossible for Phoebe to do what was right.

CHAPTER TWENTY-FIVE

His family didn't stay long, but their visit was real in a way it hadn't ever been before.

Jacob had always kept the walls up, but facing down his dad with his siblings there had shattered walls that he would never rebuild. His siblings had witnessed his darkest secrets, and they'd stood by him.

Jacob leaned against the front door frame, watching them depart. The laughter was real. The resilience of the Harts, their mantra, to always allow for joy and love whenever possible. There was too much shit in life, and the only way to thrive was to allow every ray of sunshine through they could find. That was their family commitment, and the smile on Jacob's face and in his heart as he watched them go showed how powerful it was.

He waited until the last set of taillights disappeared, then looked out across his property. The security lights were all on, letting him see across his lawn and into his woods. This fortress he'd built had been to protect against his father, and the memories of his past. But he didn't need it anymore. Even if his dad came back again, this time, Jacob knew he was more than his dad. He knew his dad couldn't hurt him anymore.

He didn't need this security anymore for himself.

But he needed it for Annie and Phoebe. Because it was their turn to get the freedom he now had.

He would never forget the way Phoebe came out of that bedroom and grounded him when he'd lost his shit after hearing his dad's voice. She'd been pure strength for him, not afraid of the man he'd lapsed into. No judgment. Just acceptance and empowerment.

Smiling to himself, Jacob stepped back and shut the door as he pulled out his phone. He called Dylan, knowing it didn't matter that it was two in the morning. Harts were always available 24/7 for each other.

Dylan answered on the first ring. "What's up?"

"My dad came by tonight."

Dylan swore. "What happened?"

Jacob walked into the kitchen, smiling when he saw the dishes from when he'd made brownies with Annie earlier. He filled his brother in on all of it, including Sienna.

Dylan got right to the point, knowing exactly why Jacob had called. "I've never been able to find Sienna before, but having the name of the man he sold her to might help. I'll start looking as soon as I'm off the phone."

"Thanks." Jacob grinned. "You're the best there is."

"I know." Dylan paused. "How are you doing? After tonight?"

"Feeling free, I guess. Free to start living."

"Feels good?" There was a hint of envy in Dylan's voice, which Jacob understood.

"Yeah. Don't give up, Dylan. Keep fighting."

"Always do." Dylan paused. "How are your newest horses?"

He knew Dylan was asking about Annie and Phoebe,

using code just in case someone was listening. "I think I fell in love with them." The words felt so real, and so fucking good. Not scary. Just deeply satisfying.

Dylan was silent for a moment. "You're kidding."

"No."

"And what about them?"

"Yeah. Same, I think." Phoebe had told him she loved him. It had been in a high-stress moment, but he'd heard those words loud and clear. Her words had unlocked something inside him as soon as she'd said them. Maybe that was why he felt so free? Not simply because of Ivan? Maybe because of Phoebe's love. Yeah. That felt right.

"Well, hell, I deserve all the credit on this one." Dylan sounded so pleased. "I had a gut feeling that you needed to go get them. Fuck, man, I'm so happy for you. Can't wait to meet them when I'm back."

"Thanks. Looking forward to it. Any word on their original owner?"

"Nope. Still looking for him. I'll keep you posted."

"Great. I'll talk to you later." Jacob hung up, swung the phone in his hand for a minute, simply breathing in how good he felt. The monster who had sat in his gut for decades was simply gone, because he'd faced down that very monster and won. And because he'd done it with the support of Phoebe and his siblings.

It made him realize he should have gone to see Ivan long ago. Leaving Ivan in his past, when Jacob had been a powerless teenager, had allowed Ivan to become bigger, badder, and more powerful with each passing day, at least in Jacob's mind.

Visiting Ivan in prison would have shed precious light on the truth, and maybe even helped Jacob find out about Sienna sooner. Sienna. His happiness faded. Was she still alive? And if so...how bad had her life been? He'd found his family and thrived in love, but what about her?

"If you're still out there, Sienna," he said aloud, "the Harts are coming for you. And we cannot be stopped." He put it out there into the universe, to his sister, in case she was listening.

Dylan would find her. He knew it. His brother had connections in every alley and dark corridor. It was what he did. Jacob could feel it. He would have answers soon, and he prayed they were good ones.

But in the meantime...

He armed his security system, shoved his phone in his back pocket, then walked down the hall to his bedroom. He cracked open the door and peered inside. The faint sliver of light cast mother and daughter into just enough illumination that he could see them. His heart tightened when he saw them snuggled together. Fuck, they were his whole heart now. Already. Completely.

Cupcake squeezed past his leg, shoving the door open, as he leapt onto the bed. Annie didn't move, but Phoebe lifted her head. She blinked sleepily at the dog, and then at Jacob.

"Didn't mean to wake you," he whispered. "We'll talk in the morning."

"No," Phoebe mumbled sleepily and wiggled out from under the covers. "I'm coming."

Jacob smiled as he watched her crawl over the blankets, careful not to wake her daughter. He held the door for her, glancing at Annie to make sure she was still asleep before closing the door behind Phoebe.

Before he could say anything, Phoebe turned to face him. "How are you doing?"

"Great. Free. Feels surreal."

She smiled. "That's how I felt after I found out my ex had died. It took me a while to stop jumping at shadows, but every day, the shadows became fainter, until they disappeared."

"Until Annie, when the danger started again."

"Until Annie," she agreed. "Any word on Annie's bio dad?"

He shook his head. "Not yet, but they'll find him. Men like that aren't smart enough to stay hidden forever."

"I know." She sighed. "Seeing you and your brothers with all the guns out, and seeing your dad, who was literally terrifying, made me realize that we're still living in danger. Am I stupid for trying to live normally? For letting Annie go to school? For teaching my class? If I ran into your dad alone, he would have been able to do whatever he wanted to me and Annie, and that's terrifying."

Jacob shook his head. "You can't live in a cave. You're right about that."

Phoebe paced away from him, heading toward the gym, which was the only other room in the house which had a door. He followed her, and she closed the door behind him when he walked in.

She sat down on the edge of the mattress that he hadn't yet slept on. "I don't want Annie to overhear us." She patted the bed next to her.

He took a seat, but didn't make a move for her. He could tell she was strung tightly, and she hadn't invited him over for physical intimacy. "What's going on?"

Phoebe pulled her knees to her chest. "Since I left my ex, I haven't actually faced any danger. It's been in the shadows, but not actually a part of my life. While it's made me scared, it's also allowed me to feel maybe a little cavalier about my safety. And now that it's Annie at risk?" She looked at him. "I would never, ever forgive myself if something happened to her. But how do I live like this? I had her hiding in a bathroom tonight, Jacob. A *bathroom*."

Jacob could feel Phoebe spiraling, just as he had earlier, so he leaned in toward her, resting his shoulder against hers. "First of all, despite everything that has happened, you have kept Annie oblivious. She had no idea there was danger tonight, and she has no idea that you're here because of her biological father. She's having an adventure and becoming more confident every day. So give yourself credit for that. It's not easy."

She nodded. "I know, thanks. I just—" She let out her breath. "You let your dad leave."

"Yeah. I'm not going to shoot him. I refuse to be that kind of man."

"But he could come back."

"He won't. And if he did, I can handle him."

She looked at him. "What if he were to come back, and you weren't here, but Annie and I were?"

He went cold at the idea. "Fuck."

She nodded. "I watched you out there with your brothers. All the guns. The look on your dad's face. He's a scary man, Jacob. Really scary. Like, monster scary."

He ground his jaw. "I know." Until tonight, he'd wondered if he'd made up how vile Ivan was, but tonight had shown him that he hadn't imagined it.

She looked over at him. "I told you tonight that I loved you."

His heart started racing. "Yeah. I heard that." He wanted to tell her that he loved her and Annie too, but he could tell she wasn't finished. She needed to speak.

"I meant that. If things kept working with us, I'd want to stay here with you. I think you would thrive with us, Annie would thrive here, and so would I."

He heard the conditional tenses she was using, and he hardened himself for what was coming next. "But?"

"But I can't raise my kid in danger. As long as your father

is alive, you bring with you a danger that's terrifying. You can't be with us all the time, and I don't want either of us to live with a bodyguard following us all the time."

He flexed his jaw. So much for not having an actual shadow team. "I'll have men trail him all the time. He won't be able to do anything we don't know about."

"What about people who work for him? People who are inspired to help him because of the amount of money at stake represented by your bank accounts? You're worth so much risk because of your money, Jacob. He's not going to stop. He's just going to find another way."

Jacob ground his jaw. "I have resources."

She looked at him. "As soon as he realizes that Annie and I exist and you care about us, he'll know we are his path to you. What would you give up to keep us safe?"

He swore. "Anything."

Her face softened, and her eyes filled with tears. "This is why I'm falling in love with you," she said. "I was talking about money, but you were talking about anything."

"Because it's true." He took her hand and tangled his fingers with hers. "I didn't keep my sister safe, and he sold her. Every day of my life, I will carry that guilt that I didn't protect her."

She tightened her fingers in his. "I know. I'm sorry."

He nodded. "We'll find out soon where she ended up. I'm hoping for a miracle, but in the meantime, my entire focus is on protecting you and Annie. As soon as Dylan told me about you and Annie, I knew that it's my calling to protect you."

She smiled. "And it didn't take me long to realize that we were meant to inject such chaos into your life that you couldn't stay the same."

"It worked." He rubbed her palm with his thumb. "I'm falling for you and Annie, and even your crazy dog," he said.

She looked over at him. "I can't stay," she said quietly. "We can't stay. Not with your father out there somewhere, looking for a way to get to you."

Resistance flooded Jacob. "We'll find a way."

"And if we make one mistake, one tiny mistake, and Annie gets caught in the crossfire, neither of us will ever forgive ourselves." She pressed her hand on his. "I think I've been lucky to be living as freely as I have, but your dad showed me that there are some risks that I need to take more seriously."

Jacob tightened his grip on her hand. "I love you, Phoebe. You and Annie and Cupcake. The Harts believe that we never let evil win. We fight until we find a way. Stay and fight."

She bit her lip. "I can't," she whispered. "Annie's my entire world. I can't take that chance. I saw your father, Jacob. He's too much." She touched his cheek. "And you know it, too."

He put his hand over hers, holding her hand to his cheek. "He isn't too much," he said again. "He doesn't get to win. To steal happiness from us. The Harts are an unstoppable force."

"How many of your siblings have guns?"

He paused. "All of us."

"Why?"

"Because we have pasts."

"Which means that even if your dad goes back to prison, all the rest of your siblings could have their version of Ivan coming for them. So anyone who is with your family is at risk."

He swore. "No, that's not how it is."

She met his gaze. "There's no risk from your past? And your siblings' pasts?"

"There's always risk," he said. "But you know that. You're the one who told me that you have to find a way to live, no matter what."

"I know. But that was before I stared evil in the eye and

realized he could be coming for my baby. My ex was a bastard and wanted to kill me, but compared to your dad? He was like a baby bunny."

Phoebe looked over at him, and he saw the sadness in her eyes. He knew she'd already decided. There was no other option for her, as a mother. His heart wanted to crack in half, but he refused to let it. He wasn't giving up now, not now that he had the chance to finally start living.

But he understood where she was, and what she was feeling.

He didn't know how he was going to get this sorted, but he knew he would. He had to, for all their sakes. He knew he was good for Annie...and for Phoebe. And they were already his world.

"Jacob," she said firmly. "We're going to leave."

He took a breath, knowing that she was in too deep to even hope for an answer, a solution, let alone look for one, so he nodded. "I understand. I'd never ask you to endanger Annie, or yourself."

She nodded. "Okay."

He cupped her face with his hand. "I love you, Phoebe. You and that beautiful daughter of yours. And Cupcake." He leaned in to kiss her before she could answer. A kiss to remind both of them of this beautiful thing coming to life between them.

She kissed him back, fiercely, almost desperately.

He pulled her into his lap, and she came willingly, settling her knees on either side of his hips while they continued to kiss, never breaking the kiss. She clasped her hands behind his neck as he palmed her hips, feeling the curves of her body under his hand. "I love touching you," he whispered between kisses.

"It's an incredible gift," she said. "I didn't think I could feel safe in a man's arms again, let alone want to be naked and vulnerable, but you give me that gift."

He grinned. "You want to be naked? Now?"

Her gaze met his. "Yes."

Need coursed through him. "Hang on." He set her to the side, then rolled off the bed. He strode into the hall, checked on a sleeping Annie and Cupcake, then left her door ajar. When he got back to their room, he locked the door. "I left her door open so we can hear her if she calls for us."

Phoebe had scooched back to the middle of the bed, and she was on her back, propped up on her elbows. "You're incredibly thoughtful. You'd make an amazing dad."

His breath caught. "I never thought about being a dad until I met Annie." He sank onto the bed beside her and pulled her into his arms. "Until you." He kissed her, using his actions to tell her how deeply he meant his words. This little trio had turned his world into chaos and rebirth in a matter of days.

He would give his life to keep them safe, but he hoped he didn't have to, because he wanted to live his life...with them.

Phoebe tugged at his shirt, and he pulled it over his head as she did the same. He ran his hand over her hips, then slid her pants down over her legs, kissing her skin with each additional inch exposed. "You're incredibly beautiful," he said. "My angel."

She ran her fingers through his hair and laughed softly. "My mom used to call me a demon. I was a handful as a kid. Kind of like Cupcake."

"Kids should get the chance to be handfuls," he said as he pulled her pants over her feet, and paused to kiss each toe.

She watched him, her eyes sparkling with laughter. "I have nice toes, do I?"

"You do. They're very kissable." He kissed the arch of her

foot. "And this part, too." Then he kissed her inside ankle-bone. "And here, as well." He raised her foot up, and kissed her along the back of her calf. "Fantastic legs, by the way."

She grinned. "I've always considered myself drop dead gorgeous, personally. Men often fall to their knees and crawl around after me, because I'm really too much for most of them."

"Not too much for me." He moved between her legs and kissed her again, deeper, pure seduction and need. "I love how much you are," he whispered. "On every level."

She locked her arms around his neck. "I can tell. It feels good."

"You feel good." He slid down her body and kissed across the swell of her breasts. Her body was already starting to feel like home, the place where he belonged, and he leaned into that allowing himself to connect with her physically, on a deeper level.

She patted his ass. "Pants off, cowboy. I want me some of this awesomeness."

He laughed and rolled off her long enough to shuck his boots, jeans, and boxers. When they came back together, with nothing between them, it felt shudderingly right.

He locked his leg over her hip, and she snuggled against him, chest to chest, entwined and touching along the length of their bodies. He kissed her again, a long, leisurely kiss which quickly ramped up into an escalating fire.

She rolled him onto his back, and sat across his hips, settling deeply. He spread his hands on her thighs, and slid them along her hips, up her ribs, and cupped her breasts. She tipped her head back and closed her eyes, fully surrendering to him, trusting him, enjoying him.

He loved her surrender, and how much it spoke to her trust of him. This was a woman who had learned not to trust men, and yet she completely trusted him, a man born from a life filled with terrible things.

He shifted her hips, and she met his gaze as she settled on him, taking him into her body. He groaned as she began to move. "You're going to kill me if you keep doing that."

"Am I?" She grinned. "You said I wasn't too much for you."

He loved her sass so damn much. "You're not. It was metaphorical."

"Was it?" She cocked her head. "I don't know if I believe you. I think you're scared of what I do to you."

"Scared shitless, yeah," he agreed, and he moved one hand between her legs. "But willing to go there."

She let out a low moan and closed her eyes as she continued to move. "Wow, just wow. Okay, you win."

"We all win. That's what love is."

Her body began to shudder, and she leaned forward, her hands digging into his chest. "God, Jacob—"

"Surrender, Phoebe. I've got you."

"*Jacob.*" His name tore from her throat, and she fully surrendered to the orgasm. His body responded, tearing out of his control, and he gave himself fully over to the connection, the electricity, the culmination into a glorious finish.

When the final shudders finally faded, Phoebe collapsed onto his chest with a groan. "I have nothing left," she said. "You literally took every last bit of my soul with that."

He laughed softly and wrapped his arms around her, holding her on his chest as he kissed her hair. "You have my soul as well, so we're even."

She sighed and rested her chest above his heart. "I want to stay here forever."

"I agree." He closed his eyes and breathed in the moment, trying to imprint her being in his arms, the sound of her breathing, the faint scent of flowers that seemed to follow her everywhere, the way his body and soul felt complete peace and contentment.

"Jacob."

"Mmm."

"Can you have Bella and Lucas spend the day with us tomorrow? And maybe your other brothers? I'd like to take Annie riding, but I'm scared to go out there now."

"If you're scared to go outside, then we're definitely going. They'll be there."

"Great. Thanks." She yawned and snuggled more deeply against his chest.

"Before we fall asleep, we need to put clothes on, in case Annie comes in."

She groaned. "I'm too tired."

He laughed and slid out from under her. He gathered her clothes, and helped her pull them on, chuckling. "You're dead-weighting it, babe. A little help?"

She didn't open her eyes. "You're a big, strong man. Do your thing."

"You're a strong, capable woman," he pointed out as he lifted her limp leg to pull her sweatpants over her foot.

"I know. I have to be strong and capable every minute of every day." She flung her arms above her head and rested them on the pillow. "I don't want to be strong and capable right now. I want to be a mushy pile of nothing but happiness right now."

He laughed. "You got it, babe. I'm on it." They were both laughing the whole time he got her dressed, battling her absolute deadweight, but it was awesome. He loved that he could do that for her, give her the chance to turn off everything but receiving help.

When they finally collapsed together on the bed, both of them dressed, and the door unlocked and ajar, he knew that he had to find a way to make this happen between them. A way to have it all.

Because now that he'd gotten a taste, he knew he could never go back to what he'd been, or what his life had looked like before Annie and Phoebe.

CHAPTER TWENTY-SIX

"THAT WAS SIX SKIPS!" Annie shrieked with delight as Jacob's rock finally sank into the gently flowing river. "Show me how to do it!"

Jacob knelt down in the water as he showed Annie how to hold the rock.

Phoebe smiled as she watched Jacob with her daughter. He was amazing. The day had been incredible.

Riding. Racing. Picnicking. Taking advantage of every bit of the glorious land the Hart Ranch occupied. They'd seen two bald eagles, seven fox babies peeking out from a pile of rocks, and a herd of local wild horses that the Harts nurtured on their ranch.

Jacob's siblings had been hilarious. They were all so funny and charming, but also the kindest people she'd ever met.

She loved everything about the day, and she knew she was falling head over heels for Jacob and his family.

Phoebe was sitting on a high rock, her knees pulled to her chest as she watched Annie and Jacob play. Lucas was standing beside him, while Tristan sat on his horse atop a distant butte, where he had a longer-range view. Colin was on his horse in the river, letting his mount cool off after a long day of riding.

"What's going on?" Bella climbed and sat down beside her. "You look sad."

"I love your brother."

Bella grinned. "That's obvious. He loves you, too. I'm happy to hear that. He's such a good man."

"I know. I trust him, which I never thought I would do again."

Bella nodded. "I know how you feel. All of us have trust issues. Jacob might be the one with the biggest challenges, and it makes me so happy that you guys found each other. I thought he might never let anyone in."

Phoebe slanted a glance at Bella. "Thanks for being so nice to me and Annie. You've been amazing."

Bella smiled. "Honestly, we all feel that you're like us. Good heart. Good person. Been through enough in life that you appreciate the good moments that come your way. We don't let many people into our circle, but you fit." She bumped her shoulder against Phoebe's. "Wait 'til you meet my sister, Meg. She's awesome. And my brothers Brody and Keegan are both married now to amazing women. You'll love them, and my brothers."

Phoebe took a breath. "I have to leave."

The smile dropped off Bella's face. "For a day? Or forever?"

"For now, at least."

Bella stiffened. "Why?" Her voice was colder now. Defensive. Protective of her brother.

"Because I have to keep Annie safe. It's my sacred duty as her mom."

Bella's jaw dropped open. "Are you kidding? You think she's safer away from us?" She pointed at the river. "Right now, she has four Hart men around her. All armed. All tough.

All smart. And she has me up here. And all my other siblings. Plus all our money. If you leave, all she'll have is you. How on earth is she safer away from here?"

"Because Jacob's dad is still out there. He knows he can't get to Jacob now, but he could get to Jacob through Annie. As long as we're with Jacob, it makes Annie a target. She's had a tough enough life so far. I need to make her life safer, not more dangerous."

Bella's jaw jutted out. "So, you're going to let an asshole win?"

"He's not just an asshole. He's a sociopath. He sold Jacob's sister. How can I possibly put Annie on his radar?"

"So, leave now then. Just go."

"I can't. Annie's biological father is looking for her—"

"So, you'll take advantage of all of us to protect Annie from a danger that comes with her, but the minute that's over, you'll take off running because you're too scared to handle what comes with Jacob? You didn't run from Annie even though she came with a possibly murderous appendage, but you're going to run from Jacob?"

"It's different—"

Bella was angry now. "How? How is it different?"

"Because Annie's a child! She needed me. I knew I was her mom the minute I met her. And I'd made a promise to her bio mom to be the one to take care of her—"

"And you didn't make a promise when you fell for Jacob? And you don't think Jacob needs you? The man lives in a self-made prison! Last night was the first time he's let any of us hug him in a decade! Maybe more! You think that's living? It's not. He might be a grown man with a lot of money and resources, but you're vastly underestimating yourself if you think he doesn't need you!"

"What if I make a choice that gets Annie killed?" she almost shouted the words back at Bella.

Bella stared at her. "Don't you get it by now? That you can't hide from danger in life? What if Jacob's dad drowns in some river tomorrow and no one finds him and we never know he's dead, but you left and never come back because of what *might* be. You could have spent the next fifty years with the man you love, but you don't, because of some imagined threat that doesn't even exist anymore? And your little girl could have had the dad who would give her everything she could ever need, including and especially love?"

Anger began to simmer through Phoebe. "I gave up my family for Annie, so I could go into hiding—"

"Do you like your family?" Bella interrupted.

"I love them—"

"You have family you love, and you gave them up because some jerk might come after you someday? Are you kidding?"

Phoebe bunched her fists. "You don't understand what it's like to be hunted by a monster, Bella. Eliana gave me, and Annie, the chance to live without fear. When you've been staring into the eyes of your husband, certain that tonight is the night he's going to kill you, it changes you forever. *Forever.* You can call me a wimp. Maybe you're right. But I'm too damned scared of how bad men can be to stand here and put Annie in the crosshairs of Ivan. I'm sorry for being scared. If you can tell me how to stop being so freaking scared, and to know how to keep my baby girl safe, then do it. Tell me."

Bella's face softened, and her mouth pursed with regret. "I'm sorry. I didn't know about your background."

Phoebe shrugged. "Do you have a magic wand, Bella? Because that's what I need."

Bella looked down at the river. "You know there's no magic wand, Phoebe. I have my own story, my own past, and it still follows me. I don't have an answer as to how to leave it behind, but I do know that the nine of us are safe because we trust each other. We set up external safeguards, and more importantly, we rely on each other. I'd never in a million years give up my family to stay safe. I'd fight for them, with them, and beside them until my last breath, because they're what makes life worth living."

Phoebe closed her eyes. God, she wanted to be a part of this family. "What if you fell in love with a man who had an enemy who would hunt down your brothers and torture them, just to hurt the man you love? Who would you choose? Stay with the man you fell in love with and let your brothers be in danger? Or leave him to keep your brothers safe?"

"My brothers come first," Bella said without hesitation. "Always."

Phoebe looked over at Bella. "That's what I'm doing," she said softly. "I have to give up the man of my heart to keep my daughter safe. If I stay with him, I add his enemies to Annie's. If I leave, then we only have her enemies, who hopefully will be stopped soon."

Bella stared at her, then slowly nodded. "Okay," she said. "I understand. But I still believe that you guys are safer with Jacob. With us."

Phoebe looked down at the river. Annie was on Jacob's shoulders as he splashed through the water. Cupcake was bounding around beside them, barking at Jacob. Annie was hitting her palms against Jacob's head with glee, while Lucas walked along with them, laughing. The deep male voices echoed across the water, and they filled her with peace, not fear.

Annie was so happy with Jacob. She clearly felt safe with him, just like the horses did, and just like Phoebe did. There was so much to gain by staying with Jacob. But what if Ivan came for them one night? It wouldn't be worth it. It wouldn't. "He's just such a scary man," she whispered.

"Ivan?"

Phoebe nodded.

Bella sighed. "He is."

"Look at that little girl," Phoebe said. "She's so happy right now. I've never seen her so free and happy as she's been since we came here. She loves the horses, Jacob, Lucas, you..."

"Maybe she's happy because her mom's happy."

Phoebe looked over at Bella. "It's not me."

"Of course it's you. You're her whole world. Don't underestimate your importance to her, as well as Jacob. You matter, Phoebe. One of the hardest lessons for all of us Harts to learn was that we matter, because we all wound up on the streets as kids. When you're a homeless kid, it's pretty easy to believe you don't matter. That you're worthless. So, we work on that together. It's important."

Phoebe bit her lip. Her yearning to be a part of this family forever was so strong it actually made her chest ache. But she couldn't stop thinking of her own ex-husband, of Sienna going missing, of Ivan's face, of the danger Annie had already experienced in her life. "I can't be that selfish," she whispered. "I just can't—"

A piercing whistle suddenly bit through the air.

Everyone turned to look at Tristan, who was on the butte. He held up his hand and made a gesture.

"Oh, *fuck*." Bella leapt to her feet. "Come with me!"

The brothers in the river went into fast and precise action. Colin kicked his horse into a gallop, racing through the water toward Tristan. Lucas grabbed Cupcake and tucked him under his arm and made a break for the waterfall at the edge of the water. Jacob started sprinting after Lucas, Annie still on his shoulders.

Fear tore through Phoebe as she scrambled down the rock, following Bella as she raced after Jacob. "What's happening?"

"I don't know yet, but that's our signal for a level five threat."

"Level five? What's the highest-level threat?"

"Five."

"Oh, God." Jacob, Lucas, and her babies disappeared into the waterfall. "Where did they go?"

"There's a cave in there. Come on! We have to be in there before the second whistle."

Disbelief and terror made Phoebe run like she'd never run before. She followed Bella through the spraying water, then ran right into her when she burst through the waterfall blindly into the cave beyond. They both hit the sand, flying across it. Phoebe scrambled to her feet as Jacob handed Annie to her. "Bella's going to show you guys this awesome secret cave. I'm going to go help Colin with his horse."

Lucas handed her Cupcake's leash and a rawhide bone. "It's quiet time for Cupcake," he said. "Keep him quiet."

Jacob gave Annie a quick kiss on the head. "See you soon, Queen Annie." He gave Phoebe a brief kiss, not lingering for even a second, before he and Lucas both sprinted out from the cave, splashing through the water.

Bella scrambled to her feet, her gaze meeting Phoebe's, full of warning. "Annie! This is a secret cave. Promise you won't tell anyone?"

Annie was frowning. "Where did Jacob go? I want Jacob!"

"We're playing hide and seek," Bella said. "We're going to go hide, and then he has to come find us. When you hear the whistle, we have until we count to thirty to hide. Then he's going to come looking, and we have to be sooo quiet, because the girls have to win!"

Annie nodded, her eyes wide. "Girls win," she whispered. She looked at Phoebe. "Mommy? Are you playing?"

"Yes." Phoebe took a breath, trying to pull herself together. "Girls win. Lead the way, Bella."

"All right," Bella said. "Annie, you and your mom start heading that way." She pointed into the depths of the cave.

"I'm going to erase our footprints to make it harder for the boys."

Oh, God. Phoebe's heart was racing like crazy right now. What was happening out there? The second whistle hadn't happened yet, which she was assuming would mean that the danger was close. Who was it? Annie's bio dad? Ivan? Or maybe the roar of the waterfall had drowned out the second whistle, and the danger was already upon them.

She wanted to ask questions, to get assurance that Jacob and the others would be safe, but she knew she had to keep Annie oblivious. "Okay," she whispered, "let's go."

"Hurry," Bella said as she began to splash water over their sandy footprints. "Jacob will be looking for us soon!"

Annie nodded and pointed. "This way, Mama!" she whispered.

"Okay, let's go." Gripping Cupcake's leash, Phoebe worked her way over the slippery rocks, heading into the shadowy cave. Was there a back way out of the cave? Or just one way in and one way out? She hated the idea of being cornered, but she had to trust the Harts. They knew what they were doing.

So, she hugged her daughter tight and kept going into the cave, where it was getting darker and darker. Could she pull out her phone to use as a light? She didn't know if it could be seen from the outside.

Bella caught up with them in few moments. "We'll be able to use our phone for light in a few minutes. We have to get around the bend."

Around the bend. Wow. Deeper into the cave. Phoebe did not like closed-in spaces, especially going into a dark, wet cave with danger hunting them. "Is there a back way out?"

"Nope."

"Okay." She took a deep breath, and tried not to think

about how the cave was narrowing, how the ceiling was getting lower. "Did the second whistle happen yet?"

"I don't know. We're too deep to hear it now, especially over the water."

Annie slid her hand into Phoebe's. "I don't like this, mama," she whispered. "It's too dark. I want to go home."

"I know, baby." Phoebe could tell that the game ruse wouldn't work anymore. Annie didn't care about winning. "Can you hold Cupcake's leash for me?"

"He's too strong."

"Not for you! You're a big pillow. Cupcake's a little pillow. He needs your help."

"Cupcake feels like a little pillow?"

"Yep."

"Okay." Annie took the leash. "Cupcake, it's okay," she said. "I'll be your big pillow. Mama's my big pillow. And Jacob. And Bella. And Lucas. We have lots of big pillows."

Phoebe smiled as Annie reassured Cupcake.

Bella turned on her phone flashlight, casting the cave into welcome illumination. "Look how cool this place is," Bella said. "I'm thinking of making it a girls-only club house. What do you think?"

"Whoa," Annie breathed, stopping in place as she stared around in awe.

Phoebe did the same, sucking in her breath. "It's magical." The ceiling of the cave stretched high now, and wide. The rock looked like it had once been a waterfall, forever preserved in rock. Stalactites hung down from the ceiling, and crevices whispered of stories and adventures long forgotten.

"What is this place?" Phoebe asked.

"Oregon is famous for its caves, but we found this one on our property. It goes for miles." Bella grinned. "Come on, there's a cool tunnel on the right that leads to another cavern."

"Wow! Is there gold? I bet there's gold. Mama, hold Cupcake!" Annie thrust the leash in Phoebe's hand. "I bet there's water in that little stream!" She ran across the rocks like a parkour expert, and Bella and Phoebe had to scramble after her.

Annie jumped in the stream, which came only up to her ankles, and then started sloshing upstream. "Where does it go?"

"To the tunnel, I told you about," Bella whispered. "I'll race you!"

"I win!" Annie took off, and Phoebe, Bella, and Cupcake splashed along behind her. It was so beautiful, and so magical, but the fact they were running was a grim reminder that they weren't here for fun. That somewhere out there, something was happening, and Jacob was in the middle of it.

Bella touched her arm. "They're fine. My brothers are excellent at hide and seek."

Phoebe looked at her, but couldn't clear the clog in her throat to answer.

Instead, she splashed after her daughter, continually looking over her shoulder to make sure no one had appeared in the cavern they were leaving behind.

But the only light was theirs, and nothing moved.

For now.

"Keep moving," Bella said. "The next cavern is the coolest one!"

They kept moving, going farther and farther into the recesses of the maze of caves, farther and farther from the danger, and farther and farther from the brothers who were risking their lives for her and Annie.

CHAPTER TWENTY-SEVEN

Jacob and Lucas ran out of the waterfall, his focus in full battle mode as he burst free. He whistled for Freedom, who immediately spun around from his napping spot on the bank and galloped toward him through the water, his ears flat back as he raced toward Jacob.

Lucas whistled for his mount, who did the same.

Jacob gripped the pommel of his saddle and swung up on Freedom as his horse raced by, not even slowing down. Lucas did the same, and then the two brothers were galloping toward the butte where Colin and Tristan were.

They reached the top, and reined their horses to a halt. "What's up?" Jacob asked as he patted Freedom's neck, soothing the jazzed horse.

Colin was already on his belly, stretched out on the sand, his sniper rifle set up, tracking their approach. "South and north."

Jacob saw three pickup trucks heading toward them from the south, and another one from the north. They were moving fast, bouncing over the rough terrain. "Not our trucks."

"Nope. I told Dylan to check the cameras."

Jacob understood. Colin hadn't wanted to take his gaze off their visitors long enough to scroll through camera footage to figure out where they had come from and who was driving.

Dylan called and Jacob answered his phone. "The ones on the south came through the woods on the east side," Dylan said. "I couldn't see who was driving."

"Fuck." Jacob and his brothers all pulled out their guns, watching as the trucks approached. Was it his dad? Annie's bio dad? Either way, someone had tracked them out into the middle of their ranch, at a river. What the hell? He'd taken precautions, but he hadn't really believed he needed them. He'd thought they were safe here. He truly had. Why hadn't his security system warned him of their breach?

"If it's my dad," Jacob said, "he doesn't want to kill me. He wants me to give him money, so I'm safe."

"And if it's Annie's bio dad, he won't kill any of you until he finds out where Annie is. I'm sending a helicopter," Dylan said. "It'll be there in fifteen."

"Move behind me," Jacob told his brothers. "None of them will shoot me, but if it's my dad, he might shoot one of you."

"No." Lucas stood beside him. "We stand together."

"No. I stand alone because I'm not in danger."

"We don't know Annie's bio dad. We don't know what he's capable of."

Jacob slid off Freedom and tossed the reins to his brother. "Keep Freedom safe. Either way, this is my battle. Cover me."

And then he started walking down the butte toward the approaching vehicles.

He didn't have to look behind him. He knew his brothers had all taken up positions behind him, their guns trained on the approaching vehicles. Colin was a trained sniper, and he could take out every driver. The others would fill in as needed.

As Jacob headed down the side of the butte, all he could think about was Annie, Phoebe, and Cupcake. Keeping them safe. Doing whatever it took to protect them.

He reached the bottom of the butte as the trucks reached him. They all stopped, but the sun was glinting off the windshield, making it impossible to see who was driving. The truck from the north arrived a split second later, kicking up dust as it skidded to a stop.

The fourth truck was off to the right, making it impossible for Jacob to watch both sets of trucks at the same time. He took a few steps back, trying to get everyone in the same line of sight.

He heard the crunch of boots behind him, and knew that one of his brothers, maybe more, had followed him down the butte. Colin would still be on top, his rifle trained on the trucks, but down at the bottom, Jacob wasn't alone.

Damned brothers. Taking risks not meant for them.

But he didn't have time to argue.

He just held his gun at his side and waited for the doors to open.

The door on the truck to their right opened first, and a man stepped out. He was a huge man. Well over six feet, muscled, bulked, with tattoos inked along his brown skin. His eyes were cold and angry, and he radiated a violence that set Jacob's teeth on edge. Jacob recognized him immediately from a photo that Dylan had sent him.

Annie's biological father.

Fury gripped Jacob. This man would never get his hands on Annie. Ever.

"Give me my daughter," the man snarled.

Jacob tightened his grip on his gun. "You're trespassing. Leave this ranch." His first goal, his most urgent goal, was to get this man away from Annie. He'd deal with getting him locked up or thrown back in prison later. Right now, he needed the man away.

Before the man could answer, the other car doors opened. Jacob glanced over as his dad got out of the nearest truck. What the fuck? How were they together?

"Imagine when we were driven out of town by my own son," Ivan said. "We're out drinking, bitching about ungrateful kids, when my new friend, Frank, overhears us talking about Jacob Hart. He comes over and tells me that Jacob Hart kidnapped his own flesh and blood. A common enemy brings good men together."

Son of a bitch. He had not seen that one coming. And how the fuck had Frank known he had Annie? Eliana had a leak, and she needed to find it fast.

Ivan raised his gun and aimed it not at Jacob, but to his right at Lucas. "You have lots of family now, son. But I have a lot of connections. You can't keep watch on all of us. One by one, your family will go down, until you're the last one standing, unless you give me what I'm owed." He nodded at Annie's father. "And my pal Frank here gets what he wants. Give him his kid. Give me my money. Or you start losing this family you care so much about."

The men on either side of Ivan raised their guns, pointing them at his brothers.

Anger coiled inside Jacob, anger built from so many years of impotence. "You have thirty seconds to get in your truck and leave," he said. "All of you."

Ivan looked around at his pals. "Anyone leaving?"

No one answered him.

Ivan grinned. "No one's leaving. What's the call, Jacob? Let my friend here have his kid? Sign me over my money? I even opened a bank account so you can wire it right in there."

Jacob didn't want any of his brothers to be murderers,

especially not Colin, who had too many kills in his past already. But he didn't see a way out of this that wasn't going to end in violence. The men standing before him were ready to kill, and he couldn't wait until one of his brothers was shot before taking action.

Everyone in his family was willing to do whatever it took to protect each other, but shooting in cold blood crossed a line he didn't want anyone to have to cross. "Put down the guns and leave," he commanded. "We won't press charges on the trespassing and assault with a deadly weapon. If we do, you'll end up in prison for parole violation."

He didn't want to let them go, but it was the first step to end the standoff.

"I'm gonna count to five," Ivan said. "And then I start shooting."

Fuck. "We have a helicopter on the way, and a sniper trained on you. You can't beat us—" He saw the man on Ivan's right twist, and he knew the guy was going to shoot Lucas. "No!" Instinctively, Jacob dove to the right to cover Lucas, and the bullet tore through his side. He stumbled, trying to keep his balance as shots rang out.

A few quick shots, shouts, and then it was over.

Every one of their visitors was on the ground, holding a foot and groaning, except for one, who had his hands up in the air, shouting, "I surrender!"

"Colin got 'em?" Jacob stumbled as Lucas caught him.

"We all got 'em." Lucas slung Jacob's arm over his shoulder. "You guys take care of those fuckers. Jacob, stay with me."

Jacob went down on his knees as pain radiated through his chest. "Where's Annie's dad? I don't see him."

Lucas looked around, then swore. "Where the fuck did he go? Colin!" he yelled. "Find the other one!"

Colin stood up, scanning the landscape. "I don't see him."

Jacob heard an engine rev, and he looked up to see the headlights come on in Annie's dad's truck. He rolled away from Lucas, pulled out his gun, and aimed for the grill and shot.

The truck went into gear and started driving right toward him.

Jacob fired again, and Lucas started shooting.

The bastard hit the gas and drove faster, the dirt shooting up. He was trying to run them down. *Fuck!*

Jacob shot again. And again. And again. He heard his brothers shooting as well, but he kept his focus on that truck, unloading his gun until finally, the truck veered off, and came to a rolling, steaming stop.

His brothers took off for the driver's side, shouting to cover each other.

Jacob tried to get up. To help.

But his legs gave out. He slid down to the ground, and rolled onto his back. His lungs felt like they were filling up, and he fought for air. Lucas dropped to his knees beside him. "The helicopter is only two minutes away. Hang in there."

Jacob grabbed his brother's arm. "Tell Phoebe and Annie that I love them. I changed my will to give them everything. Make sure it goes through."

Lucas swore. "You tell them yourself."

"Don't let Annie see me like this. We have to protect her." He swore. "Fuck. I waited too fucking long. Too fucking long to start to live."

"No, you didn't. You have time." Lucas pressed something on Jacob's side, making him gasp in pain.

"What the fuck? That hurts!"

"Get over it. The pain means you're still alive, so embrace the damned pain."

Jacob leaned his head back, resting it on the ground while Lucas worked on him. "Can't breathe," he gasped.

"Yes, you can. You have a family waiting for you. Not just us, but Annie and Phoebe. They've lost too much. You have an obligation to survive for them."

"They have my money..."

"Which means shit without you, as you know." Lucas leaned over him and grasped his face in two hands. "Look at me."

Jacob looked at him, fighting to stay conscious.

"You fight for every breath. Do not give up. Under any circumstances. Do you understand? For me. For that sweet little girl who needs you. For Phoebe, who needs you and loves the hell out of you. Got it? *You fucking matter.*"

Jacob nodded and closed his eyes to concentrate on his breathing. He mattered. He mattered. *He mattered.*

PHOEBE WAS SHOWING Annie how to skip rocks in the stream in the underground cave when she heard a piercing whistle echo through the cave three short times.

Bella let out a little whoop. "That's the all-clear sign." She raised her voice. "We're in Blue Cavern," she shouted out.

She beamed at Annie. "You want to head back out?"

"In a minute." Annie was focused on the rock, oblivious to what had been going on since they'd gone underground, but Phoebe wasn't oblivious. She was itching to get out of the cave and find out what happened. Honestly, she just wanted to see Jacob. To know he was all right.

"Come on, baby, let's go find Jacob and—"

At that moment, Colin Hart walked into their cave. He had a large flashlight, one that lit up the whole cave. He had it directed away from them, so she could see his face.

She stood up, her heart dropping. Why hadn't Jacob come to get him? "Where's Jacob?"

Colin ignored her. "Hi Annie," he said meaningfully. "What did you find in here?'

"I found cool rocks!" Annie held them up...while Phoebe's stomach turned over.

"Colin? Where's Jacob?"

Colin shot her a meaningful look. "We're going to hang out down here for a few minutes while things get cleared up."

"Colin—"

Bella put her hand on her arm. "Annie," she said meaningfully.

Were they kidding? "Colin." She snapped her fingers. "Over here. Bella, hang with Annie." She didn't wait for agreement. She just stalked away, moving fast. Her hands were shaking, and she felt like she was choking.

Lucky for him, Colin followed her. When he reached her, he took her arm and pulled her around a boulder, out of sight of Annie.

"What happened?" she whispered. "Is Jacob okay?"

"He got shot. He's being helicoptered to a local hospital."

"Oh, God." Her knees gave out and she dropped to the ground. "Is he okay?"

"I don't know."

Tears filled her eyes. "No," she whispered.

Colin crouched in front of her. "We had a medic on the helicopter. Jacob's getting treatment right now. Money buys the best, and that's what we have."

She stumbled to her feet. "I need to go with him—"

"He already left." Colin caught her arm. "He said that Annie can't know. He wants to protect her. So you have to stay calm."

"Calm?" She gaped at him. "Jacob might be dying—"

"No! He's not!" Colin cursed. "We don't talk like that in our family. We always have hope. We always believe that we can do it. He'll be fine. Got it?"

She searched his gaze. She felt his strength and his conviction, and suddenly, she fully understood the power of the Harts. The bond of this family, their resilience, their support of each other, it was unstoppable. It made her realize that she'd been wrong to believe she and Annie would be safer without them. There was a core strength to the Harts that wrapped around everyone they cared about, like a forcefield of love. She took a breath, then nodded. "Okay," she whispered.

"You need to know that Ivan and Annie's dad met up in a bar last night. Found they had a common enemy, and both showed up here."

She stared at him. "Oh, no."

"They're both dead now."

Her stomach congealed. "Who shot them?"

"Doesn't matter. It was self-defense. But there's a lot going on up there that we need to sort out. I have your horses at the entrance to the caves. The three of you are going to get on those horses and head home. Got it?"

She stared at him. "Leave?"

He nodded. "You're going to lead Freedom, and take care of all the animals for Jacob. Those are his babies and they, like Annie, are vulnerable. So, it's on you, now. The rest of us need to stay here and deal with the police. Okay?"

She closed her eyes. It felt like too much. She wanted to just fall down and cry, shudder in fear for what might happen to Jacob, process the fact that Annie's biological father was gone, which meant they were now free again, that Ivan was dead, which meant that threat was also in the past. So much to process, and she could barely focus.

Colin put his hands on her shoulders. "Phoebe. Look at me."

She did as he ordered, staring into his brown eyes. "What?"

"You got this. You're a great mom, and you're going to be able to handle this for Annie. I will keep you guys updated as soon as we hear anything. Understand?"

For Annie. She needed to keep herself together for Annie. "I got it."

"Great." He pulled her in for a quick hug that surprised her, but released her before she could lose control. He stepped away from the rock. "Bella and Annie," he called out. "Time for the horses to get home. They're tired. Let's go."

As Colin headed back toward Bella and Annie, Phoebe took a moment to close her eyes. She took a deep breath to try to calm herself. "Jacob," she whispered. "I'm not done with you yet. Come back to us. Give us a chance." She felt her heart tug, and wondered if that was Jacob, somehow hearing her. *Always have hope.* "All right, Jacob. I'll see you back at the house. We've got some stuff to figure out now." She paused. "I love you, Jacob, and so does Annie. Get back here soon."

She paused, as if she could hear an answer, but there was nothing.

She would have to go forward based on faith.

She pulled her shoulders back, lifted her chin, plastered a smile on her face, then marched back around the rock. "Annie! Shall we bake brownies when we get back to the house?"

Brownies.

They were always the answer.

CHAPTER TWENTY-EIGHT

Jacob.

Phoebe's voice drifted into Jacob's mind. He tried to open his eyes, but they felt heavy, stuck together. *Phoebe.* He tried to speak, but no words came. *I love you, Phoebe.*

I'm not done with you yet. Come back to us. Give us a chance.

He felt the urgency of her words, an urgency that pierced the growing lethargy trying to consume him. *I can't breathe, Phoebe.*

All right, Jacob.

All right? It was all right he couldn't breathe? Okay. He let go, let himself drift.

I'll see you back at the house. Phoebe's voice drifted in his mind again.

Back at the house? His house? But he was dying. He wasn't going back.

We've got some stuff to figure out now.

Stuff? What stuff?

I love you, Jacob, and so does Annie. Get back here soon.

And then she was gone. He could feel she'd left. He was alone again. Just him. No one there. *Phoebe!*

She didn't answer.

Phoebe!

Again, no answer. Panic began to beat at him. He didn't want to lose her. He didn't want to be alone. He'd been alone his whole fucking life, and he didn't want to be alone anymore. *Phoebe!* He screamed her name, in his mind, fighting for words, for voice.

"Jacob." Lucas's voice penetrated his fog. "It's me. Phoebe's not here. But she loves you. She needs you. She and that cute kid of hers. We all need you. And you have a chance for love. You owe yourself to go get it."

Go get it.

Go get it.

Go get it.

Fierce, fresh, brand-new determination surged to life inside Jacob. A will to live like he'd never had before. A commitment to life.

He was getting it.

≈

PHOEBE STOOD outside Jacob's hospital room door, taking a moment to prepare herself. She'd been warned by the other Harts that he was in rough shape, and she needed to be ready. He needed someone strong, not someone to fall apart at the sight of him.

He was going to be okay. Surgery had gone well, and he was going to be all right.

That was what mattered.

But even still, tears were swimming in her eyes as she pushed the door open and slipped inside. She caught her breath when she saw him in the bed, hooked up to beeping machines, his head turned to the side as he slept.

He looked so human in that bed, so vulnerable.

She set her purse down on a chair, then walked over and slid into the seat by his side. She slipped her hands around his, but the moment she touched him, his eyes opened.

His gaze met hers, and she caught her breath. "Hi," she whispered.

He smiled, a sweet, heart-melting smile so full of tenderness and love. "I heard you," he said.

"Heard me when?"

"You told me you loved me."

"You heard that?" she whispered, both surprised and not surprised that the words she'd whispered in the cave had made it to him.

"Yeah." He squeezed her hand lightly as if it was all the strength he could muster. "I love you, too, Phoebe. You and Annie and Cupcake. I'm not letting you go."

The tears she'd been fighting back trickled free. "I don't want to go."

He nodded. "All right." He closed his eyes. "We can build a bigger house. Find a school for Annie."

"You want us to move in with you?"

"Yeah." He opened his eyes again briefly. "I'm going to propose, but not right now. Gotta be a better story than this when people ask how I did it."

Her heart tightened. "I don't need a better story, Jacob. It's not about the story. It's about you. And me. And Annie."

His eyes closed again, but he managed a half smile. "I'm not proposing to you while I'm on drugs and almost dead."

She laughed. "It's actually a great story if you think about it."

"I can't think. I have almost-died-brain fog." But he was smiling. "I don't want to be without you. I'll be the husband you deserve. The dad Annie deserves. I can be that guy. Just want to make sure you know that."

She laughed. "I do know that."

"Even though I'm weird. I'll still be weird."

"I'll still be weird, too. And so will Annie. That's why we fit."

"Yeah." He smiled again, and opened his eyes. "Fuck it. Will you marry me, Phoebe? It's not romantic, but it's all I got right now. And I want to adopt Annie. Obviously. But had to say it."

She burst into joyful laughter. "Everyone will say we're crazy to get engaged when we just met."

"No one in my family will say that. When you've been through hell your whole life, you know when you find your peace. Doesn't take a genius."

She laughed. "This is true."

Jacob squeezed her hand. "Sweetheart, I just asked you to marry me, and you're talking about my family. You going to answer me? Because I think I've got about two more minutes until I'm asleep again."

Joy leapt through her. "Yes, you weirdo, I'll marry you."

"Yay." He pursed his lips. "Kiss me, gorgeous."

She leaned in and kissed him, laughing when he snaked his hand around the back of her head and upped the ante. "You're not almost unconscious."

"I am, but kissing you will wake up a man." He dropped his hand. "Don't tell Annie. I want to be there when you tell her she's got a new dad."

Phoebe suddenly started to cry. A new dad. Jacob said it like it was no big deal, but it was everything. "You won't even remember this the next time you wake up."

He smiled as he settled back into the pillow, holding her hand tightly. "Oh, don't you worry, sweetheart. I'll remember. I promise."

And she believed him.

CHAPTER TWENTY-NINE

PHOEBE LEANED back on the couch, her feet propped up on the front porch railing as Annie snuggled between her and Jacob. He was reading to her, and Annie was tucked up against both of them. Cupcake was on her left side, his head resting on her thigh.

To her left, Freedom and Rosa were grazing, out in the afternoon sunshine, enjoying the fresh air. The animals were close to each other, continuously touching noses and nickering to each other. Just like she and Annie had found Jacob, Freedom and Rosa had found each other. Jacob had taken down the wall between their stalls, and the two had become inseparable. Jacob had even had to slow down his rides on Freedom so Rosa could keep up, galloping freely beside Freedom, even though no one was holding her on a lead.

Freedom and Rosa both had their sparkle back, and Phoebe knew that she, Annie, and Jacob had found theirs as well. The shadows were gone, and it was amazing.

Phoebe smiled when Annie giggled at Jacob's silly voices as he read, then she looked down at her beautiful engagement ring. Jacob and Annie had picked it out together.

Three diamonds together, to symbolize the three of them as one family. It was perfect, beautiful, and quite frankly, enormous.

It was worthy of the fiancée of a billionaire, and although she didn't need it and had never dreamed of a ring like that, she absolutely loved it.

For the first time in many, many years, she felt safe. Truly safe. In her heart, as well as physically. Annie was safe, and she was becoming more confident every day. Jacob really understood how to help her, and Phoebe had learned so much from him about what Annie needed. Jacob was recovering well from being shot, they were all free to move forward and find their way.

As Jacob read, Phoebe saw a car heading toward them, winding through the driveway.

Jacob had turned off his security system during the day, so there was no alert. She watched without fear as a big black pickup truck drove toward them. "Brody's here," she said.

Jacob looked up. "Yep."

"Uncle Brody!" Annie leapt up, but Jacob caught her around the waist.

"Wait until the truck stops, princess," he said, as Annie giggled and shrieked in protest.

Brody's truck pulled up, and he got out. "Afternoon, all."

His wife, Tatum, got out of the front seat. She was six months pregnant with a round belly, but she hadn't slowed down at all. Phoebe adored Tatum, after getting over being star struck when she realized that Tatum was the very famous music star Tatum Crosby.

"Hey, girl!" Phoebe got up to welcome them as Jacob released Annie, and her daughter bolted down the steps and raced over to them. "What's up?"

"It's Hart party time," Tatum said, as she picked up Annie and swung her onto her hip. "Hey, princess. How's Rosa?"

"Good." Annie beamed at her, her hands clasped around Tatum's neck. "I want the baby now."

Tatum laughed. "Soon, sweetie. Soon."

Jacob stood up and held out his hand to Phoebe. "Come on. There's someone I want you to meet."

Phoebe raised her brows as she slipped her hand into his. "More Harts? I thought I met everyone."

"Future Harts."

"Future ones?" Phoebe groaned. "New horses? Dogs?"

"Nope." He led the way down the steps as Brody opened the back door of his truck. "Grandparents."

Phoebe frowned at him. "Hart grandparents? But none of you have parents in your lives."

"No. But you do."

Phoebe stared at him. "What?"

Jacob smiled and gestured to the truck.

Phoebe spun around and watched as her *mother* stepped out of the truck. "Mom!" She launched herself across the driveway and flung herself into her mom's arms. "You're here!"

"Oh, Phoebe." Her mom held her so tightly. "God, I missed you."

"Hey, Phoebe." Her dad leaned over and waggled his fingers at her. "I missed you, pumpkin."

"Dad!" She grabbed him and pulled him into the hug. They were all crying, and Phoebe felt like she could never let them go. "When did you guys get here? I thought you weren't coming for a few weeks."

"These billionaire boys hooked us up with their private jet," her mom said with a wink. "How could we turn that down?" She held out her arms to Jacob, who walked over and gave both her parents a huge, adorably sweet hug. "It's about time I got to meet my future son-in-law," she said. "You're every bit the handsome cowboy that Phoebe said you were."

Jacob's cheeks turned pink, but his grin was big. "Yeah, well, cowboy yes. Handsome? I'm just glad she thinks I'm worthy of her."

Rosa smiled. "We all, do, Jacob. Thanks for everything."

He nodded. "I'll always take care of her. Always."

"I know."

Henry reached over and hugged Jacob as well. "We'll never forgive ourselves for not keeping her safe the first time around," he said gruffly. "But we'll always be grateful the path led her to you."

Jacob grinned. "Thank you. I appreciate it." He smiled at Phoebe, and she saw the joy in his eyes. Just as Henry had become her dad, not simply a stepdad, when Rosa had married him, she knew Henry would be the dad Jacob had never had as well. The bond was already there.

Rosa's gaze went to Annie, who was still in Tatum's arms, watching with wide eyes. "My sweet girl. Annie. It's Grandma Rosa."

Phoebe hurried over to Annie and swung her into her arms, resting her on her hip. Annie wrapped her arms around Phoebe's neck and pressed her face into Phoebe as she carried her over to her parents. "Annie, it's Grandma and Grandpa. They came to visit."

Annie stared at them with wide eyes.

Rosa leaned in and smiled. "You remember our song?"

Annie nodded silently.

"Will you sing it with me?"

Annie nodded again.

Then Rosa started to sing the same song that she'd sung to Phoebe when she was growing up. Phoebe joined in, and after a moment, Annie did too. Then Henry joined in, and the sound became louder and more raucous, until they were all laughing and in hysterics. Annie was shrieking with laughter as she high-fived Rosa and Henry. "Lucas brought me a unicorn!! Maybe he'll bring her again for you!"

Phoebe and Jacob smiled at each other. When Jacob had been in the hospital, Lucas had come by every single day with Rainbow Sparkle to distract Annie, unicorn horn and all. That was the kind of family she was marrying into, and she knew she was the luckiest woman ever.

"A unicorn?" Rosa raised her brows at Phoebe, who nodded. "Wow. That's exciting."

"I know!" Annie tugged on her arm. "Come see my pony!"

"You bet!"

Phoebe set down Annie, her heart full as she watched Annie lead her parents over to the field where pony Rosa and Freedom were grazing. "Holy cow," she whispered as Jacob put his arm around her. "That is the most beautiful sight I've ever seen. I thought I'd never get to see my parents again, and now, they're here, playing with my daughter."

Jacob kissed the top of her head. "I have a confession to make."

"What's that?"

"I might have offered to build them the house of their dreams on the ranch, if they wanted to move here."

Phoebe spun around to face him. "Shut up."

He grinned. "I did."

"What did they say?"

"They said they'd love to."

Stunned elation leapt through Phoebe, and she flung her arms around Jacob. He'd given her everything. Freedom. Family. And now...her parents. She pulled back, searching his face. "Thank you. For everything."

He locked his arms around her waist. "It's just the start, sweetheart. We have a huge life to lead."

She beamed at him. "We do. I'm so excited to do it with you." Then she heard the roar of trucks, and she looked past

Jacob and saw a line of vehicles heading down the driveway. Lots of Hart trucks plus what looked like two catering trucks. "What's going on?"

He grinned. "It's your surprise engagement party. We had to wait until your parents arrived, but no one would wait any longer."

"Seriously?" She couldn't believe it. Every Hart was there. She knew everyone's trucks by now, and they were all there.

"We're family now," Tatum said, grinning. "And the Harts like to celebrate family at every possible moment." She threw up her arms. "It's party time!"

Then the trucks arrived and all these amazing Harts started pouring out, laughing, joking, hugging, each other, Phoebe, her parents...

She looked over at Jacob, and he grinned at her.

She was home.

≈

THE PARTY WAS WELL-UNDERWAY a few hours later. "Congrats, Jacob." Chase Stockton, the oldest sibling in the Stockton family, walked up. "I'm so happy for you."

The Stocktons were related to the Harts by marriage, when a former under-the-bridger had married a Stockton, a group of cowboy brothers who had shared the same dad, an alcoholic monster who had nearly destroyed the boys. Only by coming together had the Stocktons survived, finding their place on the massive Stockton ranch, a story that shared many similarities with the Harts.

"Yes, all of us are," Chase's wife Mira said, beaming at Jacob. "You Harts are like the Stockton men. You all are wonderful, amazing people, but you need the right partner to love you exactly as you are. I can tell Phoebe loves you that way. She's a treasure."

Jacob grinned. "Thanks. I feel lucky every day." As he spoke, his gaze went back to Brody's pool. Annie was playing with a few of the Stockton kids, while Phoebe sat on the edge of the pool with Bella and his other sister, Meg. A few of the Stockton wives were with them, including his sister Hannah, whose marriage to Maddox Stockton had brought the families together.

He used to avoid these big gatherings with all the Stocktons and their kids, but he felt differently now. He loved seeing Annie thrive with her cousins, and it made him happy to hear Annie's laughter.

Phoebe's parents were sitting under an umbrella, watching their daughter and granddaughter with so much joy.

Family. He used to barely be able to handle the Harts, but now, he was sitting here with a whole range of chaos, and he didn't feel like racing back to his truck and hiding out with his horses. So much had changed for him.

"When's the wedding?" Mira asked. "Did you schedule a date yet?"

Jacob grinned. "End of August. I'm going to send an email to both families to make sure it works." It had been a challenge to find a date when every Hart was in town without other obligations, without waiting an interminable time, but the end of August was looking good. He hoped the Stocktons were all available as well, because they were family, too, and non-negotiable.

Mira clapped her hands. "Yay! That's fantastic. We'll all be there."

Jacob smiled. "I know." And he did. He finally was able to allow the Stocktons into his life the way he'd let the Harts in. It had taken Phoebe and Annie, and the death of his father, to make it possible, but it had happened.

He felt like his life looked bright and hopeful and full for the first time.

He saw Dylan walk over and say something to Phoebe. She looked up at him, then she pointed to Annie and said something to Meg and Bella, who both nodded. She then hopped to her feet, and followed Dylan as he headed toward Jacob.

As they neared, Jacob tensed. This was it, he realized. Dylan had found Sienna, and he didn't want to tell Jacob without Phoebe being present.

Fuck. That couldn't be a good sign. "I think he found my sister," he told Chase and Mira. All the Stocktons knew about Sienna. Once Jacob had told his siblings, the word had spread, which had helped the healing.

Every Hart and every Stockton had regrets or shadows in their past, which meant they all understood. Their lack of judgment had helped Jacob begin to process his guilt for not being able to save his sister, but it still lurked.

Phoebe smiled at him and slid under his arm when he raised it to draw her against his side. "Hi, love." He took a moment to greet her, as he always did, no matter how recently he'd seen her. He kissed her, a kiss designed to remind her how much he loved her, that he would always be there for her.

It was the kiss he gave her many times a day.

She kissed him back, leaning into him for the brief moment they connected. She pulled back, gave him that special smile that still made his heart turn over. "We'll handle it," she said. "Together."

He nodded, and kissed the top of her head before turning to Dylan. "You found Sienna."

His brother nodded. "I did. Her name's not Sienna anymore—"

Jacob's heart stuttered. "She's still alive?" He'd thought for sure she was dead.

Dylan nodded. "Yep. Alive. And she's all right."

Jacob's arm tightened around his fiancé. "What do you mean, all right?"

Dylan smiled. "I mean, the man your dumb ass father sold her to was an undercover federal agent."

"What?" Jacob suddenly couldn't breathe. "She's okay? She was never—" He couldn't even say it, the words that had haunted him for so long. The terror.

"Never," Dylan said. "The agent actually ended up adopting her. He changed her name, quit the agency, and went off the grid to protect her from Ivan."

Phoebe put her hand on Jacob's chest, and he breathed into her touch, trying to control his emotions. *Sienna was all right.* "Was he a good guy?"

"From all I can find, yeah." Dylan put his hand on Jacob's shoulder. "I got her current address a few minutes ago. I don't have any photos, and she's not on social media. She's completely low profile. But it's her."

Jacob closed his eyes. "What's her name?"

"Madison Vale." He held up his phone. "I just texted you her address. She's in Montana."

Jacob looked at Phoebe, and she grinned at him. "You want to call ahead? Or just show up?"

"She might not remember me." He took a breath. "I'm not going to go mess up her life. It's enough to know she's safe. I'm not going to burden her with her past, with me."

Phoebe sighed and looked at Dylan.

"What if she's not completely okay?" Phoebe said. "What if she needs help, and you don't go? You're going to walk away without even trying?" She caught his wrist. "Besides," she said gently. "You're the most amazing man I've ever met. You're my world, and Annie's world, and if you weren't amazing, we never would have agreed to spend our lives with you. So, if you can't believe in yourself, listen to how much I believe in you."

"And the rest of us," Dylan said with a grin. "Listen to your fiancée, Jacob. She's right. Don't you dare walk away from Madison. Even if she's fine, learning that the boy she probably dreams about and doesn't even know is real has never forgotten her will be good for her. We all need to not be forgotten."

"Agreed," said Chase. "Don't underestimate how great we all are. We're all pretty fucking awesome."

They all burst out laughing, and Jacob grinned. "Who am I to deprive my sister of my greatness?"

"You're not that rude," Phoebe said.

"He's pretty rude," Dylan said.

"Not rude. Just antisocial. And now he adores everyone!" Phoebe said, trying not to laugh.

"I don't adore everyone," he said, trying to stay grumpy, just because it was fun to get Phoebe going.

She patted his cheeks. "Yes, you do. You just don't realize it yet." She turned to the party and clapped her hands. "Can I have everyone's attention?"

Jacob rolled his eyes. "Phoebe, don't—"

"Shut up, bro. This is going to be good for you," Dylan said, putting his hand on Jacob's shoulder while Phoebe somehow managed to get a family gathering of more than fifty people between the Harts, the Stocktons, and spouses, and kids to stop talking and pay attention to her.

She held up her arms. "My darling fiancé just found out where his sister is, and he hasn't seen her since she was six. He doesn't want to visit her because he feels like it will be a burden for her to know him...and all of us!"

The party broke out in raucous boos, making Jacob laugh.

"If you think Jacob is being a doofus and should reach out to her, then start dancing!" Phoebe shouted.

Dancing?

But to Jacob's amusement, the entire party started

dancing and cheering. Cowboy hats went flying in the air, and someone hit the play button on the outdoor speakers, blasting one of Travis Stockton's hits.

Phoebe turned back to him, beaming at him. "I guess that's it then. You can't overrule family."

Jacob laughed, his heart light with happiness he would never have believed was possible for him. "I'd never overrule family," he agreed.

"Madison better watch out, because she's about to get sucked into the biggest, best family that ever existed," Phoebe said as she looped her arms around his neck. But before she could kiss him, that same family started coming up, talking excitedly, asking questions, surrounding him in a way that he wouldn't have been able to handle not that long ago.

Today? He simply grinned, put his arm around his fiancé, checked on Annie, and then joined right in.

∼

WANT MORE HARTS? What happens when Madison Vale finds Lucas Hart in her living room, taking about a childhood she doesn't remember...and doesn't want to? But when her dad goes missing and Madison's in danger, Lucas is the only one she can turn to to find her dad and avoid being the next victim. One-click *A Rogue Cowboy's Heart* now!

FOR THE FIRST time in six years, Stephanie is releasing new *Birch Crossing* small-town romance! Leila Kerrigan is back in town with no time for the rebel who stole her heart long ago...but now he's playing for keeps. Treat yourself to *Secretly Mine* today or skip ahead to a sneak peek!

. . .

NEW TO STEPHANIE'S **cowboy world, and want more heart-melting cowboys?** If so, you *have* to try her *Wyoming Rebels* series about nine cowboy brothers who find love in the most romantic, most heartwarming, most sigh-worthy ways you can imagine. Get started with *A Real Cowboy Never Says No* right now. You will be sooo glad you did, I promise!

IF YOU WANT MORE SMALL-TOWN, **emotional feel-good romances** like the *Hart Ranch Billionaires*, you'd love my *Birch Crossing* series! Get started with *Unexpectedly Mine* today! Or jump in with the brand-new Birch Crossing book, *Secretly Mine*, or skip ahead to a sneak peek here!

ARE **you in the mood for some feel-good, cozy mystery fun** that's chock full of murder, mayhem, and women you'll wish were your best friends? If so, you'll fall in love with *Double Twist!*

ARE YOU A FAN OF MAGIC, **love, and laughter?** If so, dive into my paranormal romantic comedy *Immortally Sexy* series, starting with the first book, *To Date an Immortal*.

IS DARK, **steamy paranormal romance your jam?** If so, definitely try my award-winning *Order of the Blade* series, starting with book one, *Darkness Awakened*.

SNEAK PEEK: SECRETLY MINE

NEW RELEASE!

She's back in town with no time for the rebel who stole her heart long ago...but now he's playing for keeps.

Dash Stratton had just picked up his welder when he heard his name hollered from the front of the house.

Recognition flooded him, and he swore, spinning around. That voice sounded familiar, but there was no way Leila Sheridan would be at his house, bellowing his name.

But he'd thought he'd seen her in that car outside Wright's.

That was twice in the span of an hour.

What the hell was going on?

She, whoever it was, shouted his name again, and something prickled along his skin. He would have sworn it was Leila.

He set down the welder and strode out of his studio. He jerked his sunglasses down over his face, and headed across the lawn around the side of his house, moving with an instinctive urgency.

He practically sprinted around the side of the house, and then stopped dead, stunned.

Leila Kerrigan was in front of the house, her hands on her hips, staring right at him.

Emotions flooded him, so many emotions he couldn't sort them out. He couldn't take his gaze off her. She was a woman now, not a scrawny, scared eighteen-year-old. She was wearing shorts and sneakers, and a blue tank top, looking like she was ready for a day on the lake, like the old days.

She had curves now she hadn't had before, the curves of a woman. Her sunglasses were on top of her head, revealing those glorious blue eyes and dark lashes that he'd begun to think he'd imagined.

She sucked in her breath. "Dash."

"Fuck." He grimaced. That was all he could think of to say after all this time. "I mean, what the fuck are you doing here?"

Her eyes widened. and he swore under his breath. "Sorry. I'm just stunned to see you in my front yard. You look great." Suddenly, he realized why she was there.

She wanted a divorce. The time had come.

Fuck. This time, he meant it.

A cute little frown furrowed between her eyebrows. "You don't know why I'm here?"

Double fuck. Had her lawyer served him? Had he missed an email? "No."

"You don't know about Bea's will?"

He narrowed his eyes. Bea's will? Not a divorce? He was annoyed by the relief that shuddered through him. "What about it? I know I got the house, because she told me many times that's what she was doing." He frowned. "What did she put in there for you?" Was there something at the house that was for Leila? He hadn't seen anything with her name on it, but Bea might have hidden it well. "Do you need me to find something for you?"

Leila stared at him, then understanding dawned on her face, and she burst out laughing. "I swear to God, I'm going to kill Eppie. And Clare!"

Ah...Eppie. He knew what kind of chaos she could cause. "What did they do?" Eppie was as much trouble as Bea had been.

"Clare gave me a letter for you." She fished around in her back pocket, then held up a folded envelope. "I suspect she explains it here."

He didn't move. If it was a letter from Bea, he didn't want to read it, hear her words, feel her presence. It was too soon for him. "You explain it."

Leila waved the letter at him. "No, thanks. Here."

Swearing under his breath, Dash walked over to her to take it, but as he neared, he felt like his world was spinning. Leila Sheridan was back, and she was unfinished business. *His* unfinished business.

He took the envelope, and his fingers brushed against hers, sending a shock reverberating through his system. Yeah, the attraction was still there, but this time, she wasn't an eighteen-year-old he had to protect from a piece-of-shit stepfather.

She was a woman, and their age difference no longer mattered like it had when she was barely eighteen and he'd been twenty-five.

When his hand touched hers, she sucked her in breath and jerked her hand back. "Letter," she mumbled.

"Letter," he agreed, as he took a step back, folded it, and put it in his pocket. "I'll read it later."

Leila's brows went up. "You need to read it now."

"I'm good. You need anything from me?"

She stared at him. "You're as stubborn and difficult as you were back then."

"Probably."

She folded her arms over her chest. "Read the letter, Dash."

"Nope." There was no chance he was reading Bea's words right now. He missed her like hell, and he wasn't in a place to read a letter she wrote to him in front of Leila. Or anyone. Or even himself. "Anything else you need?"

She stared at him. "Really?"

"Yeah. Whatever you need." This conversation felt awkward and distant, nothing like how he'd envisioned it might be all the times he'd thought about her over the years. "Want a drink? I have water and beer." And other stuff he didn't feel like mentioning.

"Water?"

"Yeah."

She put her hands on her hips. "Dash."

"Leila."

She sighed in aggravation. "Bea didn't leave you the house. She left *us* the house."

Dash stared at her. "Us?"

"Yes." She pointed back and forth between them. "You and me. Co-heirs. We have to both live in the house together for thirty consecutive nights before either of us can do anything with it. I'm moving in now."

"No." His amusement fled. Oh, wait, he hadn't been amused by anything about her sudden appearance. "It's my house. I've been living here for the last six months. She told me it was mine, repeatedly." He'd been counting on this house, and not just for himself.

"Well, it's also half mine. I need the money from selling it, and we can't sell it until we both live here together for thirty days."

Sell it? No one was selling this house. He couldn't afford to buy out Leila. He swore under his breath, then pulled out his phone and called Clare.

She answered on the first ring. "You read the letter?"

"I'm co-heirs with Leila, and we have to live in the house together for thirty consecutive nights before we can do anything with it?" It had to be wrong. It didn't make sense.

Clare sighed. "Yes, look, I'm sorry I didn't tell you, but Bea's will specifically said Leila had to be the one to tell you."

All thoughts of his attraction to Leila vanished in a surge of irritation. He ground his jaw. "So it's true?"

"Yes, it is."

He glanced at Leila, who was watching him, chewing on her lower lip. Why did she look so damned adorable chewing on her lip like that? Why did he care? He didn't have time for this. "I need this house. You know I do."

"Thirty days, Dash. You can have it in thirty days, as long as Leila agrees to give up her share."

Fuck. He couldn't afford to buy her out. "What else is in the will that you didn't tell me? There's more, isn't there? More games that Bea put in there?"

Clare cleared her throat. "It's a rather complicated will, but that's the gist of it."

He swore under his breath. "Clare—"

"Look. You could probably contest some of the provisions, but it's *Bea,*" Clare said softly. "You loved her. She loved you. Don't you want to let her do this her way? Would you deprive her of that joy?"

"No." Dash rubbed his forehead and cursed again. Bea had changed his life in many ways, standing by him when his parents disowned him. He'd spent the rest of his life giving back to her, and he couldn't stop now just because she was gone. "I'd never let her down," he admitted grudgingly.

"Bea spent a lot of time planning this," Clare said. "It's her gift to you. Not just the house, but all of it."

Dash looked at Leila. Was Leila a gift that Bea had decided to hand him? Another chance at the woman he'd let go? He ground his jaw. A year ago, cohabitating with Leila to compete for the house would have been very different than now.

Now, it didn't work for him. "Clare, she wrote the will before—"

"No, she didn't. She updated it afterwards."

That stunned Dash into silent. "She wrote it *after?*" After his whole life had changed. Rocked to its foundation. Shattered into a thousand pieces that he was still struggling to put back together. She wrote the will *after* that had happened? *What the hell, Bea?*

"Yes," Clare said. "It's your choice, Dash. You can contest it, and drag Bea's last moments of joy into question, or go with it."

He sighed. "You're very manipulative."

Clare laughed. "I know. You're welcome. Eppie and I have to confirm every night's sleepover, so you'll see a lot of us."

Roomie. Living with Leila Sheridan for thirty days. Thirty

days in which to convince her to give him her half of the house. Not sell it to him. *Give* it to him.

Fuck. He didn't like needing charity from her. Bea's promise to give him the house had been his key to getting free. To have that compromised... *What the hell were you thinking, Bea?*

He didn't have a backup plan. He'd put everything into this house on the assumption he would get it.

And in those thirty days, he also had to avoid having Leila ask for a divorce. And...he to resist the temptation that she'd been to him for a long time.

Three bedrooms.

One and a half bathrooms.

One shower.

Hell. This was going to get rough fast.

And a part of him was looking forward to every minute of it.

How hot does it get when Leila moves in? And what secret is Dash hiding? Treat yourself today to Secretly Mine, and fall in love with Dash and Leila today by clicking here!

SNEAK PEEK: GONE ROGUE

A Mia Murphy Mystery

"So much darn fun!" Five-star Goodreads Review (Penny)

CHAPTER ONE

My phone rang just as I hopped out of Turbojet, my well-used, antique pickup truck I'd acquired along with my new business, the Eagle's Nest Marina. I saw the call was one of my new besties, Hattie Lawless, so I answered. "What's up?"

"Mia. It's been ten days since we've had to deal with a corpse. Are you getting as bored as I am?"

Alarm shot through me, and I hung up on her.

Hattie was a seventy-something race car driver who owned and operated a café in my marina. She was sassy, irreverent, and an unstoppable force, which I greatly admired. Except when it got me almost killed. Which seemed to happen a little bit too often.

She called again, and I almost didn't answer. But what if Hattie was in trouble? I couldn't take the chance. "What?"

"No one has tried to kill you in ten days either. You have to ditch your new bodyguard. I think he's repelling fun."

I hung up on her again. Hattie was like a siren. The entire world seemed to want to bend to her will, not because she tried to control it, but because it *wanted* to be her friend. If Hattie invited murderers into our lives, they would probably come.

Not that I was superstitious, but Hattie was...Hattie.

My phone rang before I managed to get it back in my pocket. I answered it as I wandered away from Turbojet and headed toward the Bass Derby town green, which was teeming with people, music, tents, and small-town festivities. "Hattie. I love you. I don't love murderers."

"Yes you do. If you didn't, you wouldn't have gone undercover for the FBI against your drug lord ex for two years."

That had not been an entirely voluntary situation for me. "They made me."

"Hey! Don't give away your power by lying to yourself like that! No one makes you do anything. You wanted to because you crave excitement, my thieving friend."

I smiled at the affection in her voice. I'd been so scared that she and Lucy Grande, my two favorite people in the world, would reject me when they found out about my criminal childhood, but my pickpocketing past had been a great hit with both of them. "I just arrived. Where's your tent?"

"Pink and white striped tent at the near end of the first aisle. Best spot of the festival. You can't miss it."

"Of course you got the best spot."

"Always," she agreed cheerfully. "The world is my playground."

Up ahead, I saw the awning in question. "I see you. Coming over."

"Awesome. Ditch Ivan in the crowds, though. Seriously."

I glanced behind me at the six-foot-four jacked-up, federal agent-type suit-wearer who had been shadowing me for the last ten days, shooting looks of "I will take you down if you mess with Mia" to anyone who came close to me. I smiled at him, but he ignored me. Ivan didn't mess around, which was a great trait in a bodyguard. "I'm not ditching Ivan. You'd be so sad if I was assassinated."

"Would I, though? That's such a complex, loaded issue."

I laughed. "Bye. I'll see you in a sec." I hung up as I merged with the crowds streaming onto the grass. Tonight was the opening night of the three-day Bass Derby Strawberry Festival, an annual event that drew people from all over the state to celebrate, culminating in the crowning of the Strawberry Shortcake Bake-Off Champion on Sunday afternoon.

How adorably small-town was that?

I was so excited. The crowds were boisterous. The tents were so cute, local vendors selling crafts, artwork, pottery, candles, pizza, sandwiches and everything else that one could create. There was a big contest tent for the competitors. Tonight was round one, the strawberry contest, where contestants would present home-grown strawberries for judging. Saturday was the biscuit contest. And Sunday was the Strawberry Shortcake Bake-Off, which was the biggie. Plus, there was a palooza of other events planned for the weekend as well.

A band was playing on the gazebo, and the local baton-twirling team was performing routines. Pickup trucks lined the parking lot, and people were tailgating with barbeques and beer. The mid-June night was warm, the evening sun casting glorious light across the water, and the adjacent town beach was full of kids and families playing in the water.

It filled my soul with all the warmth and belonging that I'd wanted my whole life.

This was why I'd turned down witness protection and moved to Bass Derby.

This was why I'd bought the run-down Eagle's Nest Marina, so that I could be here, becoming a part of a community for the first time in my life, rehabbing the marina to make it my dream.

I'd even managed to grab a last-minute volunteer spot. I was part of the team patrolling the contest tent to make sure that all the competitors had what they needed. My shift started in ten minutes, and I was so pumped. I was proudly wearing my volunteer badge, and I was pretty much giddy with excitement.

I jogged over to Hattie's tent, breathing in the scent of the fresh bread Hattie was so magical at creating. She was behind a well-stocked table, and there was a line twenty-people long already. "Hey, girl. How's it going?"

"Swamped," Hattie said cheerfully. "Niko and Cris are away at some football camp this weekend, so I'm on my own."

Nico and Cris Stefanopoulos were Greek brothers who worked in her café. They were both headed to college on scholarships, and their grandma, Angelina Stefanopoulos was raising them. As a staff member at the police station, she'd been helpful to us on more than one occasion.

Today, Hattie was sporting fuchsia hair, to match her Hattie's Café T-shirt. I didn't know many seventy-somethings who could carry off fuchsia hair, but Hattie definitely could. "Jump in and help. I'll give you free food."

Hattie never gave away anything for free, so the offer was tempting. But... "My shift starts in ten minutes."

"How long is your shift?"

"Two hours."

She shook her head. "No, that won't work. I need help now. Ditch your shift."

I blinked. "I can't. I promised I'd do it—"

Hattie leaned on the table. "I need you. I thought we were friends."

"We are friends." I would never turn down a request from Hattie, but I'd been excited at the chance to volunteer, as if I actually belonged to the community. "Hattie, I—"

"Hey!" A low voice barked out the single word.

We both turned to see three twenty-something gang member-ish dudes striding across the grass toward us, wearing heavy motorcycle boots, leather jackets, gold chains, with possible gun bulges in their jackets, and enough swagger to trigger a tidal wave in Diamond Lake.

A path had cleared, and people's jaws were open in stunned shock, clutching their babies and dogs as if the trio was there to mass murder everyone. The approaching trio was so out of place that I could practically feel the earth shifting to expel them.

The woman at the front of the line hugged her loaf of Hattie's rosemary focaccia bread to her chest. "Are they coming here? They look like they're heading here. They're not getting my bread."

As she spoke, the trio strode right up to the table and stopped, arms folded, jaws jutted out, shoulders back. Every line of their bodies said that they expected to be thrown out.

I'd spent most of my first seventeen years with that stance.

They did not tackle anyone for their bread, babies, or dogs. Instead, they focused entirely on Hattie. The tallest one spoke first. "You owe us. We're here to collect."

A woman behind me made a noise like she was slowly dying, and I heard someone whisper to find Chief Stone. I heard someone else say something about me being a drug dealer, which hurt my innocent little heart just a bit.

Hattie set her hands on her hips. "Mia? Do I owe these guys?"

I'd been with her when we'd met them a couple weeks ago. I knew what she was doing, but at the same time, I felt for these guys, because that had been me. They wouldn't interpret her response the way she meant it. I knew that, because I'd been them. "Um, guys? Vinnie?"

The tallest one looked over at me, then his brows went up. "I remember you."

More people started whispering, which bothered me a little bit. Honestly, life was so much more complicated when you cared what people thought, when you were trying to put down roots. "Hattie, for heaven's sake, stop being difficult. Vinnie, you, too. You're like two alpha dogs who want to pee on each other."

Both Hattie and the guys looked at me. "You're calling me a dog?" Hattie said.

"I am. An alpha dog, though. Top of the heap."

"A Cane Corso? I'd like to be a Cane Corso."

Of course she would choose to be a one-hundred-and-fifty-pound guard dog. "Sure."

"You're calling *me* a dog?" Vinnie didn't look as thrilled with the news as Hattie had been.

"Yes. I am." I put my hands on my hips. "Vinnie, Hattie promised you a free sandwich at her café in exchange for the favor you did. Instead, you chose to show up at the strawberry festival and try to scare everyone. But Hattie's the alpha dog, and she has to prove it by not feeding you here, since she's not at her café. So, she's going to say no to the sandwich, and then you're going to get all mad and think that no one is trustworthy. But that's a bunch of crap, because Hattie's completely loyal and amazing. We all know you're not a jerk, because you saved our lives and hers. So give it up. You two are both cute little puppies who need to go romp on the beach together instead of peeing on each other."

Everyone stared at me.

I smiled. "But Hattie needs help at the booth right now and she offered me free food to help her, so maybe you guys can make a trade."

Vinnie's eyes widened. "Work here?" He looked around, and we all did. I could see that he didn't believe Hattie would let him get behind her table, handle her food, work with customers, and take their money.

But he didn't know Hattie like I did.

Sure enough, Hattie's face lit up. She liked to nurture people with potential, and these guys were no exception. She knew goodness when she saw it, and she didn't give a hoot what anyone else thought. So what if Vinnie probably liked to steal cars in his spare time? He had a good heart buried under that gang activity, so that was all that mattered to Hattie. "Yes!" she exclaimed. "Great idea! Vinnie, get your team back here. Let's do this! One free sandwich for every hour you work the booth."

Vinnie stared at her. "You're serious?"

"I never joke about food."

Vinnie went silent, then looked at his friends. They both shook their heads and headed back down the aisle toward the parking lot. But Vinnie shrugged off his leather jacket, revealing massive, tattooed biceps that set the whispers going again. "I'm in."

Two minutes later, Vinnie and his muscles were wearing a

fuchsia Hattie's Café T-shirt that was a little too tight, a matching visor, and he was holding a credit card reader and taking money.

Hattie grabbed a muffin and handed it to me without a word.

Her way of thanks. Lucy and I owed Vinnie our lives, and Hattie was as happy as I was to offer more than a sandwich to him.

I winked at her and swiped a cookie, feeling all sorts of warm fuzzies in my heart. I was so happy to be in a position to offer belonging to someone who was an outsider, after a lifetime of being the one on the outside.

If I had tried to hire Vinnie, my marina would have paid the price in lost business. But Hattie had the power to do whatever she wanted in Bass Derby, and she'd just given Vinnie her stamp of approval.

It felt good to be a part of that.

"Mia! Hattie!"

We both turned as the third part of our trio of awesomeness, Lucy Grande, ran toward us, ducking around people. It took me only a split second to register her tension and to realize she was running hard. Alarm shot through me as she reached us. "What's up?"

"It's Rogue!"

I glanced at Hattie. "Rogue? What's wrong with Rogue?" Rogue, whose real name was Esther Neeley, was about Hattie's age. She was obscenely rich and not afraid of owning it. She was sassy, irreverent, and a member of the Seam Rippers, a local quilting group who loved margaritas, loyalty, and adventure. I adored Rogue, and she'd helped save my life ten days ago. Different situation than when Vinnie had stepped in, but equally as helpful.

"The strawberry judging starts in a half hour, and Rogue's not there. Her table's not set up. I've looked everywhere for her, and no one has seen her." Lucy looked worried. "I tried to call her, and her phone went right into voicemail."

"She should have been set up hours ago." Hattie swore. "We need to check her house. Something's clearly wrong."

Their worry was contagious. "What are you guys talking about? What table?"

"I'll drive," Hattie said. "Vinnie. You're in charge. The reputation of Hattie's Café is on your shoulders. If you blow it, I will hunt you down, and you won't like it one bit."

The gun-wielding gang leader's eyes widened, and he looked slightly alarmed. "Run your tent?"

"Yes, I'll be back soon." Hattie grabbed her keys from a corner of the tent. "Let's go!" She broke into a run, and Lucy ran after her.

They took off so fast that I had to sprint not to lose them in the crowd. They were both fitter than I was, but ten days of working out with Rogue had helped me enough that I still had them in sight when Hattie leapt into her massive, jacked-up pickup truck.

Lucy jumped into the back seat, and I grabbed hold of the passenger door and hauled myself in as Hattie hit the gas. "What is going on?" I panted as I dragged the door shut just in time to avoid taking out a telephone pole.

"Rogue has won the Strawberry Shortcake Bake-Off four times," Hattie said as she peeled out onto the main road. "The festival charter states that the championship trophy will be named after the first person to win it five-times."

"She's been entering for years, and she finally won her fourth time last year. There are four others who have also won four times," Lucy said. "Rogue wants that trophy named after her, and she's been planning for this year's festival for the last twelve-months."

"One of the four-time champions is probably going to win

this year," Hattie said, the tires squealing as she peeled around the corner. "Rogue needs it to be her."

"Why?"

Hattie glanced at me. "She used to enter with her daughter long ago. It has personal meaning for her. There's no way she'd miss out on the Strawberry Contest."

"Doing well in the first two rounds can help break a tie in the finals," Lucy explained. "Today matters."

"Rogue was planning to get there at six this morning to set up her table," Hattie added. "Presentation makes a difference."

"But her table is empty. Nothing on it at all," Lucy said. "Judging starts at seven."

I glanced at Hattie's dashboard and saw it was six thirty-three. Much like Hattie, Rogue was an unapologetic, unstoppable force, but she had the added benefit of endless financial resources. If she wanted to win that contest, nothing would have kept her from being at that table. "You don't think she changed her mind?"

"No." Hattie swung the truck into the long, white-stone driveway that snaked almost a half mile through Rogue's lakefront property. "No chance."

I pulled out my cell and texted Bootsy Jones, the only other Seam Ripper I had in my phone. *Rogue's missing. Have you heard from her?*

What? No. I'll ask around. I'm at the Festival. I'll look around here.

Great. We're at her house. I set my phone down as Hattie screeched to a stop by the front door.

Rogue's cherry red Lamborghini SUV was parked out front, with the tailgate wide open.

I was the first one out of the truck. "Rogue!"

There was no answer, but the back of Rogue's SUV was loaded with gorgeous strawberries, along with other crates containing what appeared to be table decor. I could see champagne, a velvet table covering, but no Rogue.

Hattie came up behind me. "She told me she was packing her car at five-thirty this morning."

Fear trickled down my spine. "That was thirteen hours ago."

The strawberry crates were neatly arranged, ready for transport that had never happened. The berries were a gorgeous vibrant red, plump, flawless perfection. "The strawberries look really good. Does she grow them herself?"

"Actually yes. She doesn't even let her gardener touch them. They're the best around."

Lucy was at the front door. "No one's answering." She peered through the window beside the door, then swore. "You guys! The furniture inside is knocked over. It looks like someone tore the place apart."

We all looked at each other, and then suddenly, I realized that Ivan, my bodyguard wasn't with us. "We lost Ivan."

"Well, I think that tells you a lot about how useful he'd be in an emergency, right? Because right now, I feel like there's something going on that he might be needed for."

"I agree," Lucy said. "This scene is giving me the creeps. It's like Rogue was plucked right out of her life mid-stride."

A shiver went down my spine, so I immediately cleared my throat and stood taller. Fear was never allowed to win. "It's fine. Whatever it is, we can handle it."

"Damn straight we can." Hattie pushed me toward the house. "Go unlock the door, Mia. See what's going on."

"Unlock it? I mean, yeah, I love a chance to pick locks, but shouldn't we call the police?"

Hattie put her hands on her hips. "How well did that work for us recently? Involving the police in a dicey situation?"

"That was murder!" I stared at them, horror congealing in my stomach. "You don't think—"

"Well, open the door and find out."

With the exception of Griselda, my FBI handler, I didn't trust cops to believe in my innocence. Well, if Devlin Hunt was in town, I might have texted him. But he'd been called away right after he asked me out on a date, and I hadn't heard from him since. The only one we could call was Chief Stone. The fact he was Lucy's cousin didn't mean we could trust him to do what was right and handle the situation correctly.

Quite the opposite.

Which meant if we cared about Rogue, it had to be us.

I grimaced, but pulled out my lock picks, which I now carried with me more often, because life in Bass Derby was turning out to be like that. "Make sure no one shoots us."

"They'd shoot only you. *We* don't have assassins after us," Hattie said, but she took up position next to me, facing out.

Lucy did the same as I went down on my knee and got to work.

I was sure that Rogue had an alarm, but there was no sound as the lock clicked a minute later. I pushed the door open. "Hello? Is anyone there?"

Silence.

I stood up and took a step inside. "Rogue?" My voice faded as I took in the carnage. Her house usually was in pristine condition, gorgeous, designed to emulate cozy, Maine warmth with expensive perfection. But right now, chairs were upturned. Pictures and books strewn on the floor. The rugs askew.

"Go in and check it out," Hattie said. "I'll stand guard out here."

I looked back at her. "Why me?"

She smiled and waved me inside. "You're the FBI special agent. Do your thing."

"I'm not an FBI special agent—"

"Closer than I am. Go, go."

I looked at Lucy, and she picked up a small pot of geraniums and hefted it. "I'll come with you. I'm good at throwing things."

"All right, then. Let's do this." Wishing I had my hairdryer, which I'd recently discovered was very useful as a weapon, I led the way into the front hall. I looked around and saw that the family room was open to the kitchen. "That way." I pointed, my instincts drawing me toward the kitchen.

"Okay." Lucy stayed close to me, her pot ready.

As I walked past an upturned table, I grabbed the lamp off the floor and wrapped the cord around my hand, swinging the lamp gently. It wasn't as maneuverable as a hairdryer, but all corded projectiles were pretty much in my wheelhouse these days.

We stepped into the kitchen and looked around.

"Nothing in here looks like it was touched," Lucy said. "Let's go—"

"No." I knew from my own childhood training sessions with my mom that sometimes the best distraction was in plain sight. "The front hall is a mess, so maybe someone doesn't want us to notice something in here."

"Oh...right...I forgot about that. I gotta work on my criminal mind."

We both looked around, and this time, I saw a note on the center island, with messy handwriting scrawled across the paper. I walked over and peered at it. The message was short and to the point. "I didn't do it," I read aloud.

Lucy looked over. "Who didn't do what?"

"Rogue, I'm guessing. But what didn't she do? Trash her house?" I looked around, and I saw that the pantry door was open at the back of the kitchen. Instinct made my heart start to pound. "In there."

Gripping my lamp more tightly, I forced myself to walk across the kitchen. "If Rogue jumps out of there to scare us, I'm pretty sure I'm going to have a heart attack."

"You and me, both." Lucy edged up close behind me, which I greatly appreciated—

My gaze dropped to the threshold, and fear crept down my belly when I saw something peeking out from the pantry. Limp. Lifeless. Adorned with very high heels. "Are those *feet*?"

"What? Where?" Lucy looked down. "Oh, God. *Yes.*"

We lunged for the door and yanked it open. Sprawled on the ground facedown was a fifty-something woman with raven black hair, gorgeous shoes, and a bunch of strawberries scattered around her.

"Oh, God." I dropped to my knees beside her, but the moment I touched her, I knew.

She was dead.

∽

Want more *Gone Rogue*? Go *here* to get it now!

BOOKS BY STEPHANIE ROWE

MYSTERY

MIA MURPHY SERIES
(COZY MYSTERY)
Double Twist
Top Notch
Gone Rogue
Triple Trouble
Margarita Mayhem

CONTEMPORARY ROMANCE

WYOMING REBELS SERIES
(CONTEMPORARY WESTERN ROMANCE)
A Real Cowboy Never Says No
A Real Cowboy Knows How to Kiss
A Real Cowboy Rides a Motorcycle
A Real Cowboy Never Walks Away
A Real Cowboy Loves Forever
A Real Cowboy for Christmas

A Real Cowboy Always Trusts His Heart
A Real Cowboy Always Protects
A Real Cowboy for the Holidays
A Real Cowboy Always Comes Home
SERIES COMPLETE

THE HART RANCH BILLIONAIRES SERIES
(CONTEMPORARY WESTERN ROMANCE)
A Rogue Cowboy's Second Chance
A Rogue Cowboy's Christmas Surprise
A Rogue Cowboy Finds Love
A Rogue Cowboy's Heart

LINKED TO THE HART RANCH BILLIONAIRES SERIES
(CONTEMPORARY WESTERN ROMANCE)
Her Rebel Cowboy

BIRCH CROSSING SERIES
(SMALL-TOWN CONTEMPORARY ROMANCE)
Unexpectedly Mine
Accidentally Mine
Unintentionally Mine
Irresistibly Mine
Secretly Mine

MYSTIC ISLAND SERIES
(SMALL-TOWN CONTEMPORARY ROMANCE)
Wrapped Up in You (A Christmas novella)

PARANORMAL

ORDER OF THE BLADE SERIES
(PARANORMAL ROMANCE)
Darkness Awakened

BOOKS BY STEPHANIE ROWE

Darkness Seduced
Darkness Surrendered
Forever in Darkness
Darkness Reborn
Darkness Arisen
Darkness Unleashed
Inferno of Darkness
Darkness Possessed
Shadows of Darkness
Hunt the Darkness
Darkness Awakened: Reimagined

IMMORTALLY DATING SERIES
(FUNNY PARANORMAL ROMANCE)
To Date an Immortal
To Date a Dragon
Devilishly Dating
To Kiss a Demon

ROMANTIC SUSPENSE

ALASKA HEAT SERIES
(ROMANTIC SUSPENSE)
Ice
Chill
Ghost
Burn
Hunt (novella)

A QUICK FAVOR

Did you enjoy Jacob and Phoebe's story?

People are often hesitant to try new books or new authors. A few reviews can encourage them to make that leap and give it a try. If you enjoyed *A Rogue Cowboy Finds Love* and think others will as well, please consider taking a moment and writing one or two sentences on *the etailer and/or Goodreads* to help this story find the readers who would enjoy it. Even the short reviews really make an impact!

Thank you a million times for reading my books! I love writing for you and sharing the journeys of these beautiful characters with you. I hope you find inspiration from their stories in your own life!

Love,
Stephanie

For all the women out there who need a little reminder that you're awesome, you matter, and you never, EVER need to apologize for who you are, what you want, or how you feel. Because you're amazing, exactly as you re.

ABOUT THE AUTHOR

NEW YORK TIMES AND *USA TODAY* bestselling author Stephanie Rowe is the author of more than sixty published novels. Notably, she is a Vivian® Award nominee, a RITA® Award winner and a five-time nominee, and a Golden Heart® Award winner and two-time nominee. She loves her dogs, tennis, and trying to live her best, truest life. For info on Stephanie's newest releases, join her newsletter today!

Sign me up for Stephanie Newsletter

www.stephanierowe.com

ACKNOWLEDGMENTS

Special thanks to my beta readers. You guys are the best!

There are so many to thank by name, more than I could count, but here are those who I want to called out specially for all they did to help this book come to life: Alyssa Bird, Ashlee Murphy, Bridget Koan, Britannia Hill, Deb Julienne, Denise Fluhr, Dottie Jones, Heidi Hoffman, Helen Loyal, Jackie Moore Kranz, Jean Bowden, Jeanne Stone, Jeanie Jackson, Jodi Moore, Judi Pflughoeft, Kasey Richardson, Linda Watson, Regina Thomas, Summer Steelman, Suzanne Mayer, Shell Bryce, and Trish Douglas. Special thanks to my family, who I love with every fiber of my heart and soul. And to AER, who is my world. Love you so much, baby girl! And to Joe, who keeps me believing myself. I love you all!

Made in the USA
Columbia, SC
30 May 2024

36399084R00164